The Potter *of* Paradox

THE SPIRIT SERIES

TRACI STEAD

Cover Design and Interior format by The Killion Group
http://thekilliongroupinc.com

Scripture quotation from Ecclesiastes 5:18-20 on epigraph page is taken from the Holy Bible, New Living Translation, copyright ©1996, 2004, 2007, 2013 by Tyndale House Foundation. Used by permission of

DEDICATION

This book is dedicated to my very own Jack
and Sam.
May you always turn under the hands of the
Divine Potter.
I love you, boys.

ACKNOWLEDGEMENTS

I wish to thank Kia Glosson for sharing her pottery skills and knowledge with me. It is she who said, "Pottery brings me peace."

I also want to thank Katie McAnally and Tamara Wimer for their first and second read‑throughs to offer insights and suggestions. I so much appreciated your willingness to give freely of yourselves. John David Kudrick is my editor extraordinaire who helped me bring the story to life.

I must acknowledge a special source that helped form this novel over the last several years: M. C. Richards's book *Centering* inspired me to extend the paradox and symbolism of the story.

Joe's poem recitation in Chapter 9 is inspired by Yoshida Kashichi, who wrote the poem "When Will This March End?"

Of great importance and special recognition are the city of Rome, Georgia, and its people. The women working in the Visitor Center were more than obliging and offered me free rein to look through city newspaper clippings and annals. It was a joy to visit with them. A sweet gentleman member of a local church spoke with me about pretty girls and bakeries and more. The farmer's market behind the Visitor Center was a fabulous place to find friendly people willing to talk about their special city in the 1960s. The ice storm of 1961 and Reverend Finster would not have been resurrected without their help. If you ever have the chance to visit Rome, I know you will enjoy seeing how this story came to life.

I want to thank my husband, Matt, who took pottery lessons with me, directed me to Bible resources, listened to me plan and write aloud for so long, and comforted me when the characters made me cry. Thanks, Matt, for believing in me.

More than anyone, I must thank my Lord for sharing this story with me. His Spirit hovered over our home for many, many months, prodding me to share with others a story about the unique gifts he has given each of us. I hope you will find in these pages the courage to follow the plan God has for you, even if it seems risky. Be the pot that the Potter envisioned when he made you.

Even so, I have noticed one thing, at least, that is good. It is good for people to eat, drink, and enjoy their work under the sun during the short life God has given them, and to accept their lot in life. And it is a good thing to receive wealth from God and the good health to enjoy it. To enjoy your work and accept your lot in life—this is indeed a gift from God. God keeps such people so busy enjoying life that they take no time to brood over the past.

Ecclesiastes 5:18-20

We ought not to look back,
unless it is to derive useful lessons from past
errors, and for the purpose of profiting by
dear bought experience.
—George Washington

CHAPTER 1

The box of ancient shards lay open on the tabletop. The earthy scent of ancient pottery mixed with the dusty, warm air of the college studio. It seemed my entire life spun around this one moment, like a piece of clay perfectly centered and formed under the potter's hand.

I steadied my gray head against the plate-glass window and stared through time. A boy is never a man until he can face his father with the truth. A father never sees a man until he first recognizes the truth. Truth is the clay binding father and son into an eternal mold that makes an unbreakable pot. The potter who can form that bond into a beautiful work of art has great ability. My thumb traced the faint but definite impression in the small clay fragment. A bird landed on the ledge as John Kadar swirled out of a mist of memories ...

Atlanta, Georgia: May 1961

The wind ruffled my hair while Gene McDaniels sang "A Hundred Pounds of Clay" on the radio. I sped along Interstate 75, leaving Atlanta far behind. Taking the ramp onto 411, I slowed my Chevy Corvair and switched off the radio. It had been nearly two years since I had seen my mother's sisters in Rome. Well, not Rome per se, but close to it.

I grew up in Rome, Georgia, a small town of twenty thousand or so. Daddy was a math professor at Bersher College. Mama liked city life well-enough, but she insisted children needed time to be children, and that meant walking along the river, digging worms for fishing, climbing trees, and disappearing for hours at a time.

Mama grew up in rural Paradox, a little-known community north of Rome. Every summer she would pile our suitcases into the back of the car and fling me and my little brother Sam into the backseat with a bag of sandwiches and apples and a couple bottles of Yoo-hoo. Then we headed to her family home for a couple of weeks. Aunt Lily and Aunt Rose never married, and they treated me and my little brother like their own. They never yelled when we let the screen door slam behind us early in the morning, and they listened attentively to all our adventures when we returned for dinner.

But that was years ago. Now I was grown, a college graduate, and my first job was not turning out the way I had hoped. Corporations expect results, no matter how they need to get them. The long hours, ethical questions, and stress were weighing me down. My fingertips burned red from the nail nubbins I chewed with vigor.

"Come pay a visit," Aunt Rose had begged over the phone. "Lily will make a peach cobbler, and we'll sit out on the veranda. You can tell us all about your new adventures in Atlanta. Come on; we haven't seen you in so long. Sam was here visiting last week."

Guilt always worked on me, and Aunt Rose knew it. That's how I found myself driving to the little village of Paradox, feeling the wind through the open windows, and hoping the knots in my stomach were not permanent. I stopped on Broad Street in Rome to get a cola and ease some of my tension.

"Hello there, Jack," a voice from my past called from the checkout line.

I looked up in surprise and saw an older gentleman whom I felt I should know.

"Hello. How have you been?" I asked as names and faces raced through my mind.

"Just fine." The man smiled. "I'm John ... John Kadar, from out near your aunts' place."

He paused to pull a five out of his worn wallet for the cashier. I tried to place the name, but came up with nothing.

"Haven't seen you in years, boy," he went on. "You look just like your daddy. What are you doing these days?"

"I work for a corporation in Atlanta now. I'm on my way to Paradox to visit the aunts. I have a long weekend with the holiday."

"Well, I'm sure Lily and Rose will welcome the sight of you. Stop by the shop if you get a chance." After putting his billfold back in his olive-green workpants, Mr. John gathered his bag of groceries and turned to the door.

I placed my cold cola on the counter and dug a quarter out of my pocket. "Yeah, maybe I'll see you," I called after him.

The drive from Rome to Paradox, back before US 27 was hard-surfaced, took about an hour. No one seemed in a hurry, unlike the drivers in Atlanta, and I watched the shadows and sunlight play on the tree leaves. The weeds and wildflowers waved from the side of the road as my car meandered by.

About a mile before my aunts' house, I noticed a weathered sign along the road that read: *Pottery*. A vague sense of familiarity clouded my mind for a moment, and then the haze finally lifted. *Mr. John ... John Kadar.* He was the old man Sam and I used to meet near the riverbank when we were little. He taught me how to unhook a fish.

A smile crept across my face as I recalled the first time the fish spines pierced my hand; Sam screamed to high heaven as tiny beads of blood appeared. I must have been six or seven and Sam a couple years younger. Old Mr. John, who happened to be nearby, hurried over to calm us down and show us how to safely unhook the fish. After that, sometimes we would see Mr. John along the riverbank, and he would stop to visit or share a sandwich from his metal lunch pail. My mind did some quick math: Mr. John had to be ancient by now.

I pulled into the driveway and parked in the curve under the live oak tree. Aunt Rose was sitting on the covered porch, and Aunt Lily opened the screen door just as I slammed the car door closed.

"We're so glad you are here," Aunt Rose said as she walked down the brick pavers. "I was starting to think you weren't going to come after all."

Aunt Lily stood behind Aunt Rose, holding out her arms while waiting her turn to hug me. "We just finished cooking dinner and it's all ready to be put on the table. Come on in. Oh my word, it is good to see you!"

My tight shoulders loosened just a bit as I melted into their embraces. The dark entryway welcomed me after the glaring sunshine of the highway, and I was aware of the sigh that escaped from deep within my own darkness. *Coming to visit might be a good idea after all.*

"Tell us all about Atlanta," Aunt Lily said, beaming as she filled my plate.

"Well, I work for Needler and Newman over in the art district. They sell merchandise all over the country. I keep records of incoming supplies and outgoing products. I take orders from customers, pack things up, basically whatever I am told to do." I shrugged. "It isn't what I expected when I took the job, but I guess I have to start somewhere." I couldn't help adding, "I've been there three years."

"Do you have a girl yet?" As usual, Aunt Lily went straight to the heart of their interests.

"No ..." I blushed. "I mostly just work. It's the life of a businessman."

"Well, surely you've found some friends by now. You were always such a chatty little guy," Aunt Rose said. She raised her eyebrows, prodding.

"No, really work is about all I do. Needler and Newman is one of the newer companies, and they really want to start growing. I spend a lot of time looking for new customers and encouraging old ones to buy more."

"All work and no play make Jack a dull boy," Aunt Lily said. "We'll have to do something about that." She eyed me and then passed the bowl of sweet-pickled cucumbers and onions. "After dinner we'll walk down by the river. A new family of beaver built a dam this year and they usually come out late evening."

Two plates later my gut was about to bust.

"I'm tighter than a tick on a hound dog," Aunt Lily said. "Let's wait for the cobbler." She scooted back her chair. "The veranda is lovely in the evening light. Come on out, Jack. We'll clear the table later."

The aunts led the way out, and I let the screen door slam behind me. Instantly I felt completely at home and settled. The wicker chairs and love seat were the same as when I was a kid, though back then Sam and I didn't sit on them. The porch step was always better for us with our dripping popsicles. I slouched into one of the chairs and rolled my head from side to side.

"You're so wound up," Aunt Lily said with a cluck. "I hate that you are not enjoying Atlanta. Of course, I would never be happy there either, but I thought you would like all of the excitement and bustle."

"Ohh ... I'm happy in Atlanta," I drawled. "It's just been a long few years. Business doesn't come as naturally to me as it does to some others." Another sigh escaped my heavy chest.

"Look!" Aunt Rose said. "The lightning bugs are coming out."

The first few glows flickered out of the tall grass near the trees. Aunt Lily and Aunt Rose stood, then each took one of my hands and pulled me down the stairs. We headed east toward the creek, smelling the freshness of the evening and the first cuttings of grass in the meadow.

"I remember hiding out here all day when we would visit in the summers," I said as we neared the water's edge. I chuckled. "Mr. John taught me how to unhook a fish down here. I saw him today in town. I stopped for a coke and he remembered me."

"John Kadar is a good man," Aunt Rose said. "He was gone for a long time, but he came back about four years ago." Her voice grew softer as she said, "Just about the time sweet Violet crossed the river for home."

Mama had fought with the cancer most of my teen years. She managed to see me graduate college, but she missed out on Sam's graduation. It was a hardship on all of us losing Mama like that. Daddy never spoke about it, but I knew he was hurting, missing her so much.

"Oh, Jack, there are the beaver babies," Aunt Lily said. Then she laughed, covering the sadness by pointing across the creek. A small dam of branches and logs was blocking a little tributary, and I could see the beaver-made pond behind it, glittering in the twilight. Two adult beavers were swimming with three kits in tow, their heads barely above the surface of the rippling water.

"Just up the river a ways is where Mr. John collects his clay. You say you saw him today?" Aunt Lily continued. "His pottery has been very successful. There was a write-up about him in the paper a few months ago. He goes all over the world to art shows."

"Really?" I couldn't contain my surprise. The old man in olive-green work pants traveled the world? "What does his work look like?"

"Some of it is what you call abstract, sort of flowing and weird," Aunt Lily said. "I don't much care for it. I like the practical stuff. The cobbler I made was baked in one of his dishes. We visited his shop a while back for a demonstration. He gives little talks as people walk by and then he lets you try the wheel. Rose and I did pretty well, if I do say so myself."

"Speaking of cobbler, let's get back to it," Aunt Rose said. "It's getting too dark for my old eyes down here in the hollow."

We ambled up the path arm in arm listening to the beavers smack their tails on the water. The midnight-blue sky twinkled with the first stars, and a sliver of moon lit the way. Yes, it was good to be back.

"I wish there were fresh peaches for the cobbler," Aunt Lily fussed as she carried my bowl out to the porch. "I had to use last year's canned peaches. You come back later this summer and I'll make a better one for you."

I dug my spoon deeply into the sugary crust and inhaled the warmth of cinnamon and spices. "This cobbler is the best thing I've had in ages, Aunt Lily. Mama taught me how to cook well enough to get by, but this is beyond my abilities."

Aunt Lily nodded. "Yes, your mama did right by you boys. Sam and you both get along fine, I can tell. I wish your daddy would let us help him out, though. It wouldn't be any trouble to run over to Rome and put some good food in the fridge, but he won't allow it. The last time I saw him, he was skin and bones," Aunt Lily went on, her gray hair falling out of its pins. "He needs a woman and that's all there is to it. I know he and your mama were special together, but Violet would be alright with him moving on. It's time."

"No, Lily. Joe doesn't need a woman," Aunt Rose said from her wicker chair near the door. "He needs Violet. You leave him alone and let him take as long as he needs to grieve her." She looked over at me. "Now, Jack, tell us more about your job. What do you really do all day?"

"Well, I buy and sell ceramics. Needler and Newman specializes in decorative ceramics, vases, and such. We buy the ceramics and then sell them to stores across the country. I had a contact from college who knew this guy in Santa Barbara. I just landed a big account with him last week, so we sent our stock out to his store. Jimmy, the guy at the desk next to me, does most of the buying and I do most of the selling. But I did order some nice ceramic·bead necklaces recently from a group in North Carolina. They'll be shipped to New York for selling."

"Oh my! Do you travel to all of those places?" Aunt Lily asked.

"No, no." I shook my head and chuckled. "All I usually see is my desk. Potential potters send samples to us in the mail, and we decide if they're good enough for our sales clients."

"But aren't you making any of the pottery yourself? I thought that was what you wanted to do," Aunt Rose said, tilting her head.

"I only minored in ceramics, Aunt Rose. My degree is in business. Daddy always said a man needed to be able to take care of himself and his family. Pottery just isn't going to do that."

"Well, I don't know," Aunt Rose said. "John Kadar seems to have done alright."

I gave a small nod. "Some people do okay, I guess, but most potters have other jobs to pay the bills."

"Maybe you ought to go over and see John tomorrow," Aunt Lily said. "You might want to buy some of his stuff for your company. Help John pay some of his bills, you know?" She smiled.

I shrugged. "Maybe."

The word that came to Jeremiah from the
LORD: "Arise, and go down to the potter's
house, and there I will let you hear my words."
So I went down to the potter's house, and
there he was working at his wheel. And the
vessel he was making of clay was spoiled in
the potter's hand, and he reworked it into
another vessel, as it seemed good to the potter
to do.
—Jeremiah 18:1-4

CHAPTER 2

Bethany, Judea: circa AD 30

Mariam sighed as she picked her way down to the potter's shed. Tiny shards of broken pottery littered the worn trail. It was Mariam's turn to carry lunch to Eleazar. She enjoyed lunchtime at the potter's, but the walk there was often a trial.

Men continually shattered old or broken pottery on the main roadway to line it for the horses and wagons carrying huge pots to the ports and large towns of the Empire, but the rains washed the small pieces of broken pottery over the hillside and onto the path Mariam used. She winced as another sharp edge of broken pottery cut through her soft sandals.

Eleazar had been apprenticed out to John when he was younger. It was an easy arrangement. John had been a family friend as long as Mariam could remember. He used to visit for Shabbat dinner when her parents were still living.

After their parents' deaths, Mariam and Eleazar moved into the house of their older sister Marta and her husband Jacob. Mariam hadn't minded living with Marta and Jacob, but after Jacob was killed in the tower crash in Jerusalem, Marta had become unbearable. The sisters had different interests and desires, and often their personalities exploded around them like the flashing sparks of the night fires. Eleazar knew to steer clear when the women got in one of their moods.

It was one of these moods that had Mariam sighing as she rounded the last curve to John's pottery shed. Marta had instructed Mariam not to linger at the potter's. Some local men were coming to dine this evening, and Mariam was needed to help with dinner.

It wasn't that Mariam didn't want to help Marta, but she would much prefer to sweep and wash than slave away over the hot coals of the cooking fire. The fire left hot streaks of black soot on Mariam's face and singed her hair. The men who once looked longingly at her were starting to look other ways, and the price for a night with her continued to decrease. She had not thought about the eventual decline of her business when she began working. It was a necessity born out of her disastrous circumstances, first with the passing of their parents and then the death of Marta's husband. Eleazar had been too young to understand his responsibility to find Mariam a husband, and Mariam herself was desperate to not be left defenseless or penniless again.

Pushing the door open, Mariam crept into the quiet shed. Eleazar sat at the bench scraping away pieces of clay on a delicate lamp. He was making a pattern of holes to let light shine through the lamp's sides like stars in the night sky. Mariam wished she could be a man and learn to make the beautiful pottery like Eleazar made. To be sure, her brother made many items of practicality: roof tiles, soldiers' canteens, and all of the many pots and bowls and vases. But John had taught Eleazar well, and even the practical, everyday items had some sort of beauty bestowed upon them.

John's pottery was always delicate and graceful, even if the vessel only served as a disgusting chamber pot. John told Mariam once that each piece of pottery was a piece of him, sent out to serve in his name. If the pot wasn't beautiful and useful, then John believed he had not done well. John made items for the palace in Jerusalem, and his pottery was even shipped as far away as Egypt and Spain. Eleazar was blessed to learn from one so talented.

Eleazar raised his eyes. "Shalom!" he said, then smiled at Mariam. "My stomach told me you would be here soon. What have you brought today?"

"Marta sent some of last night's stew and bread, but I popped in a couple of Julia's olive cheeses for you."

Julia was the neighbor's daughter. Julia liked Eleazar, Mariam knew, and the olive cheeses were a special treat meant for him, though Julia's father would never approve of such a union. Marta ran a tavern and Mariam was fast becoming a woman of ill-repute; she knew people were starting to talk. No self-respecting man would allow his daughter to become involved in a family like that. In any case, Eleazar didn't seem to notice Julia's interest. His mind was always on other matters.

"Mariam!" John's friendly voice boomed as he entered the room. "Have you brought some sustenance for this poor boy at last? His stomach has warned me for the last hour that you must be drawing near."

Mariam laughed and nestled into the warm embrace of John's arm around her shoulders. Another man would never hold Mariam so closely in the open, but John never seemed to notice. He was the father that Mariam missed so much.

"I made a special present for your old friend Salome," John said. "Would you like to see it?"

Mariam tensed and backed out of John's embrace. "No, Marta warned me not to stay long. She says I have to help with the cooking for tonight's guests," she said, telling the truth but avoiding the real reason: Mariam did not want to see a present to be given at a party that she had not been invited to attend. Mariam and Salome had been inseparable as young girls, but life's cruel knife had sliced them forever apart, it seemed.

John nodded. "Mm, yes, it is good for Marta to teach you these things. Someday you will be hosting parties in your own home."

"Not if she doesn't feed me first," Eleazar said. "Come on, Mariam, I'm starving!"

Eleazar was dripping as he wiped water and mud onto the clean cloth by the wash basin. Mariam began pulling out the basket's contents, and placed the dish of stew and bread on the table near the lamp Eleazar had been working on. The olive cheeses she kept tucked inside a grape leaf for Eleazar to unwrap later in the afternoon.

Usually Mariam would have stayed to visit with Eleazar and John, but today she offered her good-byes and backed out of the door, red-faced. She didn't want to admit to the men that her feelings had been hurt. She hadn't taken into account that her lifestyle would mean the loss of friendships and "appropriate" parties. They wouldn't understand.

Racing back up the path, a small shard of pottery pricked Mariam's foot and made her walk gingerly the rest of the way home. *This is all Marta's fault,* Mariam fumed, switching the blame. If Marta hadn't made such a fuss about preparing for the dinner party, Mariam wouldn't have had to hurry. Mariam frowned. Marta was always taking the fun out of life. That's why no one wanted to be around Mariam anymore: she was no fun—an ugly, smelly slave to a sister who hated anything fun or interesting.

"Mariam, wait!" a familiar voice called, interrupting Mariam's internal tirade.

Deborah, Mariam thought with a sigh.

A small-framed young woman, Deborah lived behind Marta. Mariam usually liked talking with her, but only in the privacy of the garden that backed up to their houses. Deborah had a split lip that made others look away from her. A man would never choose Deborah, and Mariam didn't want others to start associating her with such a one.

"Shalom, Deborah," Mariam called back and slowed her pace; she wasn't an overtly rude person, but she did have standards.

Deborah joined Mariam on the path, and they walked together. "Have you been to the potter's?" Deborah asked.

"Yes, I took lunch to Eleazar."

"Did you hear about Nathaniel? He came back from Melchaiah's and is all better."

Mariam looked over at Deborah. "What do you mean?"

Everyone knew Nathaniel had been taken by the Romans to work on the roads near Capernaum. A flood had washed out some of the roads and workers were few. The Romans didn't care whom they made one work with, and poor Nathaniel had been forced to labor with a leprous man. Two months later Nathaniel's legs were covered in horrid sores.

He went to visit his cousin, Melchaiah, who lived near some healing springs outside Bethsaida, near Capernaum. He'd hoped the waters would wash away the pain and disgrace.

So the springs must have helped, Mariam thought. *Good.*

Deborah smiled. "Abba went to check on the fields near Nathaniel's, and Nathaniel had him stay for a visit. He showed Abba his legs, and Abba says they are all cleared up," Deborah nearly sang.

"Good. Now if we can just rid ourselves of these Romans who steal our men and make us sick, our whole land will be healed." Mariam continued in her bad mood, fixated on her supposed friend's slight. She and Salome had been tighter than two peas in a pod, but that was before their lives changed. She knew Salome's family really belonged to the Romans; her husband was a tax collector.

They aren't good Jews, she told herself, *not like us.*

Deborah seemed startled by Mariam's angry response, but Mariam didn't care, even though she was usually tender and kind toward Deborah.

"Is something wrong?" Deborah asked.

"No ... no. I ... have a sliver in my foot and I need to hurry to help Marta. Excuse me." Mariam gave a quick nod and raced home.

Many persons have a wrong idea of what constitutes true happiness. It is not attained through self-gratification but through fidelity to a worthy purpose.
—Helen Keller

CHAPTER 3

The night was quiet except for the crickets and the occasional slap of a beaver tail echoing up the hollow. My deep slumber would have rivaled that of Rip Van Winkle. The strong sun glaring through the lace curtains startled me, and I bounded out of bed. Aunt Lily and Aunt Rose would think me a rude guest to stay in bed this long. I washed my face in the porcelain basin on the dresser and pulled on my shirt.

"Well, good morning, lazy bones!" Aunt Lily greeted me as I ran down the staircase. "Come on out to the porch. Rose has some coffee for you." She held the door open for me.

I said a quick "Good morning" to her and then obeyed, grateful there wouldn't be any hurt feelings about sleeping late.

Stepping out onto the porch, I said, "Morning, Aunt Rose. Sorry I slept so long. I guess the drive up wore me out more than I realized."

Aunt Rose tipped her cheek toward me for a kiss.

"No, I imagine you are working too hard in Atlanta and just need a break," Aunt Lily said from behind. "What you require is some relaxation. I'm going to make up a picnic lunch for us, and we'll go over to the bait shop and get some night crawlers for fishing. It's a little warm for them to be biting, but maybe we'll catch something for dinner."

"I'll stay here if you don't mind," Aunt Rose said. She leaned toward me from her seat and offered me a cup of coffee. "I don't enjoy fishing and I can have dinner ready when you get back. We'll have ham, devilled eggs, limas, and fresh rolls." She smiled, letting me know she remembered my favorites—and that she didn't trust our fishing skills.

Not long after breakfast, Aunt Lily and I headed toward Paradox in my Chevy with the windows rolled down. It had been a cool spring and the oppressive heat this day was surprising. I could already feel sweat dripping down my back. Aunt Lily had packed a large paper bag with some food and said we could get some cold drinks at the bait shop.

We passed the pottery shop and I noticed it looked closed up.

"When does Mr. John work in the pottery studio?" I asked.

"He's there most days. I imagine he is out for the holiday weekend, though," Aunt Lily responded. "He has a college girl helping some days, but maybe she went home for the summer."

I pulled into the bait shop, Hammond's Hardware, which was a local solution to driving all the way to Rome. It was Paradox's only store and met all the basic needs: hardware and tools, gasoline, stationery and stamps, a few foodstuffs, and of course, bait for fishing. It was the only filling station between Paradox and Rome.

"I'm going to gas up while we're here, Aunt Lily," I said as I pulled beside the pump.

"Alright, Jack. I'll get some cokes and the night crawlers."

A young boy filled the tank and I headed in to Mr. Hammond's to pay. I got in line behind a girl with a couple cans of tuna and a pack of saltine crackers.

"Hey, Ginny," Mrs. Hammond said with a smile. "How are things at the pottery? I haven't seen Mr. John today."

"He's fine, thanks. He went out to gather more clay. He likes it on the east side of the creek. Says it has more mottles and streaks there. I thought I might join him and bring a little lunch along. He doesn't always remember his lunch pail, you know."

"Oh yes." Mrs. Hammond laughed. "Take along some of these berries for him too. My treat."

"Well, thank you, Mrs. Hammond. I'm sure Mr. John will enjoy them."

Ginny gathered her paper bag and headed out the door as I stepped up to the register.

"Jack! Look at you," Mrs. Hammond exclaimed. "How is Atlanta? Are you doing well?"

"Atlanta's fine, ma'am, and I am too."

"So glad you're back. Sam was here last week with Lily." Mrs. Hammond craned her neck to look past me. "I suppose the two of you are headed out fishing? I see Lily's in the back picking out bait."

"Yes, she and I are going to try to catch a little something for dinner, but Aunt Rose is making a feast for us back home, just in case." I winked. "You know how Aunt Rose likes to spoil everyone with her cooking."

"She is good at that," Mrs. Hammond said. "So are you here for long?"

"No, just for the holiday weekend. I'll head back to Atlanta on Monday afternoon."

"Well, it's good to see you even for a little bit. We miss seeing your family now that Miss Violet is gone," she went on as she rang up my gas purchase.

"Yes, it's harder to get back, it seems. Daddy is busy teaching at Bersher and Sam is teaching high school now, which I'm sure you already know. My company doesn't give me much time off, but it is nice to have this weekend to visit." I paid for the gasoline and put my billfold in my back pocket.

A moment later Aunt Lily paid for the drinks and worms, and we headed out the screen door. The young lady who had bought the tuna and crackers was walking across the road as we pulled out.

"Stop," Aunt Lily said.

I slowed down as she stuck her head out the window.

"Ginny!" she called. "Are you headed to the creek? We're going fishing. We'll give you a lift."

The young woman smiled and thanked Aunt Lily, then climbed into the backseat.

Aunt Lily turned partway around toward Ginny. "I heard you tell Mrs. Hammond that Mr. John is out collecting. Maybe we can save you a little trouble and find him for you." Then Aunt Lily nodded in my direction. "This here is my nephew Jack."

"Nice to meet you, Jack—and thank you for the ride," Ginny said, then gave me a smile in the rearview mirror. "Anyway, yes, Mr. John is over to the river today collecting clay. He wants to make some more of those flowerpots he was working on last time you were by."

"Well," Aunt Lily said, "maybe we'll be able to find him and get you both to join us for a little lunch break. Jack and I are fishing, but really he just needs some slow time. Jack here works for some pottery people in Atlanta."

Ginny's eyes met mine in the rearview mirror. "Really? What type of pottery do you make?"

"Oh, I don't actually make pottery," I answered. "I work for art suppliers in their ceramics department. I'm mostly in distribution, but sometimes I help in acquisitions," I continued, thinking that I was starting to sound self-important. "I majored in business, but minored in art and ceramics, so I am hopeful that soon I can move on to the artistic side of the business. I've been there over three years now." That last part just had a way of slipping out.

"Oh." Ginny looked away from the mirror and out the passenger window.

Aunt Lily gave a knowing smile and nodded. "Yes, Jack will be making pottery again soon. I told him to talk to Mr. John and see if his company can sell some of John's work. As soon as Jack makes that deal, I bet he can do whatever he wants over there at that company."

"Well, you can talk to him about it, but Mr. John is kind of particular about selling his work," Ginny said.

The tree-lined dirt lane turned rutty and weed-strewn. I pulled over under some oaks and parked in the shade. Ginny jumped out and thanked me for the ride, then headed toward the riverbank.

"When you find Mr. John, come on over here and share our lunch. I always pack too much," Aunt Lily called after her.

Ginny waved and kept on walking. I didn't think she would bother coming back, until I noticed her sack of food still in the backseat. I grabbed the fishing poles and bait while Aunt Lily gathered a blanket and the lunch bag from the trunk, then we headed over to the bankside to look for a good spot to sit.

A large willow hung out over the water and some small oak saplings struggled nearby, a perfect place to settle down and rest in the shade. Aunt Lily threw out the blanket by the edges and then turned to me.

"Well, are you going to hook up the worms or do I have to do everything?" She grinned.

"Oh, no, ma'am. I already baited the first line for you." I laughed as I produced the first pole for her inspection.

"Well, it's good to see the city hasn't made you forget all your country ways."

"Now, Aunt Lily, you know I could never forget how to bait a hook. I learned from a professional!"

"Those days seem so long ago now." She sighed. "I sure miss your mama and you and Sam coming to visit in the summers. Those were good days. Now we hardly ever see either of you."

"Well, I'm here now," I said, brushing her comments off. "You better throw that line in before the worm crawls off."

Aunt Lily did so and then began telling me fishing stories from her childhood. Sometimes she lapsed into silence, but it was comfortable and easy. By the time lunchtime rolled around, we only had five small fish and one bee sting to show for our time. Aunt Lily said she was going to walk up the creek a ways and see if she could find Mr. John and Ginny. She pulled her floppy hat down a little tighter and headed off. Her age was beginning to show, but she was still tall and agile.

I sat on the creek side, wondering if I would be fishing and hiking when I was her age. *Probably not if I keep working for Needler and Newman,* I thought and then bit into the quick of a hangnail. I let out a gruff sigh.

"What's got you so disgruntled? Not catching anything?"

I started and snapped my head around to see Mr. John and Ginny walk in from under some of the shrubbery. They dropped several heavy pails of clay and exhaled.

I waved. "Good morning, Mr. John. Aunt Lily just went up that way to look for you and Ginny. I think she was getting tired of throwing everything back."

"Throwing them back isn't forever, you know." Mr. John smiled. "It's just waiting for the fish to be right. Next month or next fall or next year, when the time is right, so will the fish be."

"Hmm." I nodded as they joined me on the blanket. "But when you're hungry right now, waiting isn't an option."

"Ginny says Lily brought lunch, and I know Mrs. Hammond threw in some strawberries—such a good woman. So you see, today we still eat while the fish get ready."

"There you are!" Aunt Lily called, walking back down the deer trail. She plopped herself down on the blanket. "Go on and tear into that lunch, Jack. I was looking for you, John. I thought maybe you went over to the bridge."

"No, I like the clay on the other side. Remember those pots I showed you last month? The streaking comes from this clay. Each one turns out so unique."

"You always collect your own clay for your work?" I asked.

"Just some of it. I buy some clay for the really difficult pieces, but the local clay sets off the flower pots so well. Ginny is getting good at helping me collect it too, so it isn't such a hardship anymore."

Ginny blushed. "I'm just glad you let me help out. I know this internship is a great privilege."

"Internship?" I asked.

"Yeah," Ginny said, "the college tries to match up students with mentors to do a year of internship in the community. My specialization is ceramics and Mr. John agreed to help me with it."

"But school is out by now," I said.

"Yes," Ginny said. "I asked Mr. John if I could continue through the summer and get some more experience. My dad isn't too thrilled about it, but I think it's working out. Mr. John pays for my food and the Hammonds are letting me stay in a room behind the store. I help them in the garden and sometimes in the store. I think Mr. Hammond could use some more help, but I don't know much about hardware." She grinned.

"Are you at Bersher College?" I asked. "That's where I went. And my dad teaches math there."

"Yes, I'm at Bersher. I'll be a senior in the fall. What's your dad's name?"

"Joe Sharp."

"I had Dr. Sharp my first year. His wife had recently passed and—Oh ... I guess she was your mother. I'm sorry," Ginny said. "They must have loved each other a lot. He seemed so lost and sad."

"Thanks." I lowered my head. "He still seems lost and sad. We all miss Mama."

"Violet was a good woman," Mr. John said, then turned to Aunt Lily. "So I hear you didn't have any luck with the fish," he said, clearly wanting to change the subject.

"Not much." Aunt Lily blinked and then blinked again. The mention of Mama and Daddy had made her start to tear up. "But I have some bologna sandwiches and leftover peach cobbler that will do just as well. Here, help yourself."

Mr. John took a bite of sandwich and gestured to me. "You used to make some pottery if I remember your mama's stories right. She used to brag on you boys and all you did. Been throwing anything lately?"

I shrugged. "No. I spend most of my time at work. I don't even know where I would get my hands on a wheel or a kiln, anyway."

"Well then, you need to come over this afternoon and have a go at it. It'll help you relax. You look like you could use more than just a morning of fishing, though Lily surely is on the right track with you."

"I'd love to come by. What time?"

Mr. John stared at the creek for a moment, then said, "How about three? That will give me time to finish up here and get back to the shop."

"I don't want to rush you. Are you sure you have time for me today?" I asked, glancing at Ginny over Mr. John's shoulder.

"John wouldn't have asked if it wasn't good for him," Aunt Lily remarked and passed some cobbler to Ginny. "Will you be there too, dear?"

"Yes, I need to put glaze on some bisque ware before we fire it. And if Mr. John isn't back, I can get you started throwing, Jack."

"Three o'clock it is, then," I said, then smiled at Ginny.

Aunt Lily and I stayed a little longer trying to catch something worthy of Aunt Rose's dinner, but we weren't successful. Around one we headed back to the house, fishless but relaxed. Aunt Rose was sitting on the front porch looking at the mail when we pulled up.

"How did it go?"

"Not so well," I answered. "We caught several fish, but they all had to be thrown back. Today we will have ham, and this fall we will have fish."

"That sounds lovely!" Aunt Rose sounded ecstatic.

"Well, you could be a little less happy that we didn't catch anything, Rose," Aunt Lily said.

"I can't be sorry you didn't catch anything when it makes Jack want to come back again," Aunt Rose said.

"Oh, Jack will be back for some fishing before fall, or my name's not Lily Russell," Aunt Lily said. She smirked as I turned pink.

"So you had a relaxing time?" Aunt Rose asked me.

"Yes, it was a very good morning," I answered. "The trees were shady, the water calm, and the fish bit, even if we couldn't keep them. I would say Aunt Lily's plan worked out perfectly. I haven't been this relaxed in a long time."

Aunt Lily was grinning from ear to ear as she sat down next to Aunt Rose and then poured a glass of ice water. I noticed some vines had grown up to the eaves on the south side of the house, so I started pulling them down. Part of the vines twined into the rose bushes and scratched me. I hadn't thought about how much the aunts probably needed someone to come by and check on things. In my memory they were still my capable aunts who listened to my adventures and fed me popsicles. I guess everything changes, whether we take time to notice or not.

I finished up with the vines and then started carrying large tree branches out of ancient flowerbeds when Aunt Lily came outside.

"It's nearly three, Jack. You better get a move on or Mr. John and Ginny will think you aren't coming."

"Yikes! I didn't know it was that late. My mind was drifting while I worked."

"And I know just which side of the creek it was drifting toward." Her broad smile said everything she was thinking. "You better change your shirt before you go. You're covered in sweat and grime."

I ran inside and let the screen door slam behind me. Instantly the memory of Sam and me as children came rushing back. I hadn't talked to Sam in a couple of months. We weren't upset with each other; it just seemed that we were drifting apart with time and age. Without Mama here to bring us back together, we just didn't bother for some reason.

I washed my hands and face in the basin and changed into a clean shirt. I wondered why I should change shirts when this one would get filthy throwing pots, but then Ginny flashed through my mind and I knew why I was changing. She seemed like the kind of girl I would like to get to know better. She seemed confident and assured, but not bossy and belligerent—like the young women at work. Of course it didn't hurt to have wavy auburn hair and green eyes that sparkled when she spoke of her plans and ambitions.

I hurried downstairs to the muggy kitchen and pecked Aunt Rose on the cheek. "What time will dinner be?"

"Around seven."

"I'm looking forward to it. The bread smells great already. I won't stay too long at Mr. John's."

"You take your time and enjoy yourself," she called as I flew out of the kitchen and down the porch stairs.

I had decided beforehand to walk to Mr. John's, but now I was running late. I jumped into the car and took off down the dirt road. Dust flew behind me and wind blew through the rolled-down windows. Summer was just getting started and daisies along the road bowed as I passed.

I pulled into the pottery shop driveway right at three and parked next to the crape myrtle arbor. As I got out, I saw Ginny walking toward me from across the parking lot with a bundle of collards in her arms.

"Good afternoon, Jack. I was just helping Mrs. Hammond in the garden and she sent these over for you and your aunts. She said Miss Rose could fix them up for dinner pretty quick. They'll be the last of the collards with this heat," she said, fanning herself with her hand.

I could only nod, noticing that Ginny looked lovely with dirt across her brow and sweat on her lip.

She looked me up and down and laughed. "Why did you change clothes? Don't you remember how dirty potters get?"

"Oh … I was pretty smelly," I said. "I was clearing out some branches and vines at the house. It looked like several tree branches were broken off in last winter's ice storm."

"I remember that. I couldn't get out for a week. They cancelled classes at school and we had dorm parties that lasted all day. By the end of the week, we were sick of each other." She snorted, then paused at the memory. "Well, come on in. Mr. John is taking a nap, but he'll be here soon, I'm sure. I can show you where everything is. Do you have anything in particular in mind to make?"

I gave a slight shake of my head, and Ginny opened the door and led me into the cool darkness of the shop. I breathed deeply and exhaled. I had forgotten the smell of a working studio … like a dry, dusty cornfield at the end of summer, a place returning to its beginnings.

Ginny set the collards on a stool and grabbed some bats off the shelf. A bucket of water and some sponges sat next to several wheels.

"Mr. John uses different wheels depending which one suits him that day. Sometimes he stands, or sits, and sometimes he even kneels. I can't do that yet," Ginny said, smiling. "I have to stand in order to get my weight over my shoulders. Working on the small pieces, I can sit, of course."

"Really?" I said. "He kneels? That sounds awfully difficult and uncomfortable."

"A potter doesn't use the clay to make it only do what he wants," came Mr. John's voice.

Ginny and I turned as Mr. John walked in.

"He has to yield to the clay," he continued. "The potter is in charge of the clay, yes, but the clay has a mind of its own. Some people think yielding is just giving in or giving up, but actually, yielding is also gaining and getting. As I yield to the clay, the clay responds and we grow together. Sometimes the clay responds with difficulty; that clay is best worked kneeling."

"Huh ..." I said. "I never learned that in my classes at school."

"Now you see why I am continuing to study under Mr. John," Ginny said. "They don't teach you the nuances of pottery at school." A small sigh escaped her lips.

"Why the sigh?" Mr. John asked.

"Oh ... I had another call from Daddy this afternoon. He just doesn't understand why I am here this summer. He thinks I need to be back home—under his thumb."

"Perhaps it is not his thumb, but his palm," Mr. John said, but left it at that. "So ... which wheel will you use today, Jack?"

"I guess I would like to sit," I answered. "I haven't thrown in a few years probably—not since college anyway. Sitting is how I learned at school."

Mr. John gestured toward a stool. I sat down and placed the bat into the posts, then wetted it down from the bucket. Ginny was already busy wedging the clay for me when Mr. John stopped her.

"The potter must start from the beginning, Ginny. Let Jack do his own wedging."

I sliced off a bit of clay just bigger than my fist and slammed it onto the tabletop. After a few blows I remembered the rhythm of wedging and began softening the clay, warming and aligning it with the rhythmic pounding. Once the clay had been wedged and the air bubbles knocked out, I started beating it into a ball. My fingers left small dimples in the plastic clay. Finally I took the ball over to the damp wheel and slapped it onto the middle of the bat.

Mr. John had the new electric wheels. In school we'd had to use the kick-pedal kind, combining the rhythm of our feet and the rotating of the clay. The thump-thump of the electric wheel reminded me of the washing machines at the laundry-mat where I took my clothes on Saturdays.

I began trying to center the clay, holding it carefully cupped in both hands. While dripping water over my clay to reduce the friction, I noticed Ginny struggling with her own clay. Mr. John was standing over her, guiding her hands.

"See, Ginny, place your palm over the clay and support it more. With your palm, Ginny," Mr. John said and then walked over to me.

Ginny's gaze followed Mr. John's back.

"So it is coming back to you, Jack," Mr. John said. "Centering is the most difficult part of throwing, you know. Be patient and yield to the clay. Eventually it will find where it needs to be."

Yield to the clay? How do you yield to something and still be in control of it?

Mr. John sounded like more of a guru than I remembered as a kid. I kept trying to center the lump of clay, and it continued to wobble to the left. More water, more pressure, more wobble.

I looked over at Mr. John working deftly on an already centered piece. He was coning it up and down like a pro. The slick clay glistened as it rose under the guidance of Mr. John. To my left I could hear Ginny exhale as she, too, began coning her piece of clay.

I tried for twenty minutes before the clay finally nestled into its sweet spot. I began coning the clay up and up until the tip of the cone popped off in my fingers. Mr. John walked by and stuck his finger into the side of the cone and knocked it off balance. A hot bolt of anger shot through me and I had a hard time not shouting.

"Why did you do that? I just got it going," I fumed.

"You are separating the clay from itself. Part of the potter's skill is to use all of the clay ... develop it all into a useful piece of art. Clay doesn't have to be perfectly centered to be beautiful, but separating it from itself destroys the opportunity to fully develop the clay."

I bit my tongue and Mr. John walked back to his wheel with a clean bat. Ginny was giggling and forming a small cup out of her clay. I tossed the destroyed clay into the recycle bucket and went back to wedging a new piece of clay.

This time I centered a little more quickly and started coning the clay into a perfect tower under my hands. My thumb pressed down gently and the clay began to form a wide base. *Perhaps a mug for Aunt Lily's morning coffee would be nice,* I thought. She was so right that I needed to go fishing this morning. Of course, how could I forget that it was Aunt Rose who asked me here in the first place? I would just have to make another mug.

"If I make two cups, could you attach handles and fire them for me?" I asked Ginny. "I can pay you for it. I thought it would be a nice present for the aunts for inviting me out this weekend."

"Yeah, I can, but why aren't you coming back to see them again?" she asked.

"It's really hard for me to get time off from work. I would have to come out on a Friday night and leave Sunday to get back. I just can't spare the time," I said, beginning to feel exasperated again as I remembered what it took to get away for this holiday weekend.

"Oh. Yeah, I can do it for you, but let me ask Mr. John how much we should charge."

Ginny finished forming her cup and then went out back to the kiln area where Mr. John was unloading a cooled kiln. I was working on the second cup when she returned.

"Mr. John says he can take care of the mugs for you if you can come by tomorrow and cut some firewood for him. The kiln takes a lot of wood and he has a show coming up in a couple of weeks."

"I can do that. No problem. Where is his show?"

"It's in Houston. He invited me to go along, but I'm going to stay here and keep the shop open instead. Sometimes he gets customers wandering through in the summer on their way to vacation in Atlanta."

"Well then, I'll see him tomorrow afternoon. Thanks."

I headed back to the house with dirt under my ragged nails and on my pants and shirt, but I felt clean and fresh. I had forgotten how much I enjoyed making ceramics. I had forgotten what it felt like to be whole. Maybe that was what Mr. John had been talking about. I wasn't using all my clay at home—*Home in Atlanta, that is.*

"Did you enjoy yourself?" Aunt Lily asked from the front porch.

Glancing up to the shady veranda, I smiled. There was really no need to answer. I took the steps two at a time and plopped down into the wicker chair near the door. The smell of fresh bread wafted through the screen door and I could hear Aunt Rose singing as she finished up dinner.

I jumped out of my seat. "Oh! I forgot the collards that Mrs. Hammond sent." I raced down to my Chevy. "Ginny sent these from Mrs. Hammond's garden," I said as I came back up the front stairs. "Will Aunt Rose have time to make them for dinner?" I asked Aunt Lily.

"She should," Aunt Lily said. "Take them on into the kitchen and see."

I carried the bundle of collards into the house and through the hallway, trying not to drop any dirt or dust on the carpet runner.

"Aunt Rose," I said as I walked into the kitchen, "I've got a little extra for you. Ginny sent collards over from Mrs. Hammond. She thought you could cook them up with dinner tonight."

"Oh, did she? That was awfully thoughtful of her. Ginny is a sweet girl from what I've seen." Aunt Rose wiped her hands on her apron front.

"Yes, she seems sweet, but it was Mrs. Hammond who sent the collards. Ginny just carried them over to me at the pottery studio."

Aunt Rose took the collards from my hands. I knew how easily the aunts could turn a simple gesture into a lifelong commitment.

"How was the pottery lesson? Were you able to relax with Mr. John?"

"Well, I'm not sure I would call Mr. John 'relaxing,' but I did enjoy the time to throw a little. I don't think I have thrown anything since college."

"That's such a shame. I remember Violet talking about your lessons at school. She hoped you would be a famous potter someday. I guess you like business more, huh?"

"Well, I wouldn't say that, but business is probably a better plan for me. Like I said, you can't feed a family on a potter's income." I shrugged.

"Doesn't seem like you are having time to find a family on your businessman's schedule," Aunt Rose said as she washed off the collards in the sink.

"Well, maybe someday I can do both. Needler and Newman employs some potters and artists to make items for our larger commercial buyers. It's mostly molds and prints, but at least I would have a little creative outlet." I half-smiled, pleading with her to accept that answer—or maybe I was pleading with myself to believe it.

Aunt Rose brushed a wisp of hair from her face with her arm, then asked, "So what did you make today?"

"It took me awhile to get back into it. Mr. John has some odd notions about clay," I said, hoping to not give away the surprise coffee mugs.

"Notions? Like what?"

"Well, it took forever to get my clay centered. Finally I was able to cone it—you know, where you start to make a hill out of the clay?"

"Mm-hm." Aunt Rose listened as she salted the collards in a pot of boiling water.

"Well, toward the end of my coning, a nubbin of clay popped off the top of the cone. It's pretty common actually, but Mr. John came by and threw my whole clay off center. He said if I didn't use all of the clay, I would be disrupting its purpose or something like that."

"Sounds right to me," Aunt Rose said. She nodded at me, then stirred butter and cream into the lima beans.

"Well, it wasn't something that the teachers at Bersher ever cared about," I grumbled.

Suddenly my relaxing afternoon was becoming annoying. I was just fine at Needler and Newman, and business was a good way to go. Even if I never got hired as a potter, I was doing well down in Atlanta, I convinced myself. I felt determined that everyone should recognize that I was right to be there.

I told Aunt Rose I would go clean up and headed upstairs to wash and change yet again.

And what does the LORD require of you? To act justly and to love mercy and to walk humbly with your God.
—Micah 6:8

CHAPTER 4

The house was bustling with activity when Mariam arrived. Marta's sister-in-law, Helena, was chopping cucumbers for the barley salad when Mariam entered the kitchen. Helena's daughters were sweeping out the upper room for the night's guests. Marta herself was stoking the fire in the clay oven when she saw Mariam seat herself on the kitchen floor.

"What are you doing sitting down, sister? I need you to knead the dough for one last rising. I want the bread to be extra soft for Elijah's old teeth."

"I have a sliver. Just a minute," Mariam said.

Marta came over to look at Mariam's foot. She took a needle out of her sleeve and picked the clay piece from Mariam's foot.

"There, all better now." Marta smiled.

Mariam relaxed and forgave her sister's insistence on perpetual work. Mariam realized she had been angry when anger had not been deserved. *These moods pass over like rain clouds on a sunny summer day,* she thought.

"How is Eleazar getting along?" Helena asked Mariam.

"He's fine. He is working on a lamp right now. It has tiny pricks to look like stars in the night sky. Abraham would be happy to have a lamp like that."

Mariam had a soft spot for Abraham, Jacob's brother and Helena's husband. His eyes were failing him and his work as a bookkeeper in Herod's palace was becoming difficult to continue. Abraham had not taken Marta as his wife like he should have, but Marta never complained about it. She knew, as Mariam did, that he could little afford another family with the inevitable blindness in his future.

Still, Abraham checked on Marta and her siblings every day. He let her keep the house and property to run a little tavern and inn so she could support herself. Someday perhaps there would be a husband for Marta, but for now she was doing well and Eleazar would soon be a tradesman potter. He would always help care for Marta. There would be no reason for her to go the way Mariam had chosen.

Determined to make the bread tender for Marta's guests, Mariam punched down the dough in the bread bowl and began kneading it all over again. Her anger subsided by the time she was patting the dough into a ball to be placed on the baking stone.

"Thank you," Marta said, giving Mariam a little squeeze. "Why don't you go in the upper room and visit with Deborah while I finish here?"

Mariam jerked her head back and looked at her sister. "Why is Deborah in the upper room?"

"I asked her to come help prepare for our dinner guests. She came in when you were kneading the dough and went right upstairs to work."

"She won't still be here when the guests arrive, will she?"

Marta furrowed her eyebrows. "Well … yes. Why?"

Mariam grunted. "Isn't it bad enough that you and I have to help serve? Do we really have to have the neighborhood freak attend the guests? What will people think?"

Now Marta's eyes went wide. "They will think that we are kind to share our good fortune with them by preparing dinner. Mama and Abba are gone, Mariam. You must remember that you are no longer a pampered princess at Herod's table."

"Oh, I remember alright," Mariam whispered loud enough for Marta to hear.

Then she stomped out of the kitchen and headed up the stairs. Helena's young girls chased each other down the stairs and bumped into Mariam, not at all improving her mood. At the top landing Mariam drew up short. She realized she was doing it again: turning sunshine into storm. A tear trickled from the corner of her eye.

Taking a deep breath and swiping hard at the tear, Mariam entered the upper guest room. Deborah was banging pillows together to dust and fluff them. The room was neatly arranged with pillows and rugs placed around the walls of the room. Deborah had placed some flowers near the open window. Candles were waiting in a pile to be placed in the candelabras in each corner. Low benches for the food waited for the night's guests.

"Oh, there you are. Is your foot better?" Deborah asked.

"Yes, much. Thank you," Mariam said, then did her best to give a sincere smile.

"Marta said Nathaniel is coming tonight too." Deborah blushed and looked away.

Well, here is something, thought Mariam. *Deborah likes Nathaniel. Does she really hope to be loved in return? He is a man of land; he would never stoop low enough to marry the likes of her.*

"Yes, I believe he is," Mariam said. "You said he is healed?"

"Yes! Abba said Nathaniel's legs are clear and whole. There is not even scarring left from the sores."

Mariam began placing candles in the holders. "So the springs were good for Nathaniel—a blessing from the Lord."

"Not the springs," Deborah said. "Abba said Nathaniel met a man in Bethsaida. The man has a gift from God. He heals! He healed several people of leprosy, like Nathaniel, and another man who had a lame leg is able to walk again."

"Hmm. What kind of man is he, this healer, I wonder?" Mariam said. Her mind recalled the magicians and healers that sometimes stayed at the inn. They were often worth some extra attention.

Marta appeared in the doorway then and said, "Can you carry the bread to the baker's, Mariam? I have too much in the stove now, and I won't have time for it to finish baking before the guests arrive."

"Yes, of course," Mariam said.

Soon enough Mariam carried five balls of dough over to Baker Street and dropped them off. The warm aroma of baking bread filled her with a sense of hope. Perhaps the dinner tonight would be fun. The men would talk of business and their travels, and maybe she would hear some scrap of gossip.

And then it hit her.

Mariam's shoulders lifted and a smile sparkled in her eyes as she mused that some of the men would be travelers tonight, not local know-it-alls. Maybe one of them would notice her serving them and take an interest.

She left the baker's and rushed home. She had better wash her face and find a clean head covering.

The blood rushed to Mariam's cheeks as she realized what she was doing. It was up to Eleazar to find a husband for Mariam, but it couldn't hurt to put forth a little effort tonight.

*The purpose of life is not to be happy.
It is to be useful, to be honorable, to be
compassionate, to have it make some
difference that you have lived and lived well.*
—Ralph Waldo Emerson

CHAPTER 5

There's a community picnic on Monday," Aunt Lily commented as she passed the butter-topped rolls. "Will you be able to attend before you have to drive back to Atlanta?"

"Ohhh, I'm not sure. Traffic will be bad and I don't want to head back too late." I didn't relish the idea of spending the afternoon with a lot of old people who would reminisce about Mama.

"I bet Ginny will be there." Aunt Lily winked as she grinned at me.

I glanced sideways at her. "I'm sure Ginny and all of you will have a fine time whether I make it or not."

"True." Aunt Lily raised her brows. "But it would be nicer if you stayed too. We invited

Sam to come over, but he said he was going to visit your daddy."

"It will be good for Joe and Sam to spend the day together," Aunt Rose said before looking at me. "Maybe you should drive over to Rome before you head back. It would make your mama so sad to know the three of you are losing touch."

As I tried to think of a reply that didn't sound lame, Aunt Lily plowed ahead: "You could stay for lunch and then drive over to Rome for a short visit. The traffic won't be too bad until after supper. Then you could have the best of it all: us, a picnic, Ginny, and your dad and brother."

Aunt Rose let out a frustrated sigh and then rolled her eyes. "Would you leave the boy alone? He has bigger things to think of than Ginny. Just leave him alone to rest awhile." She looked at me again. "Tomorrow after church you can set the hammock up for the summer and try it out, Jack. I'll make some sweet tea and cookies, and you'll have a nice nap."

I couldn't help but smile. Cookies solved everything for Aunt Rose. "That sounds great, Aunt Rose, but I told Mr. John I would go over and chop some firewood for him. He uses a wood-burning kiln and needs to have a stockpile of firewood."

"Well, that's mighty nice of you," Aunt Rose said.

"Sounds like a very 'Ginny-erous' thing to do," Aunt Lily said, then chuckled.

"Lily!" Aunt Rose said.

"How about I help with the dishes?" I offered.

The next morning I woke with a knot in my forearms and my hands cramping into balls. It had been too long since I'd worked those muscles, and I knew I would really be in trouble that afternoon. Actually I hadn't worked many muscles at all since being at Needler and Newman. I could lift a phone to my ear with ease, but everything else was getting soft. In Rome back in the day, I had kept limber playing ball with the guys on the river levee or hiking upstream to catch some fish. I missed the freedom that Atlanta seemed to have arrested.

I walked through the dim hall toward the bathroom and listened to the kitchen noises the aunts were making downstairs. This house was awfully big for just the two of them. I wondered why they'd never married and had families. Of course, Mama moved away to have her family, so they might not have stayed to fill the house even if they had married.

I put on my nice slacks and a clean dress shirt. I had forgotten to pack a tie, but maybe since it was getting warm outside, it would be overlooked. After slapping on a little aftershave, I jogged down the back stairs to the kitchen.

I inhaled deeply. "Mmmm, coffee smells delicious," I said as I sat down at the polished old table.

"You don't smell so bad yourself," Aunt Lily said as she kissed the top of my head.

The Paradox Community Church started early as far as churches go. Sunday might be a day of rest, but the Lord meant you to rest sitting up in church; leastwise that was local opinion. The church in Atlanta started at 11:00, and I always enjoyed sleeping later and taking my time over a couple cups of coffee. At least in Paradox I was assured a big breakfast of bacon and eggs and the last of Aunt Lily's peach cobbler. I never had a breakfast like that in Atlanta.

"It's a good thing I'm cutting firewood this afternoon," I said between bites of cobbler. "My muscles are aching from making pottery yesterday. I'm really out of shape."

"A man needs to work out his frustrations with some hard work," Aunt Lily said. "Daddy always said, 'You can tell what's on a man's mind by the muscles in his back.' I didn't really understand what he meant until I saw your daddy at the hospital with Violet." Her voice trailed off at the end.

Aunt Rose cleared her throat. "You better run up and get your tie before we head out."

"Umm, I forgot to pack one." I offered my best sheepish smile. "Do you really think anyone will notice?"

"Only everyone there! Heaven's sake, Jack!" Aunt Rose said. "I think there is one in some of Daddy's things in the back-room closet. I'll go look."

"I'll come help," I said, and we climbed the stairs.

Hidden in the far corner bedroom was a closet filled with musty boxes and crates and a distinct mothball odor. Hanging from the back of the door were some ties and belts that had belonged to Grandpappy. He had been a big man and the assortment of ties all reached well below my beltline.

"Here's a bowtie," Aunt Rose said as she held up a black piece of fabric.

"I don't know how to tie one of those," I said. "Maybe I just better go without. It will be less obvious."

"To whom? Here, I'll tie it for you," Aunt Rose said. She grabbed my shirt collar and flicked the tie around my neck.

No sense arguing, I thought.

I drove us to church and parked in the grassy field beside the old wooden-framed building. When I was growing up in Rome, we attended the Episcopal church on the corner of East First Street and Fourth Avenue. The massive stone structure always had engaged my imagination, and the sun shining in through the stained glass windows held my attention between the songs and the sermon.

But the Paradox Community Church was never so austere in my memory. Mama and the aunts would march me and Sam toward the middle of the church and turn into the left pew. Then the adults would shake hands with everyone nearby, and they would all comment on how much we had grown. Mr. Norris would give Mama a hug and then pass both me and Sam a piece of Wrigley's gum. He always had a couple packs in his shirt pocket for the kids.

We would sing and pray, the preacher would stand and give a sermon, and then we would be dismissed with a final prayer. At last we would be allowed to run outside with the other children and swing on the rope hanging from the old live oak in the back where the outhouse stood.

I wondered if the rope still hung back there as Aunt Rose and Aunt Lily held my hands and shuffled us down to the familiar seat. We sidled in near Mr. John and the Hammonds, who scooted over a bit for us. The hard wooden pew was worn and smooth from a hundred years of scooting over to make room for more souls.

"How you doing, Jack?" Mr. John whispered with a smile as the welcoming announcements began.

"Just fine, thanks. I'll be over after lunch to chop your wood."

"Good, good. Take your time and enjoy these ladies' cooking, though."

We turned our attention to the front as the song leader called out the first song. The old hymns reverberated off the timeworn pine walls and filled me with a peace I hadn't felt lately. My mind drifted over the past few years. I smiled to myself as I thought, *Mama would have liked to be here today.* She always enjoyed seeing her old friends, and I knew she would have looked forward to lunch back at the farmhouse. Having Daddy and Sam here would make it complete. Aunt Rose was right: Mama would be terribly disappointed to know the three of us weren't keeping up with each other.

Mr. John went forward and closed out the service with a prayer. We stood up, and the aunts gathered their purses and gloves. I slid out of the pew and into the middle aisle.

"Oh, Jack, there you are!" came a female voice from behind me. I turned around to hear, "Mrs. Hammond told me you were at the store yesterday. Nice tie."

It was Christy. She and I went to school together over in Rome. Christy's mama came from Paradox just like my mama, and sometimes we crossed paths there as kids. She was friendly enough, but she always seemed to have a superior air about her. I never quite felt comfortable or at ease around her.

"Hi, Christy. Yeah, I came up for the holiday to stay with my aunts. How have you been?" I asked, biting the inside of my lip.

"Oh, I'm fine. I'm staying with Granny while she recovers from pneumonia. She got laid pretty low this winter during the ice storm and she hasn't perked up very quickly."

"I'm sorry to hear that," I said. "Well, I have to go now. Aunt Rose and Aunt Lily have lunch started back at the house. Maybe I'll see you around."

"Are you coming to the picnic tomorrow?" Christy asked, stepping forward and holding my arm. "I'll be there with a batch of my famous lemon cookies."

"Maybe. If so, I'll see you there," I said and then fell in behind Aunt Lily at the exit.

The silence in the car lasted about thirty seconds, just long enough to get out of the grass lot and onto the road.

"So you were talking to Christy," Aunt Lily said. "She's been helping with her grandmother this spring. Did she say if she would be at the picnic tomorrow?"

"Who, her grandmother?" I asked, trying to divert the conversation. "I don't think so. Christy said she has been quite down with pneumonia. Really nice of Christy to come and help."

I cringed as soon as I said it. I had given Aunt Lily the opening she needed.

"Yes, she is a nice girl, and you know very well that I was asking if Christy is coming to the picnic, not her grandmother. See? You ought to go too. It would be good for you to catch up with old friends."

"I suppose so, but I was starting to think about heading into Rome and visiting Daddy and Sam on my way back to Atlanta." I hadn't really considered it, but I would say anything to not see Christy.

"I think that is a wise decision, Jack," Aunt Rose piped up from the backseat.

"Yes, but there is time for both the picnic *and* a visit," Aunt Lily said.

"Lily," Aunt Rose warned, and that was that. The drive home ended in quiet reflection.

Lunch was another feast, and I decided to take a little nap before heading over to help Mr. John. Sunday afternoon naps were a tradition in our house growing up. Mama would finish up the dishes and then head into the bedroom with the shades drawn. Daddy would read the Sunday paper and lose consciousness in his armchair about halfway through Section D. He was never much for fashion or home décor. Sam and I would be left alone to do whatever we chose as long as we stayed quiet. Usually we snuck out the back door and gathered with the kids at the Little League field near the river's levee.

Now that I was a working man, I understood the lure of the Sunday afternoon nap. Back in Atlanta I usually left the dishes in the sink for later and plopped down on the couch with a game on the radio. Today I didn't have the radio playing, but the insects humming outside my open window had the same hypnotic effect and in no time I was snoozing.

I woke around 2:30 to find that Aunt Rose and Aunt Lily had retired to their rooms for their afternoon rest. I discovered a plate of cookies left on the table, and grabbed a couple before I slipped out the door, being careful not to let it slam behind me. I enjoyed the warm sunlit walk to Mr. John's studio. I wondered if anyone would be heading over to Powhatan Beach to swim that afternoon.

"Good afternoon, Jack," Mr. John said, sitting in a lawn chair under the shade of a holly tree. "How was your lunch?"

"Oh, it was mighty good. They're going to have me spoiled by the time I get back to work." I laughed.

"Nothing like good food to fill the belly, and it was good food for the soul this morning at church. What a fine day." Mr. John paused as I stopped next to him and looked around the yard. "Work is good for the soul too. Don't you think?"

"I suppose, but it sure isn't as good as a Sunday afternoon rest."

"Don't you like your work, Jack?" Mr. John tilted his head and eyed me.

"Mm, yes, I like seeing what other artists are creating, and I especially like that I get to buy ceramics for my company. I really enjoy good pottery." I paused, then said, "I just wish I had more opportunities to do some of the creating myself."

He gave a little smile. "Creating is what life is all about. We are constantly forming, molding, and reshaping this life that God has given us. Being a potter and working with clay is a special privilege. It's special both for the potter and for the clay."

"What do you mean?"

"The potter has an idea of what he wants to make. It gives him pleasure to cut into the cool clay, wedge it, and prepare it, but then especially to craft it. The clay has a purpose too. The clay cannot be forced into what it was not intended to be. It eagerly waits for its fulfillment. The potter and the clay work together, creating a thing of splendor and purpose. It is a beautiful symbiotic relationship."

"I hadn't thought about it that way before. I guess there is a special bond between the two. Anyway, I better get that wood cut for you."

"No hurry, Jack. I have enough items to show in Houston if I don't get more done in time. But since you offered, the axe is in the back of the shed. You'll see the logs that need splitting there too." Mr. John's eyes crinkled when he spoke.

"I'd like to see some of your work if I have time," I called as I walked away toward the shed.

The old axe was wedged into a short piece of pine. I grabbed the smooth, worn handle and gave it a twist. The logs had been cut with a chainsaw earlier. The smell of pinewood and the damp earth behind the shed was refreshing after my dusty walk over to Mr. John's. I split logs and piled them near the kiln most of the afternoon. It felt good to let my mind wander while my muscles worked out the kinks of worry and stress.

What did Mr. John mean by asking if I liked my work? He seemed to know something, or to want to know something, but he didn't push me. Was my irritation about work obvious to everyone, or was it just a coincidence that Mr. John asked about liking work?

Didn't I like my work?

I was doing well. I did land that client in Santa Barbara, and now I had some new prospects in North Carolina. I had talked the company into looking at more decorative pieces, like the jewelry headed to New York. Yes, I did like my work. I was just feeling awkward being back here and not having Mama around; that was all.

"Need some sweet tea?" Ginny walked around the corner of the shed, startling me. "Sorry," she said, handing me a cold glass.

I slammed the axe into a log and accepted the glass with a nod. Sitting down on an upright stump, I looked Ginny over. I had noticed her before, of course, but now she seemed different, pensive.

"Didn't see you at church this morning," I said.

"No, I borrowed Mr. John's truck and went into Rome. I go to the Methodist church there."

I smiled. "That figures. I went to the Episcopal church when I was growing up, but in high school I always went to the Methodist Youth Fellowship because they had all the pretty girls."

Ginny's cheeks pinked a little as she grinned and took a seat in the grass. "Sometimes I go to church here in Paradox, but I was meeting a friend for lunch. Her family invited me over a couple weeks ago. They know my daddy, and he wanted a report on me." She shrugged. "It was a good meal, though."

I decided to probe a bit: "You're afraid of your daddy."

"No, but he bothers me. He wants me to have a normal profession for a woman, be a teacher or a nurse. Of course the best thing in his opinion is to be a farmer's wife—end of story. He just can't seem to understand my need to be a potter. I just feel whole when I am making something." She shrugged again. "I don't know how to explain that to Daddy. So I avoid him, or worse, I argue with him."

"Sounds familiar." I sighed before I realized it.

"Your parents wanted you to be something else?" She looked up at me from her spot on the grass.

I took another sip, wanting to slow down and think before I said too much. I loved my father, and I didn't want to give the wrong impression. "We had a few rows," I said. "It wasn't much. Daddy was right that pottery is not a job that pays the bills. It was better for me to get a business degree. And it's worked out well. I still get to deal with pottery and ceramics." I tipped my head and half-smiled, hoping to convince Ginny—and myself—that I was happy.

But Ginny furrowed her eyebrows and asked, "You wanted to be a potter too? Then why didn't you do what you wanted?"

"I compromised with Daddy," I said. "I got a business degree so I can support a family someday, and I minored in ceramics so I could still study what I enjoyed. Not that I didn't enjoy business. I did—I do, but ... well, you know, it isn't quite the same." My voice trailed off as I realized what I was saying and how it must sound.

"I guess it is different for a guy, but it doesn't seem right that you can't keep on creating pottery and running a business too. Daddy hasn't forced me to change majors, though, since he says college is just an excuse to find a rich husband, anyway."

"Humph," I snorted.

"Oh, I don't mean it that way. I'm not looking for a rich husband, or a husband, or anything. I just mean my daddy doesn't see any reason for a country girl to go to college." Now she was pink all the way to her ears.

"It's okay." I laughed. "I know what you mean. My father was the same way, always preparing me for finding the right girl and getting married. I guess he just loved Mama so much, he wanted that for me and Sam."

"Sam?"

"Sam's my little brother. He's a teacher over in Rockmart. Do you have brothers and sisters?"

"One of each, but they're both a good bit older. My sister already has three kids, and my brother is getting married at the end of summer. That keeps Mama and Daddy from bothering me too much about it." Ginny grinned.

I drank down the last of the tea and handed the glass back to Ginny. "Thanks for the break, but I better get back to this before Mr. John sees me sitting around."

Ginny took the empty glass and gave a small wave. "I'll go check on Mr. John."

Half an hour later I had the logs stacked up neatly. I left the axe inside the shed and wiped the sweat off my brow with the red hanky in my pocket. Walking back around the shed, I bumped into Christy.

"Well, hello, Jack. Mr. John told me you were out back chopping wood. What a way to spend your holiday weekend." She smiled.

"Hi, Christy."

I wasn't sure if she was here for me or just passing through. I shuffled my feet and ran the back of my hand across my forehead.

"I was out for an afternoon walk and stopped in to talk with Mr. John," Christy said.

"Oh. I was chopping wood for him to pay for some pottery I was making yesterday. Well … it was good to see you."

"Good to see you too." Christy paused. "I'm still up for more walking. Do you mind if I walk back with you? I can cross over the old Sidler place on my way back to Granny's."

"Uh, yeah, that'd be fine, but I need to stop in and talk to Mr. John a minute."

I walked into the pottery shop through the store's side door. A little bell tinkled as I pushed the door closed. I was struck again by the smell of moist dust and wood smoke.

"Hi, Jack," Ginny called from the back of the shop. "A woman was looking for you a minute ago. She headed out back."

"She found me. She said she was visiting Mr. John. Is he around?"

Ginny smiled. "He's in the workshop glazing a few pieces. Go on in."

I glanced at a few of the plates and vases displayed neatly on the shelves as I walked toward the back of the shop. Mr. John was standing at a bench applying glaze to some bisque ware.

"Hi, Mr. John. I finished chopping the wood."

"Thank you, Jack. That will be a big help. Come look at my work. Do you have time?"

"Sure. Christy is waiting outside, but I have a little time, I'm sure."

Mr. John nodded and smiled. "Yes, she was in here looking for you a bit ago. I think she is lonely staying with her grandmother all this time."

"She told me after church today that her granny has been sick, but I thought she was here to talk with you."

"Maybe. We do talk sometimes. She usually walks over on Sundays and visits awhile, but today I got the impression she wanted to see you more than she did me."

I walked over to where Mr. John was working.

"These vases will be in my Houston show," he said. "Thanks again for helping with the wood. It will take a lot to fire up the kiln for these."

Four-foot-tall vases lined the bench. They looked like elegant trees standing erect in an orchard. Designs had been punched out of them to create an illusion of branches and leaves.

"Wow, Mr. John. These are amazing! Do you have any finished that I can see?"

"In the shop are a few, but you know each one is special. I can't bring myself to make the same design each time. Even the glaze helps create a unique finish to all of them." Mr. John breathed deeply and looked sideways at his work.

Ginny came in and said, "Whew, boy! You need a bath." She crinkled her nose as she walked up to us.

"Sorry," I said, feeling my cheeks turn a little red. "They always say wood warms twice: the first time when you cut it and the second when you burn it."

"There is a third warmth, you know," Mr. John said. "It warms your heart by giving beauty." He gestured toward all of the pottery sitting on the bench.

"You're right there," I said. "Will you be able to get the mugs over to my aunts?"

He nodded. "Ginny can run them by when they are ready. Go on and enjoy your visit."

I walked back out into the sunlight and saw Christy sitting in the lawn chair under the holly where I had left Mr. John earlier.

"Sorry I took so long. Evidently I don't smell so good, so maybe you better not walk with me," I said as I got closer.

"I'm used to stinky men. Remember, I have brothers." She smiled and rose from the chair.

We walked back to the aunts' house, enjoying the shady spots and the light breeze.

Christy was definitely lonely with her granny. She had been working at Pepperell Mills in town until last winter, but her parents thought she could be more helpful in Paradox. She missed town and seeing other young people.

"I do hope you'll come to the picnic tomorrow," she said, grabbing my arm. "It would be so nice to catch up some more."

The house was in view now. "I might. I haven't decided yet. I feel like I ought to go visit Daddy and Sam on my way back to Atlanta."

"Sam is in Rome this weekend? John Brown! I miss everything out here. Well, try to stay for a little while anyway ... please?"

"Maybe. I'll see you later." I waved and walked up the small lane to the house.

Why do you laugh?
Change the name and the story is told of you.
—Horace

CHAPTER 6

Mariam considered it a personal hardship that her father had died before making a match for her, his younger daughter. All of Mariam's childhood friends were already married and had children of their own. Their excitement at being in charge of a household, of belonging to a husband, of caring for children was not something Mariam could share. Eleazar seemed not to even notice that Mariam was of age. So far he didn't even seem to be aware of her "work," though Marta had started asking uncomfortable questions.

At least I don't have a deformity like Deborah, Mariam thought. *Surely someone will want me and say something to Eleazar.*

This thought renewed her heart and put a purpose in her step as she made her way back to the house from the bakery. Soon enough Mariam bounced into the kitchen.

"Can I help with anything else?" she asked Marta.

"Some more travelers just came by. Can you restock the woodpile while I see what they need?"

"Of course." Mariam gathered an armload of logs behind the tavern, still smiling to herself all the while.

Marta walked into the courtyard. Two men sat on a bench under the trellis, one's shoulders sloped and tired, the other engaged in passionate argument. Marta approached them with slow steps. She had never grown accustomed to speaking openly to men.

"May I ... help you?" Marta said, hoping it was loud enough for them to hear her.

The passionate man startled from his thoughts and offered Marta a half-smile.

"I was telling my friend here how good it would be if God would send Messiah now. I hate the Romans and the hold they have over our people."

Marta nodded. "I understand." And then she moved right to business: "Will you need a room?" *Never know whom you can trust,* she reminded herself.

"Messiah is here, I am sure. But for now we wait," the tired-looking man said to the boisterous one. Then, turning to Marta, he continued, "Yes, we will need a room and meals. We are expecting several friends in a couple of days. Are you able to manage a larger crowd?"

"I can feed as many as you pay for," Marta said, then smiled. "Beds are not as easy to come by, but I have often provided for more than we had room for. The Lord always provides." Marta looked down respectfully.

"We have heard you live alone," the tired man said.

Marta felt her body tense and she chose her words with care: "My kinsman Abraham works for Herod. He is here every night. Do you wish to speak with him?" Still the truth ... but clothed in veils for safety.

"No, no, we don't need to speak with him," the tired man said. "We bring our peace on your establishment. My name is Thaddeus and this is Simon." He gestured toward the other man. "There will be about twenty men in our group, but we are accustomed to sleeping in many kinds of places. Whatever you can provide will be gratefully accepted." Thaddeus smiled at her.

"There is a party here this evening. Will you be joining us for the evening meal?"

"Yes, if you can manage so soon," Simon spoke up.

"Certainly. My brother, Eleazar, will be home from work soon. He will visit with you in the courtyard. Please rest here awhile. I will send my sister to wash your feet," Marta said and then backed away.

"Thank you," both men said as they settled on the bench in the shade of the lone olive tree—and then began their bickering all over again.

Mariam was sweeping up wood chips when Marta entered the kitchen. "Did you get the strangers taken care of?" she asked Marta.

"Yes, I think so. They will be joining us for dinner upstairs, and then for the night as well. They have a large group that will be meeting them in a couple of days. It appears the Lord is smiling on us again." Marta's face brightened as she spoke.

Perhaps he will smile on me as well, Mariam thought. Then she hummed to herself as she started sweeping again. Marta stirred the barley salad and began cutting up the purple-and-ebony eggplants.

"Hello, sister!" called Eleazar, striding through the portico.

Mariam looked up at the brother who was now nearly a man. His jaw was square and his chest and shoulders were broad.

"Shalom, Eleazar," Marta said. "And how was work today? Mariam says you are making a beautiful lamp."

"Yes, with stars to light the night sky like Father Abraham's children," he said.

Eleazar had always been a happy boy, full of life and fun. Even the death of their parents could not keep him down for long. It was his idea to be apprenticed to John after Jacob's death. He needed to create and be busy, he had said. It was fortuitous that John had recently returned to his pottery shop. He had been gone for so long in Cairo that Marta had thought he would never return.

"And who is the lamp for?" Marta inquired.

"For anyone who needs light, of course, sister." Eleazar winked. "When will the guests arrive? I would like to go visit Matthew if there is time."

"The dinner guests will be here in about an hour, but we have some extra travelers this evening. I told them you would visit when you arrived And—Oh my heavens!" Marta said. "Mariam, I told them a while ago you would wash their feet. Quick, take a washbasin and some towels. I was so caught up in preparing dinner, I completely forgot."

"Why do I have to wash their smelly feet?" Mariam whined, but Marta's warning glance stopped her short. She took the basin and a pitcher of water and headed out to the courtyard.

The men appeared to be sleeping on the bench under the tree. Mariam walked slowly in order to get a good look at them. They were dusty and travel weary, but they looked young and healthy. Mariam approached quietly and knelt at their feet. Lifting the heavy pitcher of water, she poured a stream into the basin. The noise of the water made the men stir.

"You must be the inn keeper's sister," one of the men said. "I am Thaddeus and this is Simon."

"Shalom. My name is Mariam, and the innkeeper, as you called her, is my sister, Marta. She asked me to refresh you. May I?" Mariam asked as she reached for Thaddeus's feet.

"Yes, thank you." Thaddeus lifted his robes to his calves and placed his feet in the water. He sighed deeply and then asked, "There is a party tonight?"

"Yes."

"Is it a celebration?" Simon asked.

"No, it is just a dinner party. Marta is known for her good cooking, and often the men eat here when they have things to discuss."

You would think one of them would notice two unmarried women and want to do something about it, Mariam thought, but changed the subject instead: "Where do you come from?"

"Our group is from all over the country," Simon said. "Several of them will be here in a day or so."

"They are traveling down from Capernaum," Thaddeus said.

"Really?" Mariam said, not looking up. "One of the men who will be at dinner has just returned from there. He has a story to tell this evening."

"Then we shall enjoy our dinner all the more," Simon said as Mariam moved over to wash his feet.

Eleazar walked up then. "Shalom. I am Marta's brother, Eleazar. Did I hear you say you are from Capernaum?"

"Shalom," Thaddeus answered back. "No, our friends will be arriving from Capernaum. We have come from Emmaus."

"You will be welcome at our table; the conversation may please you," Eleazar said, his tone getting more serious with each word.

Mariam glanced up at Eleazar. *What did he mean by that?* she wondered.

"Oh? What will the discussion be about?" Thaddeus asked.

Eleazar gave a quick grunt, then said, "We are tired of the Romans. They took Marta's husband by force and then he was killed in the fall of the Tower of Siloam. Tonight we will be discussing ways to rid ourselves of their filth."

"We are familiar with such discussions," Simon said. "We may have some news to offer encouragement."

Mariam slowly rose from the ground and backed away from the men as they continued talking. She poured the water around the tree and walked back to the kitchen. She didn't know what Eleazar was getting into, and she wasn't sure what these men were up to either. Why would such a large group of them be traveling? And why would they be meeting here—in Bethany? *We certainly don't need any more trouble,* Mariam thought as her hands began to tremble. *We have lived through enough curses for three lifetimes.*

"Shalom, Mariam," John called from the portico. "Are you alright?"

"Oh! John ..." Mariam put her hand to her chest. "There are strangers here who will be having a group join them in another day or so. Eleazar said tonight's discussion is about the Romans. Do you think it is safe to have these men stay with us? There might be trouble."

"'The name of the LORD is a fortified tower; the righteous run to it and are safe,'" John said, quoting from the Holy Scriptures. "Do not judge trouble before it shows itself, Mariam." John cleared his throat. "The pot has no choice but to hold what is poured into it, but you and I are different. We have the option of what we hold within ourselves. I notice that lately you have been holding much within your pot that you should not."

"What? What do you mean?" Mariam looked away from John.

"Nothing that you do not understand, sweet girl," John replied. "Now ... where is Marta? I wanted to speak with her."

"She is probably readying the sleeping quarters. We have more guests tonight."

"I will wait in the courtyard," John responded and walked away.

Mariam wondered how much John knew.

God employs several translators; some pieces are translated by age, some by sickness, some by war, some by justice.
—John Donne

CHAPTER 7

I changed back into the shirt I wore driving up to Paradox and headed downstairs. I hadn't planned on needing so many changes of clothing for just one weekend. Turning around the base of the banister, I bumped into Aunt Lily.

"Jack, you startled me! I didn't hear you come back."

"I needed to change again. I didn't think you would want to see me just yet. Ginny said I smelled pretty bad."

"Ginny, huh? I thought I saw Christy walking across the fields a minute ago. Maybe you just missed each other."

"No, actually we walked back from Mr. John's together, but Ginny was the one who told me I stunk."

"I guess she doesn't beat around the bush." Aunt Lily laughed. "I like her. Did she say anything about the picnic tomorrow?"

"No, but Christy was asking me to go," I said as we walked into the kitchen.

I took a glass out of the cupboard and filled it with some ice water. The afternoon's work had made me thirsty, and I needed some way to distract Aunt Lily from the conversation.

"Is there any peach cobbler left over? I'm starving."

"No, you ate it all for breakfast, young man," Aunt Lily said. "I think Rose has some cookies hidden away for you, though. She was making some for you to take back to Atlanta and some to give your daddy and Sam."

"Lily," Aunt Rose said as she walked into the kitchen, "you couldn't keep a secret if it was locked up in your bureau. The cookies are packed in tins in the Frigidaire," she huffed.

I found the old butter cookie tins in the back of the fridge and pulled out the top one. It was filled with homemade oatmeal-and-raisin cookies. I grabbed a few while Aunt Rose poured some milk for me.

"Dinner will be ready in an hour, so don't fill up too much," Aunt Rose said.

"The hammock is in the woodshed if you want to set it up now and rest a bit," Aunt Lily said.

"That shounds wonderful," I said, my mouth full of cookie.

I gulped down the last of the milk and then headed outside. I walked to the end of the backyard and pulled on the big wooden doors. The hinges screeched as they gave way. It sounded like the shed had not been opened in a long, long time. I found the hammock stand covered with a tarp, probably put there several years ago based on the amount of dust on the heavy brown cover. The hammock netting was wrapped around the wooden stand.

I threw the covering off and dragged the stand out of the shed. The pin oaks near the porch would be the perfect place for a rest, so I headed that direction with it. Aunt Lily came out on the porch and offered her advice:

"We always put it out on the porch, so we can enjoy rainy afternoons. We haven't had it out in several years, though ... three, I guess. No, it's been four years. The last time we used the hammock, your mama and daddy were here. Joe helped Violet get settled in it and then he sat on the veranda with her. It seems like yesterday," she said, her voice softening.

"Would you like it on the porch? I was going to put it under the pin oaks, but I can put it up there." I started in her direction.

"No, no, you put it where you think best. Rose and I won't be using it anyway, most likely."

I nodded and then settled it under the shade. Aunt Lily helped me hook in the end pieces. A few of the threads had been frayed by mice, and I was a little unsure it would hold me.

"Don't be ridiculous." Aunt Lily frowned. "Climb on in and have a good nap. I'll go help Rose finish up dinner."

The sun was sinking low when Aunt Rose called from the screen door: "Dinner is ready, Jack. Come wash up!"

The muscles in my back and shoulders were already seizing up from my afternoon at Mr. John's. I slowly slid my legs over the side of the hammock and stretched out the stiffness in my arms. Suddenly one end of the netting gave way and I ended up on the cool grass. Laughter rang out behind me.

Christy was walking through the backyard. I turned red and felt the irritation rising in my chest. What was she doing here?

"I brought some of my lemon cookies over since you might not be at the picnic tomorrow, but it looks like maybe you are too heavy and shouldn't eat them." She giggled.

"The hammock has been in the shed for so long, the mice have eaten through it. I told Aunt Lily it wouldn't hold," I huffed.

"Let me help you up," Christy said, extending her hand.

Aunt Rose was back at the screen door now. "Christy? Is that you? How's your granny today?"

"She's fine, Miss Rose. She ate a big dinner and headed to bed about an hour ago. I thought I'd bring over some lemon cookies for

Jack since he'll miss them tomorrow at the picnic."

"Well, that's awfully nice of you. We're just getting ready for dinner ourselves. Will you join us?" Aunt Rose asked.

"No, ma'am. I ate with Granny. I don't want to intrude. I just brought these for Jack." She held out a small paper bag.

I took the bag from her just as Aunt Lily came to the door as well.

"Christy," Aunt Lily said, "you come on over and join us for some tea anyway. Your granny's in bed by now and you could use some company."

"Well, some company would be nice. Thank you."

I wasn't sure why Christy had really come— but it wasn't to deliver cookies. Sometimes during dinner she looked at me like she was thinking really hard about something, but mostly she talked and laughed with the aunts and me and seemed to be enjoying herself. She joined us on the porch for ice cream after dinner.

The lightning bugs soon made their nightly appearance. I had forgotten how much I enjoyed their flickering glow. First they sputtered to life under the shady oaks and in the higher grasses along the border to the Sidlers' fields. Then I could see them crawling out of the grass near the porch and winging their tiny lights into the air. A splash near the riverbank reminded us that it was time for the beavers to take their nightly swim.

"It's so peaceful here," I murmured, breaking into the women's conversation.

"What's that, Jack?" Aunt Lily asked.

"Sorry. I was just thinking how peaceful it is here. I don't think there is any peace and quiet in Atlanta," I said, then laughed.

"What I wouldn't give for a week in Atlanta," Christy said. "I have had enough of peace and quiet. Even Rome would be a welcome change after this spring. I miss hanging out in Hardee's Café having a coke with the gang." She sighed.

"I know it has been a long ordeal for you, Christy," Aunt Rose said as she rocked in her wicker chair, "but your granny appreciates it so much. She was so worried about having to leave her home and stay with your daddy and mama in Rome. An old body likes to feel at home."

"I know ... I know, Miss Rose, and I am glad that I can help, but I feel like I am being left out of everything. I would have loved to catch up with Sam this weekend. I only saw him a little bit when he was here last time," she said, then paused and glanced at me. "Say, maybe I could ride in with you tomorrow and Daddy could bring me back out in the evening? Granny was going to try to attend the picnic anyway, so people will be there to keep an eye on her."

"Well, uh … I suppose I could, sure. I don't know what plans Sam and Daddy have, though," I said.

"Why don't you call and see, Jack?" Aunt Lily asked.

I cringed at the thought of spending the hour-long ride alone with Christy, but it would mean a diversion when I was with Daddy and Sam. Perhaps her incessant talking would ease the tension among us. I agreed and went into the house to make the call.

The ringing on the other end continued for so long, I was about to hang up. Then I heard, "Hello?" It was Daddy's tired voice on the other end.

"Hello, Daddy," I said. "It's Jack. How are you?"

"I'm doing fine. Sam is here this weekend. He just got back from visiting some friends at Hardee's Café. You want to talk to him?"

"No, Dad, that's okay. I'm out at Aunt Rose and Lily's house. I'm heading back to Atlanta tomorrow and thought I might stop by and visit you two. The aunts told me Sam was in visiting you."

"Oh, well, sure you can stop by, but I think Sam might have plans. What time would you be here?"

It wasn't the warmest of invitations, but at least he was trying. Poor Daddy had always depended on Mama to handle family affairs. I heard Daddy mutter something and then Sam came on the line.

"Hey, Jack. Daddy says you might stop by tomorrow?" Sam's voice sounded heavy on the line.

"Yeah, I'm out at Aunt Rose and Lily's. I'm heading back to Atlanta tomorrow and thought I might stop and see you. Christy Landoff is staying out here at her grandmother's and she might ride in to visit, too."

"Really? You're seeing Christy? I didn't know that."

"No, no, I'm not seeing Christy. She's just here taking care of her granny and we were visiting. She said she'd like to catch up with you and some other friends, so if I come by tomorrow, she might ride in with me. Her daddy will bring her back out here to her granny's house."

"Well, sure, bring Christy and come on. I told the guys I would play ball with them over by the levee until noon, but then most of them are having family get-togethers. What time do you think you'll be here?"

"How about I come for lunch at 1:00? I'll need to leave about 4:00 to get back to Atlanta. Will the Bumblebee be open or are they planning to close for Memorial Day?"

"They'll probably be closed. I can whip up something here. It'll just be the four of us, or should we ask Christy's family over?"

"No, keep it low-key. I'd like to just see you and Daddy."

It was all settled in a matter of minutes, but the tension hung heavy and I felt like it took hours. Mama would have been so easy to talk to; she would have known I wasn't seeing Christy. I always felt awkward with Sam and Daddy.

Why did I agree to bring Christy along anyway? She ought to go visit her own family, I groused.

I resigned myself to a day of anxious silence and uncomfortable chatter with Christy and walked back out on the porch. Christy was looking at me, bright-eyed and smiling.

"So will it work? Should I go call my parents?" she said, practically gushing.

"Yes, Daddy and Sam said to come on over. I told them we would be there for lunch at 1:00. You should still have plenty of time to see your family too."

"Great! I'll go back to Granny's and call home to work it all out. I'll give you a call in the morning to let you know if it's good with them."

Christy picked up her empty bowl of ice cream and offered to take the aunts' bowls inside. She seemed in a hurry to be off and I was fine with that. I really didn't know how to feel about any of it.

Aunt Rose stood. "I'll take those in, Christy," she said, then took the bowls from Christy. "Jack, why don't you drive Christy back over to her grandmother's house so she won't have to walk in the dark."

"Oh, yeah ...of ... of course," I said and then pulled the keys out of my pocket. "Come on, Christy."

She followed behind me, leaping over the last few stairs. I stifled a sigh. At least someone was excited about tomorrow. I opened the car door for her and she squeezed my arm as she climbed in.

"Thank you so much, Jack. I really, really mean it."

"No problem, Christy. Come on, let's get you back."

Monday morning dawned pink and orange and quiet. Pungent coffee brewing on the stove stirred me from my nest. I threw the old quilt aside and stood at the window. I could see Aunt Lily already out for her morning walk through the small garden. When I was young, the garden took up the whole back quarter of the yard. Grandpappy always plowed it through in the fall and then tilled it up again in the spring. I wondered how Aunt Lily and Aunt Rose managed to break up the soil now.

After a quick shave I headed downstairs, where the aroma of buttermilk biscuits and sausage gravy greeted me. Aunt Rose was in the kitchen, as always, pouring apple butter in a bowl.

"Good morning, Aunt Rose," I sang as I entered, and my stomach applauded. "My mouth started watering as soon as I hit the bottom step." I kissed her on the cheek.

"I wanted to feed you well since you'll have a late lunch today. Who knows what Sam and your daddy will feed you."

She placed the apple butter on the table next to a pile of biscuits. Aunt Lily walked in a moment later carrying a few green tomatoes and a small golden squash. She plopped them on the sideboard.

"Good morning, sleepyhead," Aunt Lily said. "It's about time you were up and at it. You're losing your edge and getting soft down there in Atlanta." She pinched my cheek and then wrapped her arms around me while I sat at the table.

"I saw you in the garden. Who plows and tills for you?" I asked.

"What do you mean? I do it myself. I'm not as old and decrepit as you seem to think." She pinched my arm as she sat down next to me.

Just then a knock sounded on the back door. "Good morning," called Mr. John's familiar voice.

"Land's sakes. What's he doing here this time of day?" Aunt Lily muttered. "Come on in, John," she called from the table.

"Lily!" Aunt Rose said as she went to get the door. "Good morning, John. We were just having some breakfast. Won't you join us?" Aunt Rose asked politely.

"Well, if you don't mind, I'll take a biscuit and apple butter. I ate already, but boy those smell good."

"What brings you out so early, John?" Aunt Lily asked.

"I was hoping to take Jack with me to collect some clay before everyone heads to the picnic," Mr. John said, looking at me.

"I'm not going to the picnic," I said. "Sorry."

"Oh ... really?" Mr. John said. "Ginny thought you were planning to go before you head back to Atlanta. Well, what time do you head back? I could use some young arms and a strong back."

"I'm stopping in Rome to see Daddy and Sam for lunch. I wanted to visit with Aunt Rose and Aunt Lily some more, though," I replied, looking to my aunts for support.

"We will still be here when you get back. We have some cooking to do for the picnic anyway. You go on with John, and we'll visit some more after while," Aunt Rose said in her gentle Southern-lady way.

I changed back into the dirty clothes from my wood chopping the day before. Aunt Lily came out of the back bedroom carrying some old overshoe boots.

"These are big enough, I bet." She flashed a smile. "Daddy was a big-footed man."

I grabbed the rubbers and gave Aunt Lily a smile. Mr. John called from outside, and I raced down the back stairs. Aunt Rose was on the porch with a biscuit and sausage cake wrapped in a napkin. She gave me a quick squeeze and a kiss on the cheek.

Mr. John handed me a couple of metal pails he had, keeping two for himself. The damp dust of the road softened the clomping of my large boots as we departed. Mr. John was a walker. He said he wasn't opposed to cars and trucks, but walking cleared his mind and kept him fresh and fit. I suppose he was right because he must have been at least eighty in my judgment, but still fairly spry. We walked down the path toward the riverbank, slipping a bit on a little muddy spot created by the beaver kits. The morning sun was just heating up the day, and the dew still glistened on the high weeds in the pasture.

We walked side by side along the bank for a quarter mile until the stream narrowed enough to cross on an old foot bridge. Mr. John still looked plenty nimble, surprising me with how easily he navigated the path with pails in hand. His eyes still roved to and fro, no doubt noticing the stones and sticks strewn along the bare earth, and he hummed quietly under his breath the whole time.

We crossed the stream and headed up the other side. The ground was steeper here, and wiry Queen Anne's lace grew in spotty clumps. The sun dappled through the hardwoods, and a deer path crossed into the murky darkness on our right. Mr. John broke the silence first.

"So you're going to see your daddy and Sam, huh? How are they doing these days?"

"I guess they're okay. Daddy is still teaching at Bersher, as you know. I don't see him much these days. Sam is teaching high school over in Rockmart. We don't talk much either. Long-distance calls aren't cheap, you know," I said, hoping it at least halfway sounded like an apology.

"Then it's good you will miss the picnic today. You need to see your family. Violet would be so disheartened to know you aren't keeping up with each other."

I swallowed down a lump. "I ... I just don't get why Mama had to leave us," I mumbled, then said in a stronger voice, "We'd all be better off if she was still here."

Mr. John stumbled over some roots but caught himself, and I suggested we stop for a break. I expected him to correct my outburst like the preacher had at her funeral, but he just looked out over the flowing water. I watched a crow swoop into the nearby woods and wondered how they could be so dark when the sun was shining so brightly.

"You know, Jack," Mr. John finally said, "pain hurts. Pain has to hurt in order to save you; otherwise you just stay in the fire. Disasters and crises have meaning, but the meaning doesn't stop them from hurting."

Then he changed both pails to one hand, picked up a stick out of the water, and started using it as a cane when he traipsed off again. Trudging on, we walked in silence. I was mulling over pain and crisis and grief and sorrow when Mr. John stopped and dropped his pails with a rattle.

"This is it," he declared.

A gray clay bank stood before us. The waters had cut a small cliff out of the riverbank, exposing the fresh earth below. Tiny specks of yellow glistened in the gray smoothness, mottling the purity with individual pieces of beauty.

I ran my fingers along the silky moisture and wondered at the surprise of it all. Gathered here were flowerpots for Mr. John's shop, for Aunt Lily's windowsill, for Christy and her granny's front porch. Mr. John handed me a wire and I began slicing chunks of gray clay from the side of the cliff. Mr. John plunked them into one of the pails, seemingly oblivious to the beauty I passed him.

"I'll have that stack of wood gone in no time, Jack. I've hired the Wolfe boy down the way to chop some more for me this week. Ginny will throw this batch into flowerpots pretty quick."

"It's such an interesting mixture of colors. I can see why you chose this spot for gathering."

"Funny thing is, I wouldn't even know about it if they hadn't diverted the river years back," Mr. John said, breathing a bit heavily. "When they had so much flooding, Sidler decided to move the river instead of moving himself. That made the waters cut through this area and expose the clay below. Funny how Mr. Sidler's catastrophe makes such beautiful pots."

We walked back down the path toward Paradox carrying pails heavy with clay and hearts heavy in thought.

Those who can sin in secret
do so more quickly.
—Syrus

CHAPTER 8

Marta was on her way to the upper room to be certain Deborah had placed everything just right when she saw John in the courtyard speaking with the strangers. She stopped to ask if there was anything they needed, and John asked to see her privately. They walked to the stairs and stopped.

"Marta, I sold some special ceramics recently and—"

"No, John, you have already done enough. I know you feel obliged to help me, since you were such a special friend to Abba, but really we are doing alright."

He eyed her. "Perhaps you are doing well, Marta, but Eleazar and Mariam are struggling."

She stepped back and looked into his eyes. "What do you mean?"

"Only that they need to be watched over. You have been hiding in your grief long enough. Your parents are gone. Jacob is gone. You, however, are here. Be *here*, Marta. Be fully here."

Then John turned and walked away, leaving Marta to wonder what he meant—but she had no time for such musings now, not with such a big night ahead.

The room looked clean and inviting when Marta stepped in; the pillows were fluffed and straight, the reed mats were unrolled and carefully lined up with the wall, a small fire burned in the brazier, and Deborah had even thought to put some water and cedar bark on to scent the room. All was well, but Marta couldn't help rearranging the serving mats for the food that would be brought up. She knew where Elijah the elder would sit, and she wanted the best mats to be near him.

"Jacob would be proud," she whispered to herself.

Then she scurried down to the kitchen to continue checking on everything. She found Deborah warming the bricks that would be placed under the serving bowls. Helena was covering the last of the bread with the oiled cloths, and Mariam was sweeping up the hard·

packed floor. Even in full preparation mode, Marta had to pause and smile at the picture of domesticity.

Helena glanced up and saw Marta. "I'm heading home now. Abraham will be back by now and I want to treat his eyes before he comes to the dinner."

Marta smiled. "Thank you for your help today, Helena. You are such a perfect sister. I never have to worry with you in the kitchen. Kiss the children for me," she said as she took the bread baskets from Helena.

"I will. See you later. Bye, Deborah. Bye, Mariam. Come along, girls," Helena called.

Helena left, and Marta placed the bread baskets on the table. She pulled the cover off the barley salad and stirred it again, scraping a spoonful from the side to taste.

Perfect! Now for the pigeons.

She removed the golden birds from their spot near the oven, then Marta began to pull the meat off the bones. Shredded pigeon, eggplant, and olives were placed in each serving bowl.

"Bring me the sauce please, Deborah," Marta said.

Deborah brought over the bowl with the serving sauce, and Marta spooned it over the dishes—being sure to spoon liberally over Elijah's serving bowl.

"Make sure you place this one in front when we serve," Marta told the girls, who both nodded.

Mariam put away the broom in the corner and faced Marta. "I'm going to wash my face and change."

Marta raised her eyebrows at that and Mariam said, "I want Jacob to be proud of us."

"You're right," Marta said. "I'll go wash too. Deborah, do you want to freshen up with Mariam?"

Deborah consented and departed with Mariam. Marta sighed, smiled to herself, and then left the kitchen to wash up.

Deborah joined Mariam in her sleeping room, and Mariam untied her head covering, then began combing out her long hair.

"Let me help," Deborah said, taking the comb from Mariam's hand.

"Oh ... thank you," Mariam replied. It had been a long time since anyone had helped her with her hair, and she had to admit that it felt so relaxing to have the length of it combed and cared for.

"Do you think Nathaniel will arrive late?" Deborah asked. "He has to travel far, and he certainly has been in the fields all day."

"You're hoping to see Nathaniel?"

"Oh, yes. I am so excited about his healing."

"Of course." Mariam nodded. "He will surely share the story at dinner. Hmm ... I can make certain you serve near his side of the room."

Deborah's eyes went wide and she smiled at Mariam, then continued with the comb work.

So ... Nathaniel will be placed near the other farmers. Deborah can serve them ... and I will be free to serve the city men, Mariam thought, stopping herself from smiling at her scheme.

"Your hair is so soft, Mariam. It shines like water in the brook at Grandfather's house." Deborah sighed. "I wish I were as beautiful as you. Then maybe Abba could find a husband for me."

"Thank you, but a husband has not been found for me yet. If Eleazar doesn't hurry, I will be too old for any man!"

Deborah laughed. "You aren't that far gone, Mariam. Eleazar only thinks of you as his sister, not as someone's bride. He will realize soon that both you and Marta need husbands."

Mariam pursed her lips. She hadn't given much thought to Marta's future. It was her own that worried her, but she should have realized that Marta would need a husband too. Yes, Mariam should have thought of that. Both women were in a dreadful position.

Deborah finished combing Mariam's long locks and then fixed her own hair while Mariam tied the covering in place. Mariam sprinkled some perfume on her temple and offered some to Deborah.

"No, I can't." Deborah shook her head. "Father would not approve."

"Well, if you want to attract a husband, you may have to do more than comb your hair," Mariam said with a snort.

"Father says he will find me the right man, one who is concerned with goodness and character." Deborah looked at the floor. "But I know it will be impossible to find a man who can see beyond my face."

The finest workers in stone are not copper or steel tools, but the gentle touches of air and water working at their leisure with a liberal allowance of time.
—Henry David Thoreau

CHAPTER 9

I left Mr. John at the studio with the pails of clay and headed toward the aunts' house. Aunt Rose was waiting on the porch when I returned. Her hair was brushed tightly back into a knot, and she had some daisies fastened in the barrette. I realized how beautiful she must have been in her younger years.

"Jack! I thought you would never get back. Good heavens, don't you know what time it is?"

I smiled within. Though her looks might have dulled with time, her tongue still sliced as sharp as ever.

"I'm sorry, Aunt Rose. I was—"

"We told you to be back early. We wanted some time alone with you before you head back to Rome and Atlanta."

"Aunt Rose, it's barely 11:00. I have time to visit more." I shook my head, perplexed. "We collected so much clay that the pails were very heavy. Mr. John is in great shape for his age, but even I had to walk slowly. I left him at his place and headed right on back. I'll go wash up and we can sit on the porch for a while, okay?"

"Yes, yes, of course." She sighed and slid into one of the wicker chairs in the shade.

I jogged inside and was halfway up the stairs when I heard shuffling in the hallway above.

"Aunt Lily?" I called.

As I rounded the top of the stairs, Aunt Lily was pulling a heavy wooden box down the dimly lit hall. I pulled the shade on the stairwell window and let some light in.

Aunt Lily jumped. "Oh, Jack, you startled me. Did you see Rose? She was waiting for you on the porch earlier."

"Yes, she was still on the porch. She seemed a bit upset, though. I'm sorry I am a little late. Mr. John and I—"

"Fiddlesticks! Don't you worry about Rose," Aunt Lily interrupted. "She gets upset when things go a little unexpectedly. She made pineapple upside-down cake for the picnic, and when she was flipping it over, she somehow dropped it on the floor." Aunt Lily giggled. "Now she has to be content to only take devilled eggs and baked beans to the picnic. I told her we could scrape it off and add some frosting so no one would know, but she wouldn't hear of it." She grinned and hugged my waist. "Now help me carry this box downstairs, please."

"Sure." I reached out and grabbed hold. "Whoof! What's in here? It's so heavy." I scooted the box side to side until I could grab it off the top stair ledge.

"Just some special memories of Daddy's we thought you might like to look through."

I wrangled the trunk down the stairs and out onto the cool porch. Aunt Rose looked fidgety but seemed a little less annoyed. Aunt Lily came tagging along behind me from the kitchen, where she had grabbed a plate of Christy's lemon cookies and a pitcher of sweet tea. I plopped the box in front of the wicker love seat and grabbed a cookie. The long walk up the creek had made me hungry.

"You'll spoil your lunch, Jack," Aunt Rose said softly, but she was eyeing the box and not really noticing me.

"I'll be okay, Aunt Rose. Sam won't have lunch ready if I know him."

Aunt Lily poured tea into the glasses on the side table and handed them round. I took a big swig and then settled down to peruse the box. The first item was a pair of bronzed baby booties.

"Little Florian's," Aunt Rose half-whispered.

Florian was my uncle who had died at a year old. I never understood what it was that he died of, just some sickness, I guessed. Mama told Sam and me that she had a brother she never met, and that Grandmama never got over it. We were to never speak of him in front of her. Evidently Grandpappy didn't get over it either if this was his box of special things.

"Daddy always wanted another son." Aunt Rose sighed.

"Baloney!" Aunt Lily said. "He had all us girls and that was good enough or even better. I could fish and farm as well as any boy ever could."

Aunt Lily looked at me over the booties and smiled. She put the booties aside and reached in again. A dust-covered box of tools fell open and spilled onto the porch. I grabbed them up before any could roll away.

"Why did Grandpappy have these?" I asked, inspecting a rasp and several small chisels. I had seen similar items at school in the sculpting classroom.

"They were *our* Grandpappy's tools," Aunt Rose said. "He was a stone carver—mostly headstones. He did a lot of the work in the Paradox cemetery and even some in the Myrtle Hill Cemetery over in Rome. Grandpappy wanted Daddy to be a stone carver too, but Daddy wasn't interested. Violet tried some stonecutting for a while in high school, but it never struck her fancy, I suppose. She gave it up when she went to college. She said she wanted to be a teacher so she could make money and still be a good mother."

I handled the tools with wonder while thinking about my mother cutting delicate patterns into stone. I hadn't known that about Mama. Maybe she had wanted to carve headstones like her grandfather, but she'd been thinking of me instead. *She should have done it,* I thought.

Aunt Rose took the tools from me, and I pulled out the next item: an old family Bible. The inside cover had a list of names, a list that Aunt Rose and Aunt Lily had memorized, I soon found out. Some names meant something to them, and some were lost to time. Grandpappy's grandfather was still alive when they were little, and they remembered the stories of when he saw his wife for the first time. She was hanging laundry on the clothesline and chasing after her cousin's toddlers. They said it was love at first sight.

"Sometimes that happens." Aunt Lily smiled in my direction—another of her knowing smiles.

A ceramic vase sat nestled near the bottom of the box, wrapped in a faded red bandana. I turned it over and dried flowers floated out. The aunts laughed until I saw tears in their eyes.

"What?" I asked.

"Daddy named us girls for all his favorite flowers," Aunt Lily said. "He always kept a flower patch beside the vegetable garden. We would pick our namesakes and bring them to him." She stopped and they giggled together. "Mama would get so irritated with us, but Daddy always gave us hugs and kisses."

"He kept planting marigolds and daisies hoping for some more girls," Aunt Rose said, "but it wasn't to be. He tried planting asters one year, but Mama nearly drowned in sorrow thinking about little Florian, and Daddy never planted those again."

The bottom of the box held several ancient, mildew-encased books. Some of the pages crumbled as I turned them. In between the pages were newspaper articles, including one of Mama and Daddy's marriage announcement. Their picture was speckled and out of focus, but I could still make out their smiles. They were so happy together.

Why did it have to end so soon?

Aunt Rose finished putting all of the items back in the box and we sat on the porch for a while, quiet in our thoughts. Funny how I didn't even know the people packed away in that box in the attic, but they were still a part of my story.

Soon Christy came strolling across the lawn and up the front stairs. "Hello," she called and then waved.

The aunts broke out of their reverie and greeted her with hugs and compliments on her lemon cookies.

"Yeah, thanks for the cookies, Christy," I said, trying to start off on the right foot.

"You're welcome, Jack." Christy beamed at me over Aunt Lily's shoulder. "Are you ready to go?" she asked as Aunt Lily turned her loose.

"Yeah, let me grab my things," I said and started toward the screen door.

"I'll come help you, Jack," Aunt Rose said and followed behind. "You didn't even get to clean up after your time with Mr. John this morning." In my room Aunt Rose frowned. "We shouldn't have kept you so long going through Daddy's things."

"Nonsense, I enjoyed it. And Daddy and Sam won't mind if I'm a little dusty," I said as I threw my things in my duffel bag.

"Perhaps they won't, but Christy might not like being stuck in the car with you."

"I'll keep the windows down." I smiled. Maybe Aunt Rose had a little of Aunt Lily's matchmaking in her, as well. "Anyway, she needs to go see her family too, not just hang out with us. Maybe if I offend, she won't stay too long."

"Jack, shame on you." But she laughed, and we headed downstairs.

Christy was waiting outside with Aunt Lily. I felt so relaxed now compared to just three days ago. I hugged Aunt Lily and Aunt Rose and sincerely promised to visit when I could. I actually felt sad and disappointed to be leaving.

"Don't be a stranger," Aunt Lily said, putting on a stern face.

"Drive careful, now. And don't forget to give Sam and your dad those cookies I packed," Aunt Rose said, then waved.

I shut the passenger door behind Christy and bounced over to the driver's side. "I'll be careful," I promised, slamming the door. "I always am."

I backed the car out the driveway and turned down the dirt lane. Dust flew behind the Corvair as Christy and I waved good-bye out the open windows. I could see Aunt Rose and Aunt Lily waving in my rearview mirror until I rounded the curve by the holly trees. The roof of the old farmhouse was still visible when Christy sighed deeply and flopped back into the seat with her feet out the window.

"Oh heavenly sweetness!" she exclaimed. "Thank you so much for letting me come along. I absolutely need to get away. I love Granny, but I am shriveling up in Paradox. I can't wait to see Sam and hear how everyone is doing. I wonder who has been hanging out at Hardee's Café. The last time I talked to Bridgette—you remember her, Charlie Goodwin's sister? Anyway, she said that everyone was heading over to Powhatan Beach for the holiday. Maybe I can talk Daddy into going along and picnicking there this evening. I know it would mean I have to stay in town one night, but Granny ought to be fine this one time, don't you think?"

Christy prattled on the entire ride. I nodded a few times and offered a thoughtful "Hmm" occasionally, but she seemed fine to talk to herself. That was good because I was thinking over my weekend with the aunts. I had shown up Friday evening weary and worried. Then Aunt Lily took me fishing, and Aunt Rose spoiled me with her good cooking and attentive words, and even Mr. John had been a nice surprise. I hadn't seen him since I was a little kid spending summer vacations on the farm, splashing along the creek, climbing trees in the forest, and accepting sandwiches from a metal lunch pail. I had forgotten how much I loved Paradox.

I pulled next to the curb in front of Mama and Daddy's house. *Funny,* I thought, *that it no longer felt like my house, my home.* Yet my little apartment in Atlanta wasn't home either. It held no memories like the pale redbrick walls of this nineteenth-century relic. Perhaps the apartment was already too full of others' memories to hold mine as well. Sam stood on the front porch waving and calling to us.

Christy jumped out of the car and ran up the walk to Sam. Throwing her arms around his neck, she nearly knocked him into the shrubbery below the stairs. I could see Sam's surprise as he hugged her back and then showed her into the house. I slammed the car door shut and walked slowly up the stairs, still not expecting a happy afternoon.

Daddy was in the kitchen pulling something out of the oven as I walked in. He glanced up and half-smiled. I could hear Christy and Sam in the front room chatting about old friends.

"Hi, Daddy," I said. "What are you making?"

"Meatloaf," he answered and placed the oven mitts on the countertop. He leaned against the counter and folded his arms. "So how have you been, Jack? Did you have a nice time with Lily and Rose?"

Some anger might have been simmering beneath his comment; I couldn't tell for sure. Laughter from the front room spilled into the kitchen as Sam and Christy walked in.

"How've you been?" Sam asked, squeezing my shoulder and grinning.

"Fine, uh … good," I answered. "The aunts are well. We had a nice time," I said, turning back toward Daddy. "They wish you would visit them."

Sam nodded. "Yeah, I was there a couple weeks ago and they asked why you never visit, Daddy. Maybe they could give you some cooking lessons." Sam laughed as the beans boiled over on the stove. Sam always made meetings with Daddy calmer. He had Mama's easygoing manner.

"I thought you were going to cook lunch, Sam," I said, elbowing him in the ribs.

"The game went a little late, so Daddy took over. I've become a mean cook now that I'm on my own, though."

Daddy and Christy talked amiably about her granny and the mundane happenings around Paradox and Rome. Sam offered some updates on a few friends while we all helped plate up the food and get it onto the table. Meatloaf, brown beans, a green salad, and a can of fruit cocktail were the offerings. I added in the cookies Aunt Rose sent over for Daddy, and it wasn't too bad a meal.

"How do you like Rockmart, Sam?" Christy asked.

"I enjoy teaching at the high school, but I don't know that I want to make it home."

"Where would you like to make home?" Christy asked.

"Mm, Rome is nice, but right now I don't know that I am looking for a home. I'm thinking about joining the navy. Maybe I could be a navy admiral like John Henry Towers." Sam threw an obviously cautious glance at Daddy.

Daddy glowered at Sam. "Why would you do that?"

"I thought I could be helpful to our country. It's a man's patriotic duty, and Jack is nearly too old." Sam grinned, trying to make light again.

"Yes, it is a duty and a patriot's a fine thing to be," Daddy said, "but the situation is heating up in Asia and I don't want another Chester in the family."

Chester was Daddy's brother who died in Guadalcanal during World War 2. Daddy was still a boy at home when the news came that Uncle Chester was a casualty of war. Daddy's mama never recovered from the shock of it, and he promised her he would never join the military. Now it looked like there might finally be a continuation to the Sharp military record.

Christy looked at me across the table and quietly asked, "Who is Chester?"

Daddy wiped his face with his hanky, told Christy with forced politeness that Chester was his brother, and then excused himself from the table. He stormed into the kitchen and started banging some pots on top of the stove. Christy looked like a deer in the headlights, glancing at me and then at Sam.

"Maybe I better walk you over to your house now," I said.

Christy nodded and scooted away from the table. She said her good-byes to Sam and quietly exited through the front vestibule. I noticed the picture of Mama was still propped up on the entryway table next to the coatrack. The picture had been taken before the cancer, and her bright eyes looked straight into my soul.

Mama, we need you now.

Christy stayed quiet on the short walk down East Third Avenue. Some children were playing ball in the street, and I could smell charcoal burning in Mr. Hebb's backyard. Summer was just getting started, but it seemed like there would be a long winter to endure when I walked back home. I greeted

Christy's parents and chatted a few minutes, but then I had to return to the house. Sam would need me, I was sure.

The dishes had been cleared from the table and I could hear Daddy rattling around in the kitchen. I steeled myself and went in, expecting to find Daddy and Sam freezing each other out with cold stares and harsh, biting words, but Sam wasn't there.

"You okay, Daddy?"

"Fine, yes." I was right: the words sounded frosty.

"Where's Sam?"

"He headed back to Rockmart. Said to tell you good-bye. Had some work to do back there, he said."

Daddy seemed tired suddenly. His hair looked grayer than I remembered, his shoulders stooped and rounded. His slacks hung loosely around his waist where the belt was pulled to the last notch.

I filled the sink with soapy water and started washing the lunch dishes that were piled on the sideboard. Daddy put the leftovers in the Frigidaire and then started drying the clean dishes I placed in the drain rack. Nothing was spoken between the two of us. I didn't know what to say and Daddy didn't seem to want to talk anyway.

"So you have learned to cook a little," I finally managed. "The meatloaf was good."

"I'm not as helpless as your aunts seem to think," Daddy half-mumbled, half-growled.

I ignored his surly tone and said, "Aunt Lily said they offered to bring you some home-cooked food. It wouldn't be a bad idea; they sure fed me well this weekend. And you do look like you're losing some weight, Daddy."

"I'm just fine. I can take care of myself, but why didn't you tell me you were going to their house? You could have stopped here on your way over." Daddy looked straight at me, piercing me with his gaze.

I looked back down at the soapy water and shrugged. "I guess I figured you were busy and wouldn't want a visitor."

The dishes were finished in quietness and I dried my hands on the towel that was hanging on the cupboard knob.

Daddy put the last pot away and turned to me. "Let's go for a walk."

We walked out the front door, passing Mama's picture again, and down the porch stairs. Daddy turned toward the river. We marched in silence. As we passed the Merita Bakery, he began to speak as if from a dark tunnel:

"Sun and moon march by
Where are we going?
Slogging along under black shadowy growth
When will it end?
Terror disguises our day
Fear moves us at night
Mired in muddy Guadalcanal
Starvation is our subsistence

Bloody drops trail from our wounds
No bandages can bind our broken bodies
Suicide is the only deliverance."

My eyes grew wide, and I felt my breath catch. "Daddy, are you alright?" I stared at him.

Daddy glanced up from the sunshine‑covered walkway, then looked sideways at me. He was a man waking from a dream, pushing through the spidery cobwebs of consciousness.

"It's a poem I came across in a newspaper. Some Japanese prisoner of war wrote it. There's more than that, but it's what sticks to me, like flypaper, trapping me. Chester was there, in Guadalcanal, you know."

I nodded my head, unsure where this could be heading. Daddy reciting Japanese poetry? "I always thought you hated the Japanese," I commented more to myself than to him.

"We must try to understand what we hate. Poetry is the foundation of the soul. Knowing our enemies' poetry is one of the ways to understand why things happen. Our enemies have reasons for the choices they make. It is not enough for Sam to not be ready to settle down. He must have a solid reason to make the decision he thinks he needs to make."

"But Sam is not your enemy, Daddy."

"No." Daddy sighed. "But I don't understand him the way your mother did. Suicide is committed in many ways, my boy."

So Sam was still on Daddy's mind, along with Uncle Chester and poetry and enemies. There was more to my father than I realized. Mama would have been able to soothe Daddy's spirit, to cheer him and lighten the mood. She never would have let him think of suicide. Is that what he thought about all alone at the house?

"Do you ... think of suicide, Daddy?" I asked.

"No, Jack—not anymore, anyway."

Then we finished walking to the river in silence.

We stopped in the middle of the bridge on South Broad Street and watched the joining of the rivers. The Coosa and the Etowah flowed gently into the Oostanaula. When I was a kid, we used to have boat races on the river. We would scratch our initials on pieces of bark with our pen knives and then launch them farther down on the Etowah. Racing back to the bridge, we would take bubblegum bets on whose boat would pass under the bridge first. Now I was feeling like my boat had gotten hopelessly lost in some weeds at the side of the river and would never pass under the bridge.

Daddy slowly pulled his eyes from the water's flow and we headed toward Myrtle Hill Cemetery on the other side of the bridge. Mama was buried on the other side of the hill, but I hadn't visited the grave since her burial. Mama was never really there in my mind; she was always in the garden or the kitchen, calling me home for supper.

"Did you know Grandpappy's father was a stonecutter?" I asked, hoping to ease the tension. "He made some of the headstones in this cemetery. Aunt Rose said Mama tried stonecutting in high school, but she decided she wanted to be a schoolteacher instead."

"Hmm." Daddy nodded.

I kept on talking, trying to fill in the time until I could suggest walking back and getting on the road myself. "Aunt Rose said Mama wanted to be a teacher so she could have a family and still help out financially."

That caught Daddy's attention. "Your mother never needed to help out financially. I took good care of her. She chose to teach because she enjoyed it."

"Well, of course, but I just thought it was interesting that she thought about stonecutting too. I guess there's not much use for stonecutters anymore, though."

"She could have been a stonecutter if she had wanted to," Daddy said. "It wasn't her place to take care of us that way. She took care of us at home, like a good wife and mother should." Daddy was panting now from the exertion of walking up the hill and from being irritated by the conversation. "Someday you'll find a nice girl to settle down with and you'll understand. The men bear the burden of providing, and the women, well, they use what we provide to make life better." Daddy stopped and leaned a hand against a tree trunk to catch his breath.

"I know, Daddy," I said.

Even if it means giving up what you love to do, I thought.

After Daddy stopped breathing so hard, I suggested we head back to the house. We turned silently back to town, not even stopping to visit Mama's grave.

Mr. Hebb's charcoal grill was still fumigating the neighborhood when we returned. I stopped in the house for a glass of sweet tea and then told Daddy I needed to head home to Atlanta. He offered a few remarks to take care of myself and not be a stranger, but we both knew it had been a difficult visit. We awkwardly shook hands and I climbed into the Corvair. I waved from the rolled-down window as Daddy stood on the curb and watched me go.

On East Fourth Avenue the car started shaking and hissing. The gauge showed it was overheating and suddenly steam was pouring out the front of the hood. I pulled into the parking lot of the Colonial Grocery. I grabbed a rag out of the backseat and lifted up the hood. It didn't look good.

I decided to call Daddy from inside the grocery and see if he could come over, but the store was closed for Memorial Day. I saw a pay phone across the street by the pharmacy. I walked across and lifted the receiver; my relaxing weekend was ending all wrong.

Daddy came over and looked at the car. We figured the radiator was cracked and would need replaced. I would have to leave it in Rome, and the family mechanic would take a look at it tomorrow. The evening train to Atlanta was pulling into the station as Daddy dropped me off. I had no time to talk, but ran inside and paid for a ticket. I waved good-bye from the platform while Daddy watched from behind the gate, our second good-bye in less than an hour.

I slid into a seat and dropped my bag at my feet. I felt exhausted from the day's events and closed my eyes. *At least I won't have to stay awake for the ride home*, I thought and then tried to sleep. The rhythm of the train was interrupted by occasional stops along the route, but it was gentle enough to lull me into a sleeping stupor. When my stop was finally announced, I was red-eyed and disoriented.

I flung my duffel bag over my shoulder and scooted off the train with the other passengers. The noisy station, the cigarette smoke, the bright lights all filled my senses—leaving Rome and Paradox far behind. I walked the four blocks to my apartment and let myself into the comfort of darkness and the familiarity of my own soft pillow.

Morning arrived before I was ready, but I managed to stumble into a hot shower while the coffee percolated on top of the stove. *Some of Aunt Rose's buttermilk biscuits sure would be good,* I thought, *but now I'm back in the real world.* I jogged the four blocks back to the train station after checking the schedule I picked up last night. I was going to have a rough week of it, being up early enough to catch the train and get to work on time.

Strangers around me read their newspapers or quietly watched out the window as the city passed by. I stood holding onto a steel bar near the front of the car. I tried thinking through what to do about the Chevy, how I would get back to Rome the next weekend to pick it up, and wondered how much this would set me back. I had been planning to buy a television, but that would just have to wait a while longer. Too bad I couldn't chop wood to pay off a car repair.

Jimmy was already at his desk calling clients when I walked in thirty minutes late. "What happened to you? Too much partying over the weekend?" He grinned.

I plopped into my seat. "Hardly. My car broke down and I had to ride the train back last night from Rome. Then I had to ride the commuter in from my apartment this morning." I sighed as I rolled my chair closer to my desk.

Jimmy's client picked up the other end just then and he turned away from me as he greeted the jeweler and began the bargaining. I sighed and picked up my call list.

"Suicide is committed in many ways, my boy ..."

Daddy's words rumbled down the tracks of my mind.

Existence is a strange bargain. Life owes us little; we owe it everything. The only true happiness comes from squandering ourselves for a purpose.
—William Cowper

CHAPTER 10

The guests were gathered in the upper room. Voices and laughter floated down to the bottom of the stairs, where Deborah stood. She sighed. Walking into the room full of men was the last thing she wanted to do, but Marta had asked her to carry up some of the dishes, and Deborah was always obedient. Mariam didn't seem to be having any trouble running up and down the stairs, gathering dishes, placing new ones on the low benches, and listening in on the men while she served. Deborah had even heard Mariam laugh with the men a few times. She would never dare do such a thing.

"What's wrong?" Marta asked as she approached the stairwell.

Deborah started and then walked up the stairs, avoiding the question. The room was bright now with a fire in the grate and all of the candles lit in the corner candelabras. The smell of cedar penetrated the air even outside the room. Inside, it mixed with the wonderful aromas of the food.

After Deborah put the dishes on the serving table, she took her place on the side of the room where mostly farmers sat—where Nathaniel should have been sitting, but he hadn't shown. Deborah swallowed and tried to look relaxed. Keeping her eyes low, she glanced around the room, but Mariam caught her eye. Her friend gave a little nod to her, and Deborah smiled back. If only Deborah could be like Mariam and have such an easy manner with men. Deborah looked down at the floor again.

And where was Nathaniel?

Deborah sighed in dismay.

"You are a blessed man, Eleazar, to have such fine cooks," Elijah said. "Those who are blessed are often asked to give more, you know."

He looked at Mariam, and she blushed.

Elijah ... he's an old man, Mariam thought. *Surely he is not interested in me! But then ...*

he has sons who need a bride. Mmm … The son of a prestigious town elder would be a good husband. Mariam smiled back at him, then refilled the glasses in front of Eleazar and Elijah.

"Sacrifices are made by many these days, Elijah, the blessed and the cursed alike," Eleazar said.

What in the world did he mean by that? Mariam wondered. She finished refilling empty cups, then headed out of the room and back downstairs, her stomach starting to twist into knots. *Eleazar would not call me accursed in front of all those men … would he?* She paused halfway down the stairs. *How will I ever find a husband if he speaks of me that way? Has he heard of my activities? Have I been forever ruined?*

Tears welled up in Mariam's eyes as she hurried back into the kitchen. She swiped at her wet cheeks with her cloak sleeve and then refilled the platters and pitchers. Marta walked in behind Mariam and placed her dishes next to Mariam's. Mariam could feel her older sister's gaze on her.

"What is going on with you girls?" Marta asked. "Deborah stares up at the guest room as if a ghost will appear and now you return from the party with tears in your eyes."

Mariam dashed at her eyes again and gave a weak smile. "I guess I'm just tired."

"Are you sure you're feeling alright? I don't want you to get sick."

"Yes, I'm fine."

"I'll carry the fruit upstairs. Why don't you sit here in the kitchen for a bit?"

Mariam felt another wave of emotion bubbling up, so she only nodded and took a seat. A moment later Marta had gone back upstairs, leaving Mariam with her thoughts of a bleak future as an old maid.

The men talked on, and Deborah was filling goblets when Nathaniel came in, offering apologies for his tardiness. The men waved off his words and welcomed Nathaniel into the room with smiles. Deborah took a few quick steps to resume her position along the wall and then froze in place, her heart beating so fast that she wondered if the men nearby could hear it.

"Sit over there," Elijah said, motioning toward the seat behind Deborah. "No doubt you have had a long day in the fields. Are the crops looking good this year?"

"Yes, all is well," Nathaniel said.

"Shalom, Nathaniel," Eleazar spoke up. "It seems you are right that all is well. The news is that you have been healed—and most miraculously."

Nathaniel's face brightened and he nodded. "Yes indeed."

"Won't you tell us your story?" Elijah asked.

Deborah felt as though she could hardly breathe. What should she do? The pitchers needed to be refilled, but she wanted to hear Nathaniel's story. Then she saw Marta across the room, waiting just inside the doorway along the opposite wall. Deborah moved toward the door as if to leave, but then she thought better of it and pushed herself into a small alcove near the doorway, like some frightened mouse eyeing a fallen crumb. The men had all turned to Nathaniel. Even Marta, at the doorway with loaded fruit bowls in hand, had focused her attention on him, so there wasn't any danger of being called out for listening, but still Deborah felt guilty. She shouldn't be listening, especially since she was only here to help serve—but she needed to hear the story from Nathaniel's own lips.

Just then Mariam slipped back into the room with a full pitcher, which she set down before scurrying to her position. After she settled into place, Nathaniel started: "I went up to Bethsaida to stay with my cousin Philip. His mother is practiced in the healing arts and knows where a mineral spring is. I had hoped she would be able to help me. You know my legs had gotten so bad that I couldn't walk anymore. I took my old donkey Barsabbas and the cart, but it was a painful trip.

"Philip was not home when I arrived. His mother said he had been spending time with a rabbi. Aunt Phyllis made me comfortable right away, though, and started working on my legs. She had some poultice herbs that she thought would help prevent further spreading of the sores, and the pain did start to subside a bit. After two weeks, though, the only progress was a little pain relief."

Nathaniel paused to take a sip of wine, then went on. "Finally Philip came home. He was traveling with the rabbi, and they both came into the house. Aunt Phyllis was angry with Philip for bringing the rabbi in when I was there with the sickness, but the rabbi didn't seem to be bothered by it. He spoke with me for a while, asking how I was doing and if the leprosy was improving. I told him about being gathered up by the Romans to work on the road outside Capernaum, and he seemed very sympathetic. I could see in his eyes that he was truly concerned for me."

Again Nathaniel paused, but this time he simply stared off for a few moments. To Mariam it looked like Nathaniel had returned to that moment with the rabbi.

"Then he asked the strangest thing," Nathaniel said. "Would you believe he asked if I would like to get better?"

Nathaniel glanced around the room full of teachers and farmers, and Mariam did the same. Several of the men shook their heads; others snorted their disapproval.

"I told him that of course I wanted to get better, and he said, 'Then you are healed.' And I was! I could feel right away that the pain had eased and vitality had returned to my limbs."

A couple of the men gasped, while others murmured among themselves, with a few shaking their heads in clear disbelief. Mariam really didn't know what to think.

"Perhaps it was your aunt's work taking effect then," Elijah said.

Nathaniel shrugged. "Well, some may think so, but it was just so sudden and complete that I truly believe the rabbi did it. I don't even have any scars left from the sores. Aunt Phyllis wouldn't have been able to manage that."

"Mm, no, I suppose not," Elijah said. "So this rabbi, is he still in Bethsaida with Philip?"

"I'm not sure. I remained at the house for several more days because my aunt wanted to keep an eye on me, even though I said I felt all better. He stayed for a few more days, since some of Philip's friends wanted to meet the rabbi, and then they all left for Capernaum again. I heard that the man was healing other people in Bethsaida and Capernaum too."

"Do you know his name?" Thaddeus asked.

"Philip called him 'Jesus,' but the rabbi himself asked me not to spread it around," Nathaniel said.

"Ah! We know Philip and Jesus as well," Thaddeus said, clearly to everyone's surprise. "He is the leader of the group that will be here in a day or so. Many of us believe he is the Messiah."

Thaddeus gestured toward Simon for support, and Simon nodded, eyeing the others in a way that seemed to dare them to argue the point with them.

"Even more," Thaddeus went on, "this healing power has been given to us and to his other disciples as well."

The men laughed at this, and Mariam had to join in. Thaddeus and Simon were healthy young men, yes, but there was nothing special about them by any means. But both Thaddeus and Simon held up their hands to quiet the men.

"It is true," Simon said. "His name is Jesus and he comes in the name of the Lord. He heals the deaf and blind. He makes the lame to walk, and like Nathaniel told you, he can heal the leprous also. He teaches as he heals, and he is smarter than any of the synagogue rulers. He is kind and gentle, but he is a leader."

More side talk and whispers broke out until Elijah raised his hands. "Well, if he is as good as you say, I'm sure we will hear more of him soon," Elijah said. "Still ... though things turned out well for Nathaniel, it is not common that our people safely return from these Roman demands. Some Council members believe it would help our people's cause if we had a little uprising to make ourselves heard."

"Elijah, please, not now," Eleazar said, and then he glanced around the room with a tilt of his head to indicate he didn't want the women to be part of such a conversation.

"No, Eleazar," Elijah said. "The time has come. The Romans are becoming more demanding every day. Something must be done—and soon!"

"Hear hear!" most of the men chorused.

And with that, Mariam knew she had no interest in staying for such rabble-rousing. She gathered up an empty pitcher and plate, then left the room, hoping that perhaps she'd caught the eye of at least one of the men.

As voices and tempers flared among the men, Marta completely forgot about the fruit bowls she held as she let out a gasp. Her hands shook and her knees felt weak as she stood there in the doorway, barely noticing as Mariam rushed by her with empty serving ware.

So this was what John meant! But ... no! How could my baby brother be involved in this ridiculous talk? The Romans are an irrepressible force. They kill those who threaten uprisings. She shook the thought from her mind and clenched her jaw. *I'll talk this over with Eleazar later. He can't be too involved yet. Tonight will not be ruined by this news!*

Forcing a smile, she walked the rest of the way into the room and set the bowls down, nearly knocking them over in the process. Marta stood up, maintained her forced smile, and tried to calm herself, but some of the men spoke with such wrath.

Oh, Eleazar!

Deborah was not fooled by Marta's smile. She had heard the gasp that escaped Marta when Elijah began his fiery talk. Deborah's own joy over Nathaniel's healing became short-lived.

Poor Marta! Deborah thought. *She must be so upset by this news. Eleazar is surely in danger.*

Deborah caught Marta's eye and held it for a second. Marta's understanding of the situation and the price it might cost were fully expressed in that look, and Deborah could only offer a silent prayer for the woman she respected so much.

Marta's eyes welled as she looked away from Deborah, and then she swept out of the room. She couldn't be so transparent, so emotional, in front of all these men.

Entering the kitchen, Marta found Mariam morosely sweeping crumbs into the pail for chicken scraps. Marta groaned within. *Enough of all this melodrama already!*

"For the sake of all that is good, what is your problem?" Marta nearly shouted.

Mariam, though, didn't even look at Marta. She only gave a teary sigh. Marta huffed and turned for the courtyard. She needed some fresh air.

Leaning against the old olive tree, Marta breathed deeply of the cool night air. Stars were beginning to appear in the darkening sky. Marta tried praying, asking the Lord what to do, but the words fell from her as tears of despair and desperation. Was Eleazar to be taken from her like Jacob and Abba and Mama? It seemed so unfair.

A large hand touched Marta's shoulder, and she snapped her head around.

"Oh, John! I'm sorry, have I neglected the room too long? Deborah is supposed to be helping." Mariam put on a smile as she wiped her face with her apron.

"No, the men are fine. I felt tired and thought a little fresh air might help. It seems I am not the only one who needed some quiet solitude."

Marta blurted out a sardonic laugh as she felt the tears welling up again. "Why must the Romans bother us, John? Why can't Messiah rescue us and save us from this calamity?" Her tears ran freely now and she felt a shudder course through her.

John squeezed her shoulder, then let go. "Messiah will come when the time is right, but even when he comes, rescue will cost each of us in some way. The Lord relies on us to stand up for what is right." He paused until Marta looked him fully in the eyes. "Eleazar is a good man," he said.

Marta sniffled and nodded. "I know he is good, but he is not a man. He is still a boy. I need him. He might get hurt, John, and then what will I do?"

"You will do what any child of Abraham does. Obedience is not easy, but it is honorable. You must bring honor to God."

Marta looked at the ground and let her shoulders sag. "I know I should want to be honorable, but this obedience is too much. I have already lost my husband, and Abba and Mama. I have Eleazar and Mariam to look after. What will become of me and Mariam if something happens to Eleazar? Why can't those horrid old men see their injustice? Why...?" Marta let her voice trail off. John was a good listener and an old family friend, yes, but maybe she was saying too much. What if he went back to the guest room and shared what she said?

John again rested his hand on her shoulder. "Do not worry. I will not share your comments," he said, reading her mind. "You are frightened and deservedly so, but if anything happens to Eleazar, you know I am here. I will always be here for all of you."

Marta took in a breath and stood a little taller, attempting to smile as she did so. "Thank you, John. You have been a dear friend to our family. Abba always said I could lean on you in times of trouble. Now ... I should go make sure Mariam and Deborah are watching over the men. Those girls are flighty this evening."

If you paint the leaf on a tree without using a model, your imagination will supply you with only a few leaves; but Nature offers you millions, all on the same tree. No two leaves are exactly the same. The artist who paints only what is in his mind must very soon repeat himself.
—Pierre-Auguste Renoir

CHAPTER 11

Yes, this is Jack Sharp," I began, my hand jamming the receiver against my ear to capture the faraway voice on the phone. "I'm calling to schedule your next shipment of Needler and Newman ceramics."

"One moment, please."

The California accent on the other end of the line made me smile. *Wonder what she thinks of my Southern drawl,* I mused.

"Jack," an older male voice said on the line, "this is Mr. Carter. I'm glad you called. We won't be needing any more shipments from Needler and Newman."

"Oh? Was there something wrong with your last shipment?"

"Not particularly. We just decided as a company to focus on paintings and sculptures and to drop our ceramics line."

I could feel my hands begin to shake. "Surely there is space for pottery in your store," I said. "I recently engaged a ceramics jeweler whose work can easily be showcased in a small glass cupboard. Perhaps you would like to see some of his work."

"I'm sorry, but we really have already made the decision," Mr. Carter said. "If I hear of anyone else in Santa Barbara looking for ceramics, I'll pass along Needler and Newman's name. Thank you for your service all this time. Good-bye."

"Thank you ... Good-bye," I managed as the line clicked. A cold sweat trickled down my back.

"Fantastic!" Jimmy exclaimed. Then he began asking for shipping information, and I could hear him typing up the forms in the cubicle next to me. At least one of us was doing well. I bit my thumbnail and wondered whom I should call next.

Two days later, on Wednesday, I negotiated with some New York jewelers who thought the commission was too high on our end. I explained that all our commissions were the same, and that it really was the industry average, but they were emphatic that I lower it by two percent. I promised to speak to Mr. Needler about it.

I waited until after lunch, hoping he would be in a good mood. The secretary informed Mr. Needler that I was in the waiting area and would like to meet with him. I heard him sigh over the intercom; that couldn't be a good sign.

"Good afternoon, Mr. Needler," I said.

"Jack, I'm glad you came by. I was going to send for you anyway. I see that you lost the Santa Barbara account this week. You are responsible for distribution as well as acquisitions, you know," he said as he looked over a manila file folder. "You acquired some good ceramics for us, Jack, but you haven't been holding up your end of the selling. We need you to push the product more, especially the in-house wares."

"Yes, sir." I nodded. "The company in California made a complete change, sir, and is no longer carrying anyone's pottery. They offered to give our name to other sellers. I don't think it had anything to do with Needler and Newman."

He looked up at me. "Of course it didn't. That's not the point, Jack. You have to fight for the customer. Show them why they need to keep selling ceramics in their store. Convince them that it is in their best interest."

"Yes, of course. I'll try calling them again," I said just as a sharp pain pierced through my left eye.

"That will be all," he said as he closed the folder with a snap.

"I'm sorry, Mr. Needler, but I ... uh ... need to talk to you about another matter."

He leaned back in his chair and gave a small nod.

"I've been speaking with a group of jewelers in New York City. They insist that the commission is too high on our part and that they need a two-percent increase on their end."

Mr. Needler's eyebrows began arching and I knew it wasn't going to go well. When his nostrils also flared, I hastened to explain.

"I know what we are giving is the national average, but since they are in New York, we get a higher mark-up from them. The extra two percent is easily made up in that difference. Maybe we would even gain some other clients in New York when they discover the deal."

He leaned forward and put his elbows on his desk. "No, Jack. We can't give in on this point. You will just have to convince them that the commission is non-negotiable."

He rose and then held open the door for me. I muttered gratitude as I slunk out of the office. The large oak-paneled door nearly slammed behind me.

I worked until ten every night that week trying to make up for my mistakes. I called friends and colleagues hoping to unearth a new market in some untouched city, but I had no luck. Even the local potters were uncooperative. I toured the studios on the west end of the building, but came away sad and discouraged. The work was unoriginal and lacked the flamboyance that might interest the Santa Barbara dealers in rethinking their decision.

On Thursday morning a box of ceramic oil lamps lay open on my desk. The potter that sent the sample enclosed a handwritten note: *You recently purchased some ceramic pieces from my neighbor. I am wondering if you would be willing to look at my work. I am not a professional potter. It just brings me peace.*

The note went on to describe the type of clay used, the firing method applied, the artist's experience, and her contact information. But those lines ... *I am not a professional potter. It just brings me peace.* They burned into my brain.

Peace was far from me. I had worked late every evening hoping to leave early on Friday to pick up my car, but try as hard as I might, I had no success in gaining a new client the entire week. Jimmy, sitting not ten feet away from me, had landed three large buyers.

On top of it all, the car repairs were going to eat deeply into my savings, and I wondered why I was working so hard when it was barely enough to cover my expenses.

Peace ... It was a mystical mirage dangling from the end of a line floating far, far in front of me. How unfair it seemed for this female potter to offer her peace when she probably had a husband at home covering the daily necessities.

Ginny doesn't know how good she has it, I thought.

Electrical pulses raced down my spine. What had made me think of Ginny? She was a good potter already from what I could tell, and she was working toward a degree, right? *How is that any different than Mama choosing between being a stonecutter or a teacher?* Ginny was willing to help with the costs of a family and do all of the hard work of pottery and family life. The memory of Ginny's sweaty brow and her dirty nails while handing me collards for Aunt Rose's table made me recognize the jealousy that was wrapping itself around my heart.

Ginny was doing what she wanted, and it probably brought her peace. I was trying to transform my job into what I wanted it to be, and peace was resting back in Paradox. I shook my head to clear my thinking.

Suddenly I realized Paradox held the solution to my problems: Mr. John. John Kadar was a professional potter. And on top of that, he was an old friend. Certainly I wouldn't need to worry about contract and commission changes with Mr. John. I let out the air that seemed to have been building up in me all week and looked forward to my trip to Rome, and especially to Paradox.

I called Aunt Lily that night to see if I could stay over the weekend again. I wanted plenty of time to warm up Mr. John and to look over his inventory. Aunt Lily sounded plenty pleased to be seeing me again so soon and assured me I would always have a bed at their house.

I called Daddy to tell him I would not be spending the night on Friday, but he never answered the phone.

I'll stay for dinner and then head over to the aunts' house. He'll be glad to not have me all night, anyway, I reassured myself.

Friday afternoon couldn't come soon enough. Jimmy teased me about finding a girl back home, so I knew my excitement to head out was obvious. Mid-afternoon, I dropped a note off with Mr. Newman's secretary letting him know I had a good lead on a potter with some unique pieces, then finally closed up shop for the day. The train ride was enjoyable and didn't take nearly as long as I remembered. The thought that I should probably visit more often entered my mind but was quickly dismissed.

Daddy was standing outside the station waiting for me as planned. His sagging slacks and rumpled shirt made him appear older than his years. A smile played around the edges of his mouth, but it didn't reach his eyes. I gave him a quick hug and he grabbed my duffel bag from my hand.

"I parked over here. How was your week?" Daddy asked, pointing me toward his car.

"It was rough, but I think I got it figured out. I'm going over to the aunts' house tonight so I can visit with John Kadar tomorrow. I'm hoping he will let me sell some of his ceramics." I slammed the car door shut and smiled over at Daddy.

"You're not staying the night here?" he asked quietly.

"No. I tried calling you last night, but you never answered. Anyway, I really hope Mr. John will let me pick up some of his work. It might be what I need to get the Santa Barbara account back." I winced as I remembered the reprimand I took from my boss just days earlier.

"Oh, well, I wish you could stay, but I understand. A man has to work to get ahead in life." Daddy sighed.

"I bet you could come with me," I said on a sudden whim. "The aunts kept talking last weekend about wishing you would visit. We could call them before dinner."

Surprisingly Daddy didn't quickly object; he just stuttered over some feeble excuses, and before I knew it, he had agreed to call Aunt Lily and Aunt Rose. We stopped first at the auto shop and collected my car. Then Daddy offered to treat me to dinner at the Bumblebee Café.

Open-faced roast beef sandwiches steamed on the plates in front of us as Daddy and I caught up on the week's events. It had been a long time since we easily carried a conversation between us, and I was enjoying the lighthearted banter.

"Have you heard from Sam this week?" I asked, sliding a huge forkful of mashed potatoes and roast beef into my mouth.

Daddy's knife rattled against the plate as he tried to cut into the sandwich. His face became a cloud of fear and fatigue.

"What's wrong, Daddy?" I asked, already knowing the answer: Sam had made his decision.

"Sam called last night. He turned in his final grades at the school as well as his resignation. Seems he had already signed up when he was here last week."

The words hung in the air between us like heavy birds unable to fly.

"Are you alright?" I asked.

"Of course. He's a grown man. He has to decide these things himself. I walked out to talk to your mama about it after he called. She didn't seem surprised. She always understands you boys better than I do."

He spoke as if he and Mama had a real discussion. I didn't know what to say, so I took another bite of potatoes and gravy instead. The waitress came by and filled our coffee cups. Daddy seemed in his right mind, but after last week's talk about suicide, I just wasn't sure what to think.

Finally I ventured, "Daddy, you and Mama don't really talk. You know that, right?"

Daddy looked at me and grinned. "Your mama and I have been talking for over thirty years. No little thing like death is going to stop that. Don't worry, Jack, your father hasn't lost his mind." He paused, looking thoughtful. "You know a few of the kids over at the college sometimes get into a little trouble." He looked at me like he expected me to understand. "They smoke stuff to get some sort of mystical experience. Some people don't think there's a difference between the drug-induced vision and the real honest-to-goodness visions. The difference, I suppose, is what you expect out of the vision."

He looked away, then said, "I don't need drugs to have a vision. Your mama only left me in body. Her spirit is still here," he said, looking at me and patting his hand over his chest.

"You've missed her, though. You've lost a lot of weight."

"Well, yes, I have missed her—and her cooking." He laughed. "But she isn't really gone, Jack. She'll be back, and until then I go talk with her over on Myrtle Hill."

There was more to my father than I had ever known. Mama would have been pleased that he and I were having dinner together. *No, I told myself, Mama IS pleased we're dining together.*

Daddy paid the check and we drove back to the house. He called Aunt Lily and Aunt Rose, and they were naturally delighted to have him come with me. Daddy packed an overnight bag, and we headed out in my newly repaired Corvair.

"Joe! Jack! It's so good to see you two," Aunt Lily greeted us before we could even get out of the car.

The porch light was on and Aunt Rose was standing at the top of the stairs waiting for us. We grabbed our bags and headed toward the house with Aunt Lily's arms wrapped around both of us.

"Joe, you look good tonight," Aunt Rose said when we got to the top of the stairs.

"It must be the darkness," Daddy said. "It's good to be here, Rose."

Aunt Rose hugged me and stood back. "And, Jack, oh my! We are excited to have you back so soon. I'm sorry about your car, but I'm glad it means you can come back again. Come on in." She motioned us inside.

We put our things inside by the stairs and then followed the aunts into the kitchen.

"I have some pineapple upside-down cake, if you'd like a slice," Aunt Rose said.

"Well, I don't know," I said. "Is it frosted?" I looked at Daddy and whispered, "If it is frosted, then she dropped it on the floor." I snickered.

Aunt Lily hooted and pinched the soft flesh under my arm.

"No, it isn't frosted, young man," Aunt Rose said. "It is a fresh cake and has never once been on the floor. Now, do you want a slice?"

Cake and coffee were passed around, and then we headed out to the porch to enjoy the last of the lightning bugs. The frogs and crickets were joining in the nightly revelry, and occasionally we could hear the beavers smack their tails.

I sighed. "It's just so peaceful here."

Aunt Lily grinned in the wicker chair across from me. "Jack, I'm surprised to see you here again so soon. I understand the car broke down, but I just thought you would stay in Rome. We're happy to have you, mind you, but I was wondering if maybe a certain female person caused you to return so quickly."

"Actually I'm returning for a male person, Aunt Lily."

Her eyebrows shot up.

"I lost some clients at work this week. I'm hoping to talk Mr. John into letting me sell some of his work. It would be good for his business, and would help me out of a bind too."

"Hmm. I don't know," Aunt Lily said. "John is a little funny about his work. He's pretty careful about who shows it, anyway. Of course, he knows you and trusts you. Are you going over tomorrow to talk with him?"

"Yes, first thing in the morning. Well, first thing after some of Aunt Rose's buttermilk biscuits," I said with a smile at Aunt Rose. "I sure missed those this week. I had to get up so early to catch the train to work that I only managed coffee for breakfast all week."

The smell of frying bacon and percolating coffee brought me to my senses. The morning was gray and drizzly outside my window, but I expected that the sun was shining at the bottom of the stairs. I could hear the aunts and Daddy talking as I neared the last step.

"You haven't visited since Violet left us," Aunt Lily was saying. "You know you are the only brother we have, Joe. We still want to be a part of your life, as well as Jack and Sam's lives."

I heard Daddy let out a long breath. "I know, I know. I've just had trouble figuring it all out, Lily. I always took care of everything. I provided for Violet and the boys. I have always done well at my job. I just didn't know what to do when I couldn't fix Violet, couldn't make her better. I've been so angry. No, not completely angry," Daddy said. "I've been confused. I realized I don't know the boys all that well. Violet did all of the raising; I just disciplined and provided for them. Now it's like I don't know my own family and they're gone. Gone more than Violet is, to tell you the truth." At his last words Daddy's voice lowered as dark clouds covered my sunny-morning hopes.

I stood there, listening and wondering how many times I had added to Daddy's confusion.

Certainly I had been gone all the years since Mama's death.

"But, Joe," Aunt Rose said, "they aren't gone. They're just distant, and distance is never further away than once we turn around. Perhaps the distance is closing; Jack and Sam were with you on Monday."

"Well, that didn't go so well either. Seems Sam has joined the military, the navy. If anything can put distance between people, it's the military."

Feeling guilty for eavesdropping, I called out a "Good morning" and finished walking down the stairs. Aunt Rose stood to pour me a cup of coffee, and Aunt Lily swatted me as I walked behind her to my spot at the table.

"Sleep well?" Daddy asked over his coffee.

"Like a baby." I spread butter on two biscuits and reached for the apple butter. "What time do you think Mr. John will be up and about?" I asked no one in particular.

"Oh, he's up by now, if I know John." Aunt Lily nodded. "He doesn't sleep long; of course, old people rise earlier than young ones."

"Hey, I had a long week! It's just so much easier to sleep here for some reason."

After a quick bath and shave, I headed out to see Mr. John. The rain had grown steadier, so I drove the car. Aunt Rose asked me to stop at Hammond's Hardware and pick up some seeds on my way back. All the way to town, I rehearsed what I would say to Mr. John.

I parked next to the leafy arbor and ran for the shop door. The *OPEN* sign showed in the window, and a metal bell tinkled as I walked in. "Runaway" was playing quietly on the radio.

I walked down the first aisle and looked over the wares. On the left were some more of the tall vases with tree branches cut out of them. One had some long reeds and a few peach blossom branches arranged in it.

I heard footsteps behind me that weren't Mr. John's, and so I turned, eager to see Ginny.

"Oh, Christy. Uh ... Hi. I mean, hello. I didn't expect you here," I said.

"Good to see you too, Jack." Christy smirked. "Mr. John suggested I work here a few hours each day. With summer upon us, the tourist season is picking up. Granny still needs someone around to cook and check on her, but she doesn't need me all of the time. This gets me out a little bit. What are you doing back here so soon anyway?"

"Well, I was hoping to visit with Mr. John. Is he around?"

"He's in the studio. You can go on back; I'm sure he won't mind," she said as she jerked a thumb over her shoulder.

"I know where it is," I said and headed back toward the studio door.

Mr. John was working on the wheel when I entered. His paper-thin eyelids were gently closed and he appeared to be whispering to himself as he shaped a wide bowl.

"Good morning, Mr. John," I said.

"No talking," he whispered.

I didn't know if I had offended him and should leave, so I stood there shifting my weight from one foot to another. After a couple of minutes, Mr. John slowly opened his eyes and a smile spread across his face.

"Jack, so good to see you. What brings you back here so soon?"

I cleared my throat. "I wanted to talk to you about some of your work. I hope I didn't interrupt you too much."

"No, Jack. Don't you remember shaping takes more focus than throwing? I have to give shaping my full attention. I close my eyes to feel for the lumps and flaws. Our eyes can be so deceiving."

"Yes, of course. I remember. Do you need to keep going? I can come back later, if that's better." I wanted to make sure Mr. John was in a good mood before putting my proposal out there.

"No, I always have time for you. So what's up?"

"Well, I told my boss about your work, and I thought maybe I could talk you into producing some pottery for our warehouses. I assured him you have some very unique pieces," I said, hoping not to reveal my dire straits.

Mr. John pursed his lips, then shook his head. "No, Jack. Thanks, but no. I enjoy doing shows and letting people see my work, but it isn't made to sit unseen in warehouses. I like selling here in the shop. But ... I don't think that is the only reason you came back to visit." He looked at me—more like looked *into* me.

I sighed. "Actually I'm pretty desperate to get some of your pieces signed on. It was a rough week at Needler and Newman, where I work. I lost a couple of big contracts."

"Well, why didn't you say so from the start? We're old friends, Jack. Of course I will help you out."

"You will?" Relief washed over me.

"Yes, but I have some conditions to my offer."

"I'll see what I can do, but our contracts are basically fixed forms."

"I think you can agree to my demands." Mr. John smiled. "I will follow the standard contract, but I also want you to work in my shop every other weekend for the duration of the contract."

"Um, okay. Doing what?"

"If you are going to sell my pottery, I want to make sure you understand it. You will practice your methods under my tutelage, and if I am gone, Ginny can work with you."

"There may be some weekends I have to work," I said as I peered around the studio. "What happens if I can't make one of the weekends?"

"You'll have to make it up on another weekend, or you can take time off of work at Needles and Nuisance."

I couldn't tell if it was a purposeful mistake or not, but I chose to keep quiet about it. Working with Mr. John might be a fun diversion from the city, and with the heat of summer coming on, getting out of town regularly seemed like a good idea anyway.

"Okay, I agree to your terms," I said, nodding.

We shook on it, and then I spent an hour watching Mr. John work on the bowls. They would be casserole baking dishes when he finally finished. I was impressed with his dexterity and speed. He turned out several dishes and then looked at me.

"Do you want to try today or wait until next time?"

"I'll wait. I'd like to check out your inventory and get an idea what we can plan on purchasing for the first lot."

"Sure. Christy can show you around the store. I have some larger items stored away in the woodshed. I plan to take them with me next week to Houston, but I can add more to the show from other work if you want those items."

I laughed; Mr. John was so kind and easy to deal with. "I wish all of my clients were so congenial."

I walked back out to the shop floor and began looking at Mr. John's items. Coffee mugs lined the top shelves; bowls, plates, and platters were on the middle shelves; and larger pots and vases were stacked on the lower shelves. Mr. John appeared to like blues and greens the best, but some ceramics were glazed in golds, reds, browns, and purples. The walls were reserved for specialty items like lamps, pitchers, and the huge decorative vases. Many had intricate designs cut out of the walls or imprinted into the sides or inside the bases. Lifting several pieces, I noticed Mr. John's signature was a thumbprint morphed into a bird.

Gathering several smaller mugs, bowls, and candy dishes, I placed them on the front counter. I told Christy I would come back later with some boxes and then jogged over to Hammond's Hardware through a light rain. Mrs. Hammond was at the counter helping some little kids pick out penny candy. She looked up with a smile and waved, then went back to the peppermint and lemon sticks.

I wandered through the aisles at the back of the store looking for the seeds I'd been instructed to buy. The dim light filtered through the front windows and barely reached its fingers into the shadowy corner of seed packets. Some onion bulbs were laid out in old wooden drawers on the floor, and Mr. Hammond had some tomato starters in paper containers next to the onion bulbs. I grabbed a container of tomatoes on impulse. Perhaps I would be able to grow some in the window of my apartment.

I scoured the seed packets and found what Aunt Rose had sent me to get: marigolds, black-eyed Susans, and daisies. I grabbed a packet of each, and then my eyes fell upon the colorful blue-and-purple packet of asters. I wasn't sure how the aunts would feel about it, but I thought for the sake of Grandpappy I should buy those too.

I walked up to the counter with my hands full of flower packets and tomato plants. The kids and their candy were gone. Mrs. Hammond waited patiently at the register, beaming at me.

"Good morning, Jack. I'm very glad to see you back so soon. I bet Rose and Lily are beside themselves. They miss you boys so much, you know. They always talk about how well you're both doing, you and Sam."

"They're awfully sweet ladies. And Daddy came with me this time."

I wasn't sure why I had offered that piece of information, but Mrs. Hammond continued in her friendly way: "Oh, it would be so good to see Joe. Please tell him to stop by if he has a chance. I haven't seen him since—" Mrs. Hammond stopped herself and glanced up at me with sad eyes.

"Since Mama's funeral? I know. I think Daddy is starting to rejoin the world. He isn't over Mama's death by any means, but he's able to talk a little about it now. I'll let him know you asked after him."

"Please do, Jack. Mr. Hammond and I always liked your mama and daddy."

Mrs. Hammond put the seed packets in a small brown bag. "Do you want the tomato plants in the bag or will you leave them out?" she asked. Then, as if she just noticed what I had bought, she asked, "Did Lily's tomatoes fail? She always has such a green thumb with them."

"No, Mrs. Hammond, those are for me. I thought I would try to grow them at my apartment in Atlanta. It might not work, but I thought I'd try anyway." I smiled at her, though I was thinking it was probably a foolish way to spend my money.

"Well, good luck with them," she said as she handed me my packages. "Make sure you tell your daddy we'd love to see him."

"Whoops, I nearly forgot! Do you have any boxes lying around that I could have? I wanted to carry some of Mr. John's ceramics back to Atlanta with me."

"Oh, Jack." Mrs. Hammond clucked. "I just gave all of them to Ginny. She was going back home this weekend."

"That's okay," I said, trying to hide my disappointment—which had nothing to do with not getting some boxes. "I can wrap them in some newspaper. See you later, Mrs. Hammond. And I'll be sure to pass your greetings on to Daddy." I waved as I walked out the screen door, letting it swing back harder than I'd intended.

I trotted through the rain to my Chevy, wondering why it should bother me that Ginny had gone back home. Ginny had seemed so self-confident, so assured. I guess I just hoped that she would fare better than I had in standing up to a father with different expectations than her own.

With a sigh I placed the paper bag and the tomato plants on the floorboards of the backseat and headed back in to the pottery shop. Mr. John, in his clay- and water-splattered work clothes, was rearranging some items on the middle shelves. He turned and smiled when I walked in the door.

"There's my new partner looking like a wet duck!" He grinned. "Have you come back already to start working? I didn't expect you so soon." He wrapped his arm around my shoulders and patted my face with his other hand.

"No, I ran over to Hammond's Hardware. I was hoping they would have some boxes I could use to pack some of your ceramics in the car, but evidently Ginny took all of them."

I looked at Mr. John, hoping he would offer some information, but he just nodded his head and turned toward Christy.

"Christy, would you go look in the back of my truck? I think I have some boxes left in there," he said, then turned back in my direction. "I picked up some boxes at the

Colonial in Rome last week. I need to ship some items to Houston this week. Oh, listen ..." Mr. John started humming as the radio played the piano theme music from the movie *Exodus*.

Some friends and I had gone to the theater to see it last winter. Some of the girls at work had been all agog over Paul Newman, and Jimmy and I agreed to go with them one night. It wasn't bad for a love story; at least there was still some fighting and action involved anyway.

Mr. John was watching me closely, as if he could read my mind. "You saw it, didn't you?" he asked. "What did you think of the end when Ari says that someday Jews and Arabs will live in peace?"

I shrugged. "I don't know. Seems to me they've been fighting more than they've been peaceful. I don't think the US will ever be the ones to bring peace."

"That's just it, Jack. Peace isn't an international policy. And love? Love is not just some doctrine for pacifists and pansies. Love and peace are real spirits who live in all of us." Mr. John's face seemed young and vibrant as he spoke.

Behind Mr. John, I saw that Christy was back, holding three boxes stacked inside each other. She walked up a little closer and cleared her throat.

"Here you are Jack," she said as she eyed the again-humming Mr. John.

I took the boxes from her and walked toward the counter where I had placed the dishes I was interested in. Mr. John kept humming along with the radio. Christy wrapped pieces of pottery in newspaper and handed them to me.

"Do you think he's right?" she asked, not looking at me or Mr. John.

"About what?" I asked.

"That peace and love live inside us. That governments won't be able to force peace." Christy seemed anxious, almost flustered.

"I suppose. Does it matter?"

Christy looked at me with tears brimming in her eyes. "Sam," was all she said as she stared at me in obvious disbelief.

My head jerked up and I looked her in the face. That was the moment I knew that Christy was in love with Sam.

"Sam will be alright," I said as I put my arms around her. I pulled her close and offered a prayer for all of us. "God will keep him safe. We can't lose him and Mama both."

The rain stopped by lunchtime. Now the afternoon sun warmed my face as I lay in the repaired hammock. *Should have put it up on the porch like Aunt Lily said,* I thought. A fly buzzed around my head despite my shooing it

away, so I finally gave up on my afternoon
nap. Aunt Lily had taken Daddy fishing while
I was at Mr. John's, and now they were
cleaning fish for dinner. Aunt Rose was in the
kitchen, singing and making macaroni salad
for tonight's feast.

I wandered across the backyard and looked
over Aunt Lily's garden. Cucumbers were just
forming on the vines. The pole beans were
sending runners up the wooden tripods, and
two-foot-high tomato plants displayed white
and yellow blooms. The ends of the garden
were capped with varying flowers just
beginning to show their colors. My favorite
violets were interspersed among the smaller
flowers, reminding me of the way Mama was
always there for me, no matter where I might
be.

Aunt Rose came out on the porch and called
for me to join her. She handed me a cold glass
of sweet tea and settled on the wicker chair
near the door. I chose the top step and leaned
my back against the banister beam. The ice in
the glass clinked as I swallowed a long
draught.

"Was your visit with Mr. John successful?"
Aunt Rose asked.

I had been surprised that she didn't ask
about it earlier at lunch. I felt nervous about
revealing my plans.

"Yes, it went quite well. Mr. John agreed to
contract with Needler and Newman if I would
agree to a contract with him."

I stared into the glass of tea, grasping what had happened. I was contracted to Mr. John for as long as I needed him to help me out. I was the one being helped, I realized. Mr. John was far superior to any of the potters I had dealt with yet, and he certainly didn't need to deal with our upstart company.

Aunt Rose eyed me. "Can you keep your end of the agreement? Mr. John can be demanding at times."

I smiled. "I'm pretty sure I can handle it … if you will help me."

"Me? You know I'll help any way I can, but how?"

"Well …" I began, thinking how to explain, but then Daddy and Aunt Lily came around the side of the house with a bowl full of water and cleaned fish.

"Woo boy! Are we going to eat well tonight, Jack," Daddy hooted. His face and neck looked sunburned, and he wore suspenders with his old work pants. He wiped his balding head with his handkerchief and then stuffed it back into his pants pocket.

"Your daddy still knows something about fishing," Aunt Lily said, smiling. "I was afraid he had forgotten all the things Violet taught him, but he's still cooking in all his pots."

"All the pots!" Aunt Rose hollered as she jumped from her chair. "I forgot the potatoes were still boiling." She ran to the screen door, letting it bang shut.

"Good heavens, Rose. Don't get all worked up," Aunt Lily called after her as she entered the house a few steps behind Aunt Rose.

Daddy sat down next to me and I handed him the rest of my tea. He smiled, ran his arm across his brow, and then gulped down the last of the tea. He looked strong and healthy.

"It's good for you to be here. You look better," I said, not very loud. I had never spoken to my father like that before—like a friend.

Daddy looked at me and then out toward the creek. "I used to walk with your mama down to the water. She especially liked to go in the evening. Lightning bugs would sparkle and she would hold my hand. Those were good times to be here too." His voice cracked, but he went on. "When she had the cancer so bad that she couldn't walk anymore, Lily would pack blankets around her in the trailer—you know she was so thin and bony—and I would drive the tractor down to the river. We would sit there together in the trailer as the lightning bugs began to crawl up the tall weeds and start their show. As sad as it was that she couldn't walk and hold my hand, it was still a good time."

Daddy and I sat there on the steps together. He had never shared intimacies with me. It was like the Japanese poetry and suicidal thoughts: a startling insight into a man I barely knew.

"You know, Jack, you're right. It is good for me to be here." He paused, then added, "And it's good for you too."

Fried fish, boiled buttered potatoes, home-canned green beans from last year, and macaroni salad were heaped in serving dishes on the sideboard buffet. The table was covered with a white crocheted cover, and the dishes were the good ones reserved for holidays. A vase of wild daisies and Queen Anne's lace rested in the middle of the table.

"Whew! You girls are going all fancy on us," Daddy said.

"Well, it isn't every day that we get such good-looking company for dinner," Aunt Lily said.

We all sat down and held hands. Daddy said the blessing and then Aunt Rose served each of us from the sideboard.

"You are good-looking," Aunt Rose said, "but the real reason we are celebrating is that Jack got his contract."

Daddy turned and slapped me on the back. "Congratulations, Jack. I'm sorry I forgot to ask about it."

"It's okay. I was just getting ready to tell Aunt Rose about it when you and Aunt Lily came with your pile of fish. That was a pretty big deal too. I didn't catch any that were worth keeping last week."

"So what did Mr. John say?" Aunt Lily asked. "I'm very surprised he agreed to do it."

"Well, he did have some demands," I drawled. "Nothing I can't handle, but I could use your and Aunt Rose's help." I raised my eyebrows and looked at the two of them.

"Our help? What in the world can we do?" Aunt Lily asked.

"Whatever it is, Jack, you know we will help if we can," Aunt Rose answered.

"Well ..." I paused, thinking again about the best way to ask so much of them. *Straightforward is always best,* I thought. "Mr. John has agreed to sell to my company if I will agree to work with him every other weekend while he is contracted with us."

The aunts' eyes lit up.

"Oh, Jack! That's wonderful," Aunt Rose cheered.

"Your mama would be thrilled," Aunt Lily said.

"But how can we help with that?" Aunt Rose asked. "We aren't very good at pottery."

"Oh, no. No, I'm sorry," I said. "You can help by letting me stay here when I come to work for Mr. John."

Aunt Lily laughed. "Jack, how silly!" she said. "Of course you will be welcome to stay here. It will be nice to see you more often, and it will give Rose an excuse to cook more."

Aunt Rose brought me my plate and gave me a hug about the neck. A peck on the cheek was the only answer I needed from her.

*Perhaps a man's character is like a tree, and
his reputation like its shadow; the shadow is
what we think of it; the tree is the real thing.*
                    —Abraham Lincoln

CHAPTER 12

In the kitchen Deborah stared at Mariam. "Is it true?"

Mariam swallowed and her hands perspired. *She found out my secret!* she thought, but simply said, "Is what true?"

"That the healer, this Jesus, will be staying here?"

Letting out a relieved breath, Mariam thought, *So that is what interests her: not Nathaniel himself, but the healing—the healer.* "Mm," Mariam replied, "they are expecting more men, so I suppose it is true." She paused and looked at Deborah. "Do you ... think he will heal your lip?"

"I doubt that Father can afford his gift," Deborah said, then sighed. "Nathaniel is a man of wealth. My family is not so blessed."

"Well ... there are ... ways ... of getting money," Mariam said, then thought, *I doubt that you could make much with that face, but you might get enough.*

Naïve Deborah shook her head. "Father doesn't have anything to sell. Everything goes for the taxes anyway." Her eyes filled with tears.

"Perhaps we should speak to Thaddeus and Simon. They may know what he charges, and then we will figure out a way to help you." Mariam smiled and put a hand on Deborah's arm, hoping it would be enough to calm and reassure her friend.

It wasn't: Deborah leaned forward and fell into Mariam's arms, holding on for dear life, it seemed. What had Mariam gotten herself into now?

Hope was all that Deborah had; it would have to be enough for now. She and Mariam waited hand in hand at the bottom of the stairs for the guests to leave.

The night had grown chilly, but Deborah's shivers came from anticipation and fear. *Can this healer really do what they say? Can he help me? Can I afford him? What if he can help, but I can't afford it—what then?* It was too much to imagine and she leaned into

Mariam for support. Mariam gave her a small smile, and then both of them looked upstairs at the sound of men talking.

Ben and David sauntered down the stairs and eyed the two women. Mariam glanced down, Deborah noticed. The two men stopped near the women as the other men filed off the stairs behind them

"Mariam," Ben said, "we would be happy to stay a while longer. If we put a veil over her face, your friend can earn a little too." He laughed and so did David.

Deborah wasn't sure what they meant, but she knew it was not a compliment. She was used to being insulted, even feared, but time never took away the pain.

Mariam's hand squeezed Deborah's so hard that Deborah looked at her. Mariam's face had grown red, her jaws clenched.

"What makes you think she would want to take care of the likes of you?" Mariam asked.

Towering over them, Ben said, "Well, our money was good enough for you, little Miss Whore. Why wouldn't it be good enough for this piece of trash?"

Deborah's eyes grew big as she now began to understand the men's insinuations. She let her hand fall from Mariam's grip.

"Mariam?" Deborah gasped.

"Can we help you with something?" Simon asked, coming down the stairs just ahead of Thaddeus and Eleazar. He stared at Ben and David, who shrugged and walked away. They were known as good men, Deborah knew; both betrothed to girls in Bethany, and could not risk incrimination.

Deborah looked first at Simon and then at Mariam. Choosing to ignore the inappropriateness of the first conversation and the possible inappropriateness of the desired one, she said, "This ... This Jesus, the healer ... how much would he charge for ... to heal a split lip?"

"Do you want to be healed?" Thaddeus asked her.

Deborah felt her chest swell with another surge of hope. "Yes, sir, very much, sir!" But then reality crashed in like a great wave, and Deborah looked down as she wrung her hands. "But I don't have much money. My father cannot pay a lot." The tears threatened to spill over onto her cheeks.

"There is no charge, sister," Thaddeus said, smiling as he spoke. He placed his thumb over the hole that fractured Deborah's face and cupped her chin with his long fingers. "May the Holy Lord, the Father of all that is good, bless you with wholeness and health."

Deborah couldn't help it; the tears she had held back for so long, the pain, the embarrassment, the shame, all of it tore loose from her broken spirit in one deep groan. No man but her father had ever touched her face or looked at her with such concern or spoken over her with such grace. She dropped her head and broke into uncontrollable sobs.

Mariam placed her arm around Deborah's shoulders and tried to comfort her. Eleazar moved to separate Thaddeus and Simon from Deborah.

Eleazar glared at them. "That is enough. You should not play with a young girl's weaknesses. Leave at once!"

"Perhaps you should look at the girl first," Simon said.

Deborah turned her tear-stained face toward Mariam. She saw Mariam's eyes light up, and her smile was contagious. Deborah reached her hand to her face. Her breath caught and she began crying all over again. She turned, and now Eleazar saw her face, whole and complete. He started apologizing to the two men.

Thaddeus stopped Eleazar. "Only faith can heal like this. If the girl had not had faith in the Lord, she would not be healed. Our God has returned to his people, and he comes with power and glory. Wait until Jesus arrives; then you will see what real miracles are."

In a gush of tears, Deborah tried to offer her thanks to the men. After they encouraged her to praise the Lord for this blessing, she rushed home, with Mariam and Marta following, to tell her family the good news. Deborah's father demanded to see the healers and so the entire family traipsed back to Marta's house, a gaggle of singing and dancing merrymakers. When they arrived, Eleazar was talking with

Thaddeus and Simon, while John sat nearby listening.

Deborah's father approached the men and knelt before them. "Please accept my humble thanks," he said. "I haven't much, but here is what I have." He pulled out a small pouch of coins. "You will also come to dinner at our house, and we will pay your bills here at Marta's."

Thaddeus shook his head. "Thank you for your thoughtfulness, but it isn't necessary. We have received this gift freely, and we freely give to others. It is not our power that healed your daughter, but the power that Jesus has bestowed upon us."

"Who is this Jesus?" Deborah's father asked.

"He is the Messiah," Thaddeus answered, "and he will be here in a day or two. He will be happy to meet you and teach you the ways of the Lord."

*Those who restrain desire, do so because
theirs is weak enough to be restrained.*
—William Blake

CHAPTER 13

I arrived early to work on Monday, grateful to have my car back. Jimmy pulled in behind me and raced to catch me at the stairs.

"Jack! Did you hear the news? We got a raise!" Jimmy called.

I stopped and waited for him to catch up. "What do you mean?" I asked.

"Needler and Newman, both of them, they came out on the floor Friday evening before we quit work and told everyone." His voice rose as his hands flew through the air. "The company did well in the first quarter and they felt like we could be compensated for it. You should have been there."

"Really? A raise for everyone?" I asked, barely able to imagine it since my depressing week last week. "I doubt that includes me. I had such lousy luck last week."

"It's for everyone, even you. What's one week, anyway? You just hit a rough patch. You'll do better this week. You'll see." Jimmy grinned and I couldn't help doing the same.

I spent the day photographing Mr. John's ceramics to show clients what we could offer. Mr. Needler came out mid-afternoon and told me about the raise and looked at the cut-out vases. He was obviously impressed and shook my hand on signing such a great potter.

I stopped at the local hardware store on my way home that evening to pick up some pots for my tomato plants. The store was well-lit, organized, and stocked, but the cashier was a teenaged boy more interested in popping his gum than carrying on a conversation with me. I realized I liked Hammond's Hardware because my purchase always came with a free smile and a friendly chat.

I walked next door to the grocery and picked up a steak. *Might as well celebrate my raise,* I told myself, *even if I am all alone.* By the time I got home, it was getting late and I nearly burned the steak trying to cook it too quickly on high heat. I sat down at the table, turned on the radio, and listened to the news on the public radio station.

After dinner I arranged the plants in their new pots and set them on a small table in front of the window. I forgot to place a pan under the pots, and when I watered them, the liquid flowed right through and flooded the table. I grabbed a few kitchen towels and sopped up the mess. *Hardly a night to remember,* I thought. The aunts were right that I needed to make some friends.

The next two weeks passed quickly, assembling packages, filling orders, answering calls, and speaking with potential buyers. Jimmy was enthralled with some new girl on the second floor and kept taking smoke breaks to see her. The three of us went out for burgers one evening after work, but it wasn't much fun being the third wheel. By the time my first scheduled weekend with Mr. John rolled around, I was ready to leave town.

I packed my bag on Thursday night and left it in my car Friday while I worked. As soon as work ended, I headed toward Paradox, trying hard not to speed down the country roads in my exuberance. How odd that Paradox should be considered home. For three years Atlanta had been home, and before that Rome had always been home, but now as I contemplated my coming weekend, I found myself thinking of Paradox as home. *That would excite the aunts.* I smiled.

Once I passed the signs for Rockmart, I tore into the peanut butter sandwiches I had packed for my dinner. *Should have called Sam and arranged to meet him,* I thought. *Next time, perhaps.*

A few apples and cookies later, I was pulling into Rome's Colonial Grocery on Fourth Avenue to buy a cold Coca-Cola. The Friday night crowd was strolling toward Broad

Street to catch the latest show at the DeSoto Theater. I waved to several people as I jumped out of the car. Stretching after the long drive, I ambled into the grocery for my drink.

"Jack, is that you?" Sam's voice stopped me in the second aisle.

I turned to see Sam—and Christy—flagging me down from the register counter. I grabbed a bottle of Coca-Cola out of the cooler and walked back to meet them.

"Daddy said you were headed to Paradox this weekend, but he didn't think you were stopping in Rome," Sam said with a hint of accusation. "Have you seen Daddy yet? You could go with us to the show."

"No, I'm just stopping for a drink before I head on out to Paradox. The aunts are expecting me. Hi, Christy."

"Jack." She nodded.

"Are you not staying with your granny anymore?" I asked her.

"Oh, I am, though she doesn't need me as often now. I'm still helping Mr. John out at the shop too."

Sam smiled. "I thought Christy could use a break, so I picked her up this afternoon in Paradox. It's supposed to be a good movie tonight. I'm heading back to Rockmart tomorrow, so I don't guess I'll see you. Daddy told you I joined the navy?"

"Yeah." I looked at my feet. "When do you head out?" I asked, more out of duty than interest or concern. *What is wrong with me?* I wondered. *Sam's my brother ... used to be my best friend.*

"I haven't gotten definite orders yet, but it looks like it will be July or August."

An awkward pause ensued—filled with Christy's confused gaze.

"What's wrong with you two?" she asked. "You're acting more like strangers than brothers."

We paused, both grimacing a bit.

"Nothing," Sam finally mumbled.

"No, nothing's wrong," I said. "Well, I better go."

I paid for my drink while Sam and Christy walked out of the store and over toward the DeSoto. I passed them when I left and waved out the window. I could feel Mama pinching the underside of my arm, but I kept on driving to Paradox.

Aunt Rose and Aunt Lily were waiting, sitting on the porch, sweaters draped around their shoulders, when I pulled up. "You shouldn't have waited out here," I called as I grabbed my bag out of the passenger seat. "It's chilly tonight."

They both rose and waited at the top of the stairs to hug me tight and then squeezed my waist one more time.

"Oh, it's so good to have you back again. I could definitely get used to this," Aunt Rose said.

"Well, I hope so, since I'll be here often from the responses I'm getting at work."

We spent the last hour of the evening catching up on my life in Atlanta, Aunt Lily's garden, and the people I remembered in Paradox. Aunt Lily told me that Mrs. Hammond brought them their mugs and some fresh strawberry jam she had canned that week. I wondered what had happened to send Ginny away, but I didn't ask. The night was getting late and I needed to be up early.

Coffee and bacon woke me in the morning before the sunshine even had a chance to break through the open window. The night had gotten cooler than I expected, and I was burrowed under the quilt. Work awaited me, I knew, but the promise of breakfast and hot coffee kicked me out of the bed. I grabbed my jeans off the chair and threw on a light flannel shirt.

Aunt Rose was at the table reading her Bible, but Aunt Lily was already outside tilling the weeds under in the garden. The hum of the tiller motor barely reached the kitchen. I piled bacon and scrambled eggs on my plate while Aunt Rose poured me a cup of black coffee.

"Sam dropped by for a few minutes yesterday," she said. "He was picking up Christy to go to a movie."

"Yes." I cleared my throat. "I ran into them at the store in Rome."

"He told us he joined the navy. Said he leaves this summer sometime." Aunt Rose looked at me with curious eyes.

"Mm-hmm," I said, grabbing another forkful of bacon from the serving platter. "July or August, he thinks." I didn't have any more information to share, but I felt like Aunt Rose was waiting for more.

"He seemed proud to be joining up. I hope Joe can come to grips with it." Now she eyed me.

I snorted. "That's not likely to happen."

"Your daddy loves you boys. He just wants what is best for you." Aunt Rose sipped her coffee and then turned back to her morning Bible reading.

I finished up my breakfast and gulped the last of the coffee. I wasn't sure Daddy wanted what was best for us as much as he wanted what made him comfortable, but I didn't know if that was fair either. I kissed Aunt Rose good-bye, waved across the yard to Aunt Lily, and walked to Mr. John's place.

Smoke was drifting across the lawn when I reached Mr. John's. I walked over to the area with the outdoor kiln and saw Mr. John loading more wood on the fire. The heat felt comfortable in the chilly morning air, but I was sure by afternoon it would be a hot job to keep the kiln going.

"Good morning, Mr. John," I said, breaking the silence.

"Hello, Jack." Mr. John grunted, pulling a heavy log from the stack. He threw the log on and then stood back to survey me. "Are you ready to work?"

"Yes, sir."

He nodded toward the studio. "Head on into the shop. The clay is set out on the counter. You can start wedging and practice your throwing while I check on a few things."

"Will Ginny tell me what to do?" I asked, trying to avoid having to ask straight out about her.

"I'm telling you what to do, Jack. Now get on in there." Mr. John seemed preoccupied, so I quietly headed toward the pottery shop.

The smell of dust and dampness calmed my spirit. *Perhaps Mr. John is just tired,* I thought as I sliced a slab from the plastic-encased block of gray clay. I banged the clay on the wooden counter, wedging out the air bubbles, softening its stubborn hardness, and then finally patting it into a ball. By the time Mr. John joined me in the studio, I was wetting the bat and preparing to throw the clay onto it.

Mr. John nodded toward me, and then headed over to slice off his own piece of clay. I was coning my clay between the ball of one hand and the palm of the other when Mr. John started talking: "This is the time of preparation—when you can talk to the clay, perhaps make an impression on it as it begins to grow under your hands. Once the clay's spirit has been brought into alignment through the wedging, it will join more closely to the potter as he centers."

I listened to his soothing voice and continued placing pressure on the cone. Soon it would be ready to open up with my thumb.

"When you are working on the potter's wheel, you only touch the clay at one spot," he continued quietly. "Yet as the wheel turns the clay, the whole is being touched."

Certainly I already knew this. What was Mr. John trying to say to me? I wondered. Did Mr. John really want to teach me pottery, or was this contract a way to preach to me some guru mumbo-jumbo?

As I started opening up the clay to form the bowls we would be working on that day, Mr. John continued with his hushed speech.

"Ginny isn't here today. She went to visit her family for a few days. She's attending a bridal shower for her brother's fiancée."

A happy sensation traveled from my spine out toward my fingers as the bowl suddenly sprang to life in my hands. I couldn't help smiling, but I kept looking at the clay beneath me.

"Ginny told me you chose to be a businessman at your father's request." Mr. John continued centering, never looking up from his own piece of clay, always watching, always focused. "Ginny's father hasn't demanded she not be a potter, but he makes his wishes known in other ways. Like a piece of clay on the wheel, he only touches one part of her, but all of her is affected." Mr. John finished speaking as he added water to his clay with a soft sponge.

"She told me she would make her own decision," I said, surprised at the defensive tone in my voice. "I think it's great that she is doing what she wants to do, even if it means going against her father. There's nothing wrong with a girl being a potter."

"How is Ginny's situation different than your own?" Mr. John stared at me as the cone of clay circled under his hands.

"Potters don't normally make enough money to take care of a family," I said, reprising all my old arguments. "A businessman has many other options than a potter or an artisan."

"Do you remember the day you first tried throwing with me? The day I poked your clay and made you start over?"

I turned red from embarrassment and a little leftover anger. "Yes."

"Why did I do that?"

"You wanted me to use the entire piece of clay. I thought it was thrift on your part, but you said the clay should not be separated."

"That's right, Jack. Separating ourselves from our full potential makes us only part of a person. If that clay had been intended to be a foot-tall candelabrum, but you only made it eight inches through your mistake, the clay would never be what it was intended. The light would never shine the way it was meant to."

"So you think I'm not using all my clay? Is that what you're saying?"

Mr. John threw the question right back at me: "Do you think you are?"

The days of questioning what I was doing at Needler and Newman came hauntingly to mind. The times I watched Jimmy nail a deal or effortlessly make a sale while I struggled next to him floated through my memory. I had hoped to be able to create some pottery in Atlanta, but all I had been able to do so far was find a market for other people's creations. At times I did feel like my light was flickering on a too short candlestick.

I never replied to Mr. John. I finished my bowl, ran the metal wire underneath it to break it free from the bat, and then began a new bowl. Mr. John never tried to make me talk, and his silence was easy, not accusatory. I was on my third bowl before I spoke again.

"What did you mean when you said Ginny would be affected in other ways by her father?" I asked, suddenly remembering where this conversation had begun.

Mr. John walked over to my wheel and stood watching my hands as I worked. "Remember the time to talk is during coning. Shaping is slower than throwing; it takes more focus."

I turned my attention back to the bowl, but my mind wandered back to Ginny. I saw her auburn hair shining in the sun as she told me her dreams and plans. I heard her good-humored sniffing and saw her nose curl up at me after the end of a long day chopping wood. I remembered her description of her brother and sister, of her mother and her father. I understood her irritation and reluctance to stay at home.

"Jack!" Mr. John's voice startled me. "That one can be tossed out. You lost your focus."

I looked down at the bowl swirling under my hands. It looked fine to me: round, moderately deep. I didn't understand what was wrong with it. I looked at Mr. John, but he just sliced the clay from the bat and threw it back into the recycling vat.

"Start over, and stay focused," Mr. John said.

"But it looked fine."

"It looked fine on the outside, but the inside was heavy and dark. The potter cannot become distracted during shaping."

How could he tell?

Christy came in to work at ten o'clock. She looked fresh and vivacious in denim pants and a flowing blouse.

"Did you enjoy the movie?" I asked.

"Yes, it was good. You should have watched it with us." She smiled as she put on a work apron.

"I think you and Sam were fine without me." I winked.

Christy blushed and then went about her work rearranging shelves, dusting the front window displays, and greeting the customers starting to trickle in from the weekend tourists. Most people wanted to watch me and Mr. John working on the wheels, and he was generously accommodating. They asked questions, and he always patiently answered.

"Where do you get your mud?" a young girl asked, peering into the bucket of discolored water next to the wheel.

Mr. John smiled. "We have to use clay for pottery. Do you make mud pies?"

The small girl smiled back and nodded.

"Do they ooze all over and make a mess when you bake them?" He grinned.

The girl's eyes grew large. "Yes. I set them on the stone wall near the coal shed, but they always slide off the back. Sometimes they stay put on the leaf pans, though."

"That's why we use clay," Mr. John said. "There are many types of soil, but clay has an inner strength to it. That strength allows it to be molded and shaped, and lets it stand up to the heat when we fire it in the kiln."

"How do you put on handles?" asked an older gentleman who had stood by listening while his wife shopped in the store.

"The clay has several stages before it is complete," Mr. John said. "After Jack here finishes his bowl, he will place it on the drying shelves. After a few days, depending on the weather and the temperature in here, the clay will be at what we call the 'leather' stage. That's when we can use some slip—sort of a very watery clay mixture—and attach appendages. Pottery takes a long time to develop. Often I have no idea what it will end up being. I have to wait for the clay to tell me."

That sort of conversation always made me uncomfortable, like maybe Mr. John was losing his marbles, but the gentleman tilted his head, stroked his chin, and nodded.

"Sort of sounds like my life," he murmured.

Maybe he's losing it too, I thought.

The small group of people drifted off and the thrumming of the wheel stopped. Mr. John patted my back and congratulated me on a good day's work.

"You will be sore tomorrow, Jack, but you worked hard. By the end of our contract, you will be an accomplished potter."

"Thanks, Mr. John, but I'm not sure how much I am learning. With people coming in all of the time, I don't get to ask you for much advice."

"The first step, Jack, is centering. Centering takes a very long time to learn. You have managed in your studies at school, and somewhat here, to center the clay. But centering is a test, a practice that is not often perfect. What you must first learn is to identify when the clay is off center and how to coax it back into the center. You can't give up on the clay when it is being difficult. Remember, you must yield yourself to the clay and let it speak to you."

Mr. John turned to wash his hands, leaving me more befuddled than ever.

"Will you be staying over tonight at your aunts' house, or are you headed back to Rome?" he asked over his shoulder.

"Oh, umm, I'm staying at the farmhouse. I never thought about staying with Daddy," I said, more to myself than to Mr. John.

Mr. John shook the dirty water from his hands and held my own in his strong grasp. "Yielding and listening," he said and then walked out to the shop floor to give Christy final instructions.

I spent the night with the aunts and went to church in Paradox the next day. I hadn't realized how much I missed the familiar hymns and prayers, and I even enjoyed visiting with the old people. Sunday lunch was a picnic along the riverbank. Aunt Rose brought two old quilts and threw them out in the shade of some hardwoods, where we enjoyed cold fried chicken and biscuits with Mrs. Hammond's jam. All of us napped afterward, listening to the birds and insects in the lazy afternoon. Atlanta and work seemed so far away, but duty called, and by late afternoon I was tossing my bag into the back of the car.

"Be careful," called Aunt Rose.

"See you soon," Aunt Lily said.

I waved from the open window and headed on my way. The daisies and wildflowers were higher now, obstructing the view as I turned from the one-lane road onto the main thoroughfare. The sky was beginning to cloud up making it easier to drive without the sun glaring through the windshield.

As I neared Rome, I considered Mr. John's words again. *Yielding and listening to clay?* It sounded like malarkey to me, but if it made Mr. John feel better, I would attempt to somehow yield and listen to dirt. My attitude would need some yielding as well, I realized.

I needed to make a pit stop by the time I was in Rome, so I drove by the house, hoping Daddy would be in. I pulled up to the curb and spotted him sitting on the front porch reading the paper. He lowered the paper and waved.

"Jack! How are you?" He slowly raised himself from the rocker, his pants sagging around his waist. "I didn't know you were stopping. I was just fixing to have a BLT. Will you join me?"

"Oh, I wasn't staying—just needed to make a pit stop. I've got to get back home. Work tomorrow, you know." My words seemed rushed and distant.

Daddy's face drooped like his pants and I immediately felt guilty. I glanced at my watch. "Well, it's not that late after all, and I could use a bite to eat or I'll just have to stop somewhere."

"Come on in," Daddy said as he patted my back. "I'll get everything out." He walked toward the kitchen.

I was surprised to find Daddy could so adeptly assemble sandwiches and even had devilled eggs and a gelatin salad made. We talked over dinner about my work in Atlanta and at Mr. John's. Daddy asked if I had learned anything helpful from Mr. John.

"I don't know. He seems a little odd, to tell you the truth. I thought he would teach me skills to use with the clay, but instead he says things like I have to listen to the clay and yield to it."

Daddy wrinkled his brow and looked at me. "What do you suppose he means by that?"

What I wanted to say was that I thought Mr. John was a little nuts, but just then a bird flew into the kitchen window.

Daddy turned around in irritation. "That bugger has been flying into the window for a week. He starts in the early morning at my bedroom window, and as the day progresses, he moves to the kitchen window. He's driving me insane."

"Have you tried putting something in the window?" I asked as the juvenile mourning dove kept throwing itself at the window.

"Yes, I have put things in the window, taken things out of the window, opened the window, stood outside the window. Nothing works. Every day it comes back and starts all over again. He's very persistent; I have to give him that." Daddy sighed.

We finished eating and cleared the table while the bird kept flapping into the window, sometimes sitting on the edge and pecking on the glass. I thought it was funny, but Daddy had evidently had enough of it. Daddy suggested we go for a short walk before I had to sit so long in the car, and I agreed.

Without intending it, we ended up back at the cemetery. The clouds had continued to darken the sky, and the air was sticky and still. From the top of Myrtle Hill, we looked over the town and rested. The veterans' graves were clustered in one area with Private Charles Graves's monument. Touted as "America's Known Soldier," he was a bit of a town legend in Rome. Private Graves was a casualty of the Great War and had been buried in France. The government wanted to bring him back and bury him alongside the Unknown Soldier in Arlington, but his mother wouldn't hear of it. She had waited long enough to get her boy back home, and she wasn't having him far away from her again.

Looking down on Private Charles Graves's resting place, I thought about Sam. Daddy must have been thinking the same thing.

"Sam goes to boot camp in July or August," Daddy said, staring toward the war memorial. "He'll start out at the Great Lakes and then go to Rhode Island for Officer Training School.

It's so far away but still closer than he will be later."

"He'll be okay, Daddy."

Daddy looked up at me and smiled faintly. "That's not something any of us knows, Jack. I learned that completely with your mother." Daddy paused in deep thought; I waited patiently. "There are things in life we don't like, and we can't do anything about them. And there are things in life we can do something about. Sam is a grown man who needs to make his own decisions. I don't like the decision he is making, but I can try to understand it." He paused a minute more to stare out over all of the soldiers' graves. Somewhere among them was Uncle Chester's grave; it had to weigh on Daddy's heart. "It's like that Japanese poet, Jack. I'm sure I don't like him, or anyways I don't like his people, because they killed my brother. But when I try to understand him, when I read his poetry, I can't help but appreciate him a little. It's when we have to read the poetry of our enemies that we start to understand them. Remember?" He smiled at me again. "I guess I'm going to have to pay attention to Sam's poetry."

The evening was getting dark quickly and lightning started flashing over near Oak Hill. A rumble of thunder put us on alert just as the wind picked up. Once again I never made it to see Mama's grave, I mused as we headed back home, quickening our pace. Back at the house I gave Daddy a hearty handshake and left him waving on the porch as I raced to beat the storm.

*The soul should always stand ajar, ready to
welcome the ecstatic experience.*
—Emily Dickinson

CHAPTER 14

The dusty group of travelers appeared two days later. News of the healings of both Nathaniel and Deborah had spread throughout Bethany and into nearby Jerusalem. Thaddeus and Simon were speaking to the town elders near an olive grove when the men wandered into town.

"There he is now!" exclaimed Simon, pointing toward a man of about thirty.

The man walked amid a group of strange assemblage. Boys as young as fourteen and fifteen poked at each other while older men of forty or so listened to the healer. Women dressed in varying degrees of wealth were in the group too. They all appeared to be on a holiday pilgrimage like so many others who passed through Bethany at different times of the year.

Simon and Thaddeus excused themselves from the elders and trotted out to meet this Jesus and his band of merry men. Eleazar, standing in the doorway of the potter's studio, watched as the men embraced and greeted one another.

John approached the doorway from behind Eleazar. "John, what do you think of all this?" Eleazar asked.

"I think it is time to gather clay. Come along," John responded as he handed the digging tools to Eleazar.

They hauled the sledge around to the grassy field and headed toward the water.

"Thaddeus and Simon say he is the Messiah," Eleazar said, not ready to let it go. "Do you think such an inexperienced man can lead us against the Romans?"

John gave a faint smile. "Eleazar, there will always be rulers and there will always be oppression. Wars will never cease as long as the Earth endures. Those who fight most vehemently, most violently, and most victoriously, often never lift a weapon."

The tall grasses swished around Eleazar's legs as he neared the water's edge. John was a wise man, no doubt, but Eleazar did not always agree with him. How were they supposed to rid themselves of the Romans and take their rightful inheritance of the land if they were not to conquer the Romans by force? Elijah was a town elder and he could see force would be necessary.

The muddy stream flowed across some rocks and trickled away to the desert. Eleazar usually enjoyed the jaunts to collect clay, but today his thoughts disturbed the tranquility like school boys throwing rocks at birds in flight.

"What do you see?" John asked as he motioned to the creek bank.

"Clay," Eleazar answered, bewildered.

"Pots, lamps, basins, pitchers, platters ... These are the things I see. You must learn to look past the obvious and expected, and see the possibilities that exist. If you cannot see possibilities, you will get mired down in the clay and be stuck forever in the same place."

"What do you mean?"

"There is clay in Israel, certainly, but there is clay in Rome as well. It does not take war to make pots, lamps, basins, pitchers, or platters. It takes work and love," John said and then shrugged.

Eleazar knew better than to push John. He often spoke in riddles that Eleazar had difficulty following, but the more time he spent at the potter's shack, the more the riddles uncoiled and displayed their wisdom. Eleazar still believed fighting was necessary, but maybe John's riddle would prove to be a strong fortress.

By the time Eleazar finished at the shop that day, a large crowd had gathered at Marta's. Eleazar found no room to pass through the front door, so he went around to the back of Deborah's house and jumped the low wall around the garden—and came to a halt at what he saw.

Sick and crippled people filled the courtyard. Eleazar's eyes followed a blind man being led by a young child toward the healer whom Simon had pointed out earlier.

The healer stood under the olive tree, placing his hands on the people and praying in a manner unlike the teachers of the synagogue. He was speaking to the people about turning to the Lord, but he spoke of caring for each other, not about tithing and sacrificing. He encouraged the men and women to help one another, and to praise the name of the Lord.

Abraham and Helena spotted Eleazar by the wall and called to him. "Eleazar! Shalom!" Helena said.

Eleazar smiled and waved, then headed over to them. "Marta will make a lot of money off this crowd," he said as he drew near. "I didn't think there were supposed to be so many."

"There aren't so many with Jesus," Helena said. "It's just that the people join in and follow hoping to be one of the healed ones." Helena's eyes gleamed as she looked at her husband. "Like Abraham!"

He nodded. "It's true." Abraham was smiling from ear to ear as he took Eleazar by the shoulders and turned him. "Look in the olive tree. There's a bird on the fourth branch up. I can see it. I can see it clear as day, Eleazar!" He laughed and clapped Eleazar on the back.

Eleazar felt his eyes get big. "Abraham, that's wonderful!"

Soon enough Eleazar joined in the celebration. *Maybe that kind of power can defeat the Romans without weapons,* he thought.

Soon it was time for dinner and Jesus dismissed the crowds. He and his disciples climbed the stairs and settled on the reed mats for dinner. Eleazar sat among the men and listened as Jesus talked to them about what they had been doing over the last few months. Thaddeus and Simon told Jesus about the kind way Marta, Mariam, and Eleazar had treated them while they stayed in Bethany. Jesus looked at Eleazar and smiled.

"You have a fine family, Eleazar," Jesus said. "Thank you for sharing your blessings with us. I hear you are a potter."

"An apprentice, yes. John the Potter is teaching me."

Jesus nodded. "John is an excellent potter. I have admired his work for a long time. He so clearly sees the purpose of each piece of clay."

Eleazar agreed, and the conversation turned to the other disciples and their travel adventures—but Eleazar's mind lingered on Jesus and his comment about the clay.

Preparation for old age should begin not later than one's teens. A life which is empty of purpose until sixty-five will not suddenly become filled on retirement.
—Dwight L. Moody

CHAPTER 15

The time until my next session with Mr. John seemed to fly. I kept making a lot of sales. The North Carolina pottery was taking off with a new client in New York, and I added another one in Boston. And Mr. John's pottery was doing so well that I needed to call in another order. I'd finally made a good decision when I took on Mr. John's work. Life was looking up. Success was finally within my grasp.

I reached for the phone and dialed the number for Mr. John's studio.

Christy answered the phone. "Hello?" her voice vibrated across the line.

"Christy, it's Jack. How are you?"

"Jack," she said warmly, "how good to hear from you. Is everything alright? You're still coming up this weekend, aren't you?"

"Yes, everything is fine. I just need to put in another order with Mr. John. My customers want more supplies. Is he around?"

"No, sorry. He had to run into Rome for some supplies himself. Can I take a message?"

I left a list of items that were selling quickly and confirmed again that I would be up that weekend. I was about to hang up when she stopped me.

"Jack, I won't be here this weekend. I'm going back to Rome for a couple of weeks."

"Oh, well then, I suppose I'll see you next month. I guess your granny is doing better?"

"Yes, Granny is all better now. The warmer weather has her doing just fine. But, Jack, I won't be back to Paradox. I'm staying in Rome for a couple of weeks before I leave for training. I ... I joined President Kennedy's new Peace Corps," Christy said. "I'm going to Ghana to be a teacher."

Shocked did not even begin to describe my reaction. Little Christy Landoff from Rome, Georgia, was going to Africa? Who would have imagined that?

"Wow, Christy. That's ... great," I managed. "So when do you leave?"

"I go to Colorado for some training in a couple of weeks. Then I leave with the first group at the end of August."

I finally mustered the courage to ask what I was really thinking: "What made you decide to do that?"

"Well," she said, "I applied several months ago. I had volunteered at the Marine Armory downtown. My cousin was activated there during Korea. Anyway, I was volunteering there some evenings after work until Granny got the pneumonia. I guess volunteering, and then helping Granny, made me want to be able to do more." She paused a second and then went on. "I had sort of changed my mind, though, because Daddy doesn't approve of girls going off so far. But then I heard you and Mr. John talking about peace and love not being a political pact. I thought Mr. John might be talking more to me than to you, but however it was, I decided for sure then. The world will be a better place if we start helping each other instead of hurting each other."

The line went quiet. How wrong I had been all of this time thinking Christy was a snobby, shallow girl. "I'm sorry," I said out of the blue.

"For what?" Christy asked.

I hesitated, then said, "That I won't get to see you anymore." A fib when said, yes, but then I realized it was the truth. I would miss Christy.

Needler and Newman always closed the entire week of Independence Day, creating a forced vacation. It was my time to work with Mr. John again anyway, so I decided to spend the entire vacation in Paradox. I was looking forward to a week of quiet, throwing pots, and visiting family. I even used my first pay raise to buy some new fishing equipment.

I arrived Friday night to a surprise: Daddy sitting on the front porch with Aunt Lily.

"Welcome back," Aunt Lily called as Daddy walked to the car.

"Jack, it's good to see you," Daddy said. "Rose and Lily invited me last night. I thought we might go fishing when you're done with Mr. John tomorrow."

"That would be great, Daddy. I actually bought a new rod and some weighted bobbers so I could fish this week."

Daddy seemed relieved. He took the bag out of my hand and walked up the brick pavers to the house. Following behind, I noticed there was a little less sag to his pants. *Maybe he is coming back around,* I thought.

Aunt Lily gave me the traditional squeeze and peck on the cheek before she started in. "So, Jack, have you found a girl yet? You've been down in Atlanta long enough now. When are we going to get some little ones running around here?"

"I don't know, Aunt Lily. Maybe I'll stay an old bachelor, and Daddy and I will come haunt you and Aunt Rose."

"Jack Joseph Sharp! You better watch yourself or I'll turn you over my knee." Aunt Lily swatted at me.

"What has he done now?" Ginny said, laughing as she came out the front door, followed by Aunt Rose, who was carrying a plate of ice cream sandwiches.

I felt the blood rush up my neck and didn't know what to say. "Hi, Ginny," I squeaked.

"Good evening, Jack." She smiled politely. "Sorry I missed you last time."

"How was the wedding shower?" I asked, recovering my composure.

"Wedding shower?" Aunt Lily jumped in.

"For my brother," Ginny said. "He's getting married in August. The bride's church had a shower for them a couple weeks ago and I went."

"That was nice of them," Aunt Rose said.

"Will you be in the wedding?" Aunt Lily asked. "You know the saying, 'Always a bridesmaid, never a bride.' You're not getting any younger, you know."

"Lily!" Aunt Rose said. "She's still in college. Ginny is too young to be thinking about getting married. She has other things to be concerned about."

"For heaven's sake, Rose, I'm just playing with her. Remember, I'm the oldest single woman here." Aunt Lily winked at us. "A woman can do whatever she wants. She doesn't need a man. But the right man and the right woman together is a sight to behold. Isn't it, Joe?"

Daddy smiled at Aunt Lily and nodded. I was surprised to see the wan, gray look of the last several years beginning to fade. Or perhaps I should say Daddy was beginning to brighten.

"So will you be in the wedding?" Aunt Lily asked again.

"No." Ginny smiled, helping Aunt Rose pass around ice cream sandwiches. "It's just a small wedding. Her sister will be in it and my brother's friend from work." I took the treat from Ginny and thanked her. "I'm allowed to bring a friend, though," she said, stopping to stand in front of me. "I thought I would take Christy. We've become friends at Mr. John's studio, but she'll be gone by then." Ginny looked at me.

"Oh? Where will Christy be?" Aunt Rose asked, settling herself into the wicker chair. "Is she going back to work at the mill in Rome?"

"No, ma'am," Ginny answered, still watching me.

"She's joining President Kennedy's Peace Corps," I said, staring back at Ginny. "I talked to her earlier this week. She leaves in a couple of weeks for Colorado and then on to Ghana, Africa."

"Little Christy? She's just a girl," Daddy cried. "What is becoming of the world?"

"She's nearly as old as I am." I grinned. "Anyway, she has good reasons, Daddy. She wants to bring peace to the world. I think she has been reading poetry." I turned my eyes on Daddy, and he caught my look.

He nodded and moved the conversation along. "So, Ginny, what will you do after college?"

"I hope I can work with Mr. John," she said as she looked at her bare toes. Glancing up at the aunts, she added, "I really like Paradox. The Hammonds are very good to me, and so are the two of you. It's such a pleasant place." She looked at me and then ducked her head. "I thought about going to Atlanta, like Jack, but I just don't think it's for me."

"Have you tried it?" I asked. "I mean, have you have been to the Art District to look around? They usually have openings for potters and artists." I shrugged, not wanting to betray the excitement that burned in my chest at the possibility.

"Yes, some of us at Bersher rode the train down. I just didn't care for it. Too much noise, and I don't like all the crowds."

"Mm, I guess you get used to it," I replied. "I didn't notice it too much until after I started coming back to Paradox. When I got back to Atlanta on Memorial Day, the lights and noise seemed so intense. It's not Paradox, that's for sure," I said with a half-smile.

"Who named it 'Paradox,' anyway?" Ginny laughed. "I think it is a perfect place."

"Don't you know the story?" Aunt Lily asked. "You're in the midst of celebrity, my girl. Our family goes back almost to the beginning. Back in the early 1800s, Paradox was actually named 'Paradise.' Henry Sidler founded it. Those are his fields next to ours. He brought his bride from Atlanta to join him in building a port town along the Oostanaula River. Old Henry thought this was the perfect spot for a ferry and barge system to deliver goods downriver, but Henry didn't know that the Oostanaula flooded quickly and often. His ferries and barges were constantly stranded on the flood plain. The year they spotted a steamboat paddling by where the barn stood was when old Henry changed the small community's name from Paradise to Paradox and turned to cotton like the rest of the South."

"Are you serious?" Ginny asked. Her eyes darted from Aunt Lily to Aunt Rose. Aunt Rose puffed out her chest like a wise old owl.

"Yes, ma'am. They've got a picture of it over in the Rome courthouse," Aunt Rose said.

"Anyway, Henry's son, Lloyd, married our grandmother's cousin, Susan, from Atlanta. Susan invited Grandmommy to stay with her and help after the babies started coming. That was how our grandparents met. Daddy's grandfather owned this farm next to the Sidlers'. We're far enough away from the river that the flooding wasn't too bad for Grandpappy. He grew cotton too. Mama and

Daddy stayed in Paradox all their lives and left the family place to me and Rose. I guess we just never wanted to be anywhere else," Aunt Lily finished with a catch in her throat.

"There they are." Daddy pointed, ending the sentimental story. The first lightning bugs were rising toward the night sky. "I think I'll walk down to the river," Daddy said. He placed his ice cream wrapper on the tray and hoisted himself off the divan. I wasn't sure if I should stay or join him.

Aunt Lily saw me start to open my mouth and gave her head a short shake. "Enjoy yourself, Joe," she said and then turned to Ginny again. "Do you think you can make a living here in Paradox?"

"Well ... it will take awhile," Ginny said. "I'll have to rely on Mr. John's contacts and expertise, but Jack has been getting a lot of orders for us lately. Mr. John has let me create some of the items Jack has shipped off, and I think the tourist trade in the summers is promising. Mr. John has agreed to help me set up a vendor booth at the Coosa Valley Fair this fall too." She paused, and her shoulders drooped. "Daddy thinks I'm crazy, but I think it can be done. Mr. John has managed." She seemed to give her last excuse with that and took a small bite of her ice cream sandwich.

I felt drawn to say something. "If you want it badly enough, it will work out. You are a gifted potter already."

Everyone sat quietly watching the lightning bugs and finishing their ice creams. The clouds drifted across the sky, covering over the moon and then letting it reappear. *Ginny is right,* I thought, *Paradox is peaceful and pleasant.*

Aunt Lily yawned and cleared her throat. "It's starting to get late. I'm going to head in to bed."

"Me too," Aunt Rose said, "if that's alright with you, Ginny. Jack is young enough to stay up if you want to stay longer."

"I'm   sorry,"   Ginny,   said,   looking embarrassed. "I shouldn't have stayed so long. I'll go on home now." She rose to go.

"Did you walk here?" I asked, looking around.

"Yes, Miss Rose asked me to come for dinner," she said. "I had a nice visit with the ladies and your father." She smiled. "Thanks again for dinner, Miss Rose, Miss Lily."

Ginny started for the stairs as the aunts said their farewells. A cloud covered the moon again and temporarily darkened the porch.

"I better walk you to the Hammonds'," I said.

"It's okay, Jack." Ginny chuckled. "I'm not afraid of the bogeyman."

"No, Jack, you walk her back to the Hammonds'. She shouldn't be out alone," Aunt Lily said.

Ginny didn't object again, so I followed her down the stairs and headed out the driveway. The night was pleasantly warm with a gentle breeze. The clouds traveled across the moon and dimmed the occasional star, but the midnight blue sky still blazed with light.

"Well, that's one thing Paradox has got Atlanta beat at," I said, jerking my head toward the sky above.

Ginny looked up. "I would miss the stars, for sure. They're pretty bright back home too."

"Do you think you would ever want to move back there?"

We walked slowly, talking of her dreams for a prosperous pottery business. She believed Paradox was situated better than her hometown in the highlands. She was right in thinking that Mr. John could help her both artistically and economically.

In the distance we could hear Daddy talking down by the riverbank.

"The beaver kits must be getting big," I said, based on the number of tail smacks I could hear.

"Is your father talking to the beavers?" Ginny smiled in the dimming light.

We stopped and listened a minute when the name "Violet" drifted across the field.

"No," I answered softly, "he's talking to Mama. He told me they used to walk to the river in the evenings and watch the lightning bugs."

"He still misses her," she said, "but he looks more alive than when I had him in Math class a few years ago."

"He still talks to Mama like she is right there. I thought he was crazy for a while, but I think he just can't separate himself from her. I guess they really did become one, like the preacher says."

We walked a while longer and then Ginny started telling me a story: "Thursday there was a little boy in the shop with his mother. He was probably three years old, I suppose. Anyway, he was singing a little song, but I couldn't understand him properly, and he was picking up the lamps at the end of the aisle. You know, the ones with the pinpricks in them?"

I smiled my acknowledgement.

"Well, I guess the little guy thought he was some sort of Elvis Presley rock-and-roll star or something, because he started dancing around while he was singing and knocked over the lamp on the edge of the shelf. It broke all to pieces."

I laughed. "I bet he got in big trouble."

"His mama started to scold him, but Mr. John was there when it happened. He stopped the mother and told her it was okay."

"What? He said that?"

"Yeah. Then he said it wasn't the image of the lamp that he loved, but the image that lives after the lamp is broken. The woman looked at him kind of like he was simple or something." Ginny snorted.

"Sometimes he is."

Ginny slowed almost to a stop and shook her head. "No, Jack. You just have to understand Mr. John. He sees being a potter as his life, not his trade. He told the woman that the lamp was imperfect, but he had enjoyed it anyway. And now that it was broken, he could live with the memory of the perfect lamp that he thought it must have wanted to be."

I started feeling pretty sure Ginny was just as cracked as Mr. John.

She looked at me sideways. "Jack, your father loved your mother. He doesn't need her to be here; he has her memory. Her lamp may have broken, but he still has her memory, and to him it is perfect."

Soon enough the mile-and-a-half walk to the Hammonds' place was over before I realized it.

"See you tomorrow, Jack," Ginny said, touching my arm. Then she walked into the house and quietly closed the door before I could speak—although I wasn't sure what I would have said anyway.

I rose early the next day. A foggy mist clung to the river valley and the dim twilight seemed sadly silent. I found Daddy on the porch holding a cup of coffee and staring into the distant fog.

"Good morning, Daddy," I said quietly as I sat down next to him with my own mug.

"Jack." He smiled briefly and then continued staring.

"Did you sleep well?"

"No, not so much. Your mama kept me up."

"You were talking to her last night by the river, weren't you?" I looked sideways at him, keeping my eyes lowered. I still didn't think it was right for him to be having these conversations with Mama, but what Ginny said last night was starting to sink into my thick head.

"Yes." He cleared his throat. "Yes, I was. Jack, your mother thinks I should visit you in Atlanta. Would it be alright if I came down one day to see where you work?"

I turned in my seat to look closely at him. "Really? I mean, of course it would be, Daddy. You can visit anytime you like. But ..." I paused. "How did Mama tell you that exactly?"

Daddy glanced at me and shook his head. "Jack, when you're married to someone as long as we were, you hear them even when they aren't there. Your mama talks to my heart. I suppose some might say it is my conscience speaking to me, but I know it's Violet. I don't think she will ever be silent."

We sat in the still morning until the sun rested on the edge of the world, ready to break the dawn. I wasn't sure whether to believe Daddy or not, but he didn't seem insane. He seemed calmer than usual and certainly he looked healthier. Who was I to say he couldn't hear the love of his life?

Taking another sip of coffee, Daddy tried again: "Jack, I know I have been distant with you over the last few years. I relied on your mother too much to rear you and Sam. I'm not sure if maybe Mr. John wasn't talking to me when he told you to yield and to listen. I think I need to listen to you more often and to Sam too."

I sipped my coffee, my mind churning through all of this. Mr. John's malarkey might not have been helping me with my craft, but maybe it was helping in other ways.

"Let's go fishing, Daddy, before I have to head over to Mr. John's."

Brilliant light rays shone across the yard as the sun forced itself above the horizon. We gathered our poles and grabbed a bit of cheese out of the fridge for some bait. The foggy mist was beginning to lift from the water. Wet grasses slapped against our legs as we walked through the field toward the riverbank. Daddy hummed a familiar tune and then broke into song:

> *"Soon, the bright homeland adoring,*
> *We shall behold the glad dawn;*
> *Lean on the Lord till the morning,*
> *Trust till the night is gone."*

I remembered Mama and her sisters singing that as they worked in the garden. Aunt Lily's alto would support Mama and Aunt Rose's soprano parts. I joined Daddy on the chorus:

"Home of the soul
Blessed Kingdom of Light
Free from all care
And where falleth no night
Oft in the storm
We are sighing for Thee
Beautiful home of the Ransomed
Beside the Crystal Sea"

We didn't catch many fish, but Daddy and I had a good time anyway. We sang and joked. I told Daddy more about my work and the people there. He told me about some changes at Bersher and what they might mean for him. Then we gathered our poles and the bucket of fish, and walked back up the path to the house. It seemed as if the night was long gone, the day had dawned, and Daddy and I were home at last.

*While I thought that I was learning how to
live, I have been learning how to die.*
—Leonardo da Vinci

CHAPTER 16

Marta yawned in the morning light. Dawn came much sooner than she wanted. It had been a long night waiting on the men upstairs. Many had fallen asleep on the floor, but others had moved out to the courtyard and slept under the olive tree. She could see them wrapped together in their robes like swaddled babies when she went to the cistern for water. She resigned herself to the idea that caring for traveling men was the closest to babies she was likely to come. *Why did you have to leave me, Jacob?* The dawn of day could never reach the darkness that lived inside her.

Marta brewed a weak mint tea while she sliced fruit and bread. Breakfast was not included in her guests' fees, but their leader had done so much for Abraham. Marta felt it was only right to feed them a morning meal.

Jacob would want her to do it. She placed some dried figs and dates on one of the platters and carried it upstairs.

"Excuse me, sir," Marta spoke in a hushed voice, not wanting to disturb the men's sleep. "I brought some food for your breakfast." She entered the room and noticed Jesus was standing near the window, surrounded by his sleeping disciples.

"I passed an olive grove yesterday," Jesus said. He turned toward her, smiling. "I was thinking it would be a quiet place to pray. Would you like to join me?"

"Me, sir?"

"Yes. You do pray, don't you?"

"I ... used to. Now I only stand in silence. I don't know what to say anymore."

He nodded. "Silence is a good place to start, Marta. And thank you for the food. You have been very kind to us."

Marta bowed her head. "It is you who have been kind." Then she walked out the door, regretting a tiny bit that she hadn't accepted the healer's invitation to join him for prayer.

The evening brought new droves of lame and sickly people to the inn. It was not only the news of Nathaniel and Deborah's healings that brought them now, but the scores of other people healed of illnesses and disease the night before. The courtyard was crowded with the poor and maimed, and Eleazar felt overwhelmed by the sickening odors that flooded the small, walled garden.

Suddenly the crowd near the door parted and a murmur of contempt broke out. Abraham led the way, followed by a man clothed in fine robes. It was Chuza, the manager of Herod's palace. He pulled a small cart behind him. A bound woman sat on cushions in the cart, foaming at the mouth and hurling curses at Chuza.

Abraham and Chuza fell at Jesus's feet as the crowd hushed. "Please, lord," Chuza said. "Abraham has told me you are a healer. My wife, Joanna, is plagued by a demon. She has to be bound in order to not hurt herself or others. We never know when the demon will attack. Please, can you help us?"

"Don't help the likes of them," someone yelled from the crowd. "They work for Herod!"

Squeezed between two beggars with a remarkable odor, Eleazar waited to hear what Jesus would say to that. He had his own regrets that Abraham worked for Herod, but he comforted himself that it was Herod's books Abraham looked after. Perhaps Abraham was able to keep Herod a little honest, Eleazar liked to reason.

Jesus never said a word to the protestor, but instead turned toward the bound woman and untied her. "Your bonds have been released. Return to the Temple and offer your sacrifice," Jesus said.

Eleazar watched as Joanna's distorted face relaxed and her curses turned to praises. She fell out of the cart and knelt at Jesus's feet while Chuza declared his loyalty.

Marta entered the courtyard then and motioned to Eleazar. He reluctantly left the scene and joined her.

"I ran out of firewood," Marta whispered. "I have the evening supper prepared, but I need more wood for tomorrow."

"I'll go to the kiln and gather some," Eleazar said and headed out toward John's shop.

John was stoking the fire at the kiln when Eleazar arrived. The pungent smoke filled his nostrils and stung his eyes. The slow fire would burn hot for a week in order to create the hard ceramics that John was known for.

"Good evening, John," Eleazar called as he neared the older man. "Marta is out of firewood again. I told her I would get some from you. I can go cutting again tomorrow if that satisfies you."

John looked up from the fire. "Shalom, Eleazar. Of course that will be fine. I'm surprised to see you here this evening, though. I thought you would be listening to the healer."

"I tried, but there is such a crowd, you can hardly get in the door. I'm not so sure I would like what he has to say, though."

"Why is that?"

"He cast out a demon from Chuza's wife—you know, Herod's manager. I don't know who this healer is, but he can't be Messiah. Messiah will save us from the oppressors, not help them," Eleazar said, even as he felt his face redden and his fists clench.

"Eleazar," John said slowly, "where is the best place to get our clay?"

Eleazar shook his head and furrowed his brow. "By the group of cedars ... but why?"

"Do we get our clay anywhere else?"

Now Eleazar gave a small nod, still wondering where John was going with this. "There is a spot farther down, near Zebedee's goat field, but there is so much litter in that clay, it takes a long time to sift it and tread it."

"Yes, exactly so. Why do we bother to get the clay from Zebedee's field if the clay by the cedars is the best?"

"The clay by the cedars centers easily on the wheel, but the clay in the goat field makes unique designs when we fire it."

Now John looked back into the fire. "You are only a piece of clay," he said. "Chuza's wife is also a piece of clay. It is not for us to decide which clay is to be used, but only that we will use it. Every piece of clay deserves a chance to become a useful piece of pottery. Does it not?"

Eleazar stifled a grunt, then gathered a load of wood into the carrying strap and lifted it to his back.

"Some pots are only intended for offal and dung," he nearly spat.

With each step up the trail to the tavern, the wood pile grew heavier.

"I need to make deliveries in Jerusalem for John today. Would you like to go?" Eleazar asked his sisters.

The crowds were now long gone, following Jesus through the countryside. Bethany was quiet again, and Eleazar was thinking of Elijah's suggested riots.

Marta smiled. "No, I told Helena I would help her with some preserving today. The Lord has blessed her garden this year. It will take a lot of drying to get it all done. You two go, and I will go another time."

Mariam couldn't help but smile at the thought of enjoying a day of leisure and distraction with her brother. Eleazar said he planned on stopping at Saul's house after his deliveries. It had been nearly a year since Eleazar had seen his old friend Saul, he told the women, and he wanted to see how his former companion was doing.

"Saul has a young sister you would like— Elizabeth. You remember her?" Eleazar said to Mariam.

She nodded, recalling how young Elizabeth was last she saw her.

"Maybe you and Elizabeth can sew together while I make the deliveries, then I can join you at the house and we all can visit."

Eleazar left his cart near the city gate and led Mariam through the narrow streets to Saul's house. Saul was not home, but Elizabeth assured them that he would be back for lunch. Elizabeth then offered to entertain the men after Eleazar's deliveries were made. It was agreed that Mariam and Elizabeth would visit at the house and prepare lunch for Saul and Eleazar. Soon Mariam was left alone with Elizabeth.

"I haven't seen you in so long," Elizabeth said. She pulled a bench closer to the window for some light as they prepared to sew. "I can remember when you still lived in Jerusalem. I've seen Eleazar around quite a bit, though. I guess it is harder for a woman to go far from home. You will marry soon, I suppose?"

"I don't know." Mariam shrugged. "Eleazar hasn't made any arrangements yet. But what did you mean? Has Eleazar been visiting Saul when he makes deliveries?"

"Sometimes, but usually I see him when a meeting is planned for that evening."

"Meeting?"

"Simon, Matthew, Zechariah ... You know, all of the young freedom fighters." Elizabeth said it as if she were buying flour at the millers: *"Give me some spelt, some barley ... oh and some poison."*

But Mariam could only gasp. "Freedom fighters! What is Eleazar doing with them?"

Elizabeth looked up and stared at Mariam. "Didn't you know? I thought you knew. Oh no! Please don't tell Eleazar that I let the secret out. Oh no, I thought you knew."

Mariam shook her head. "No, I didn't know! And I won't tell, Elizabeth, but I am concerned. Aren't you worried about Saul? What if they get caught, or hurt, or worse?" Mariam shuddered.

"Yes, I'm concerned, but we need to be freed from the tyrants. Saul would gladly give everything if it meant that our family would finally be free."

Mariam and Elizabeth worked quietly then, sewing and sharing shallow gossip. Mariam was afraid to plunge too deeply into the waters. *If something happens to Eleazar, what will become of me and Marta?* The thought was too disturbing to pursue.

Eleazar returned before Saul and sat outside in the courtyard while Mariam and Elizabeth finished the small details of the meal.

"When will Eleazar announce your engagement?" Elizabeth raised her voice, standing near the open window and winking at Mariam, perhaps thinking that Eleazar could be prodded a bit.

"Men don't often tell women what is going on." Mariam grinned, looking down at the grapes and cheeses that she was arranging around some small figs.

"I guess that's true," Elizabeth said, and she gave Mariam a slight hug. "And I am sorry again. I thought you knew," she whispered just as Eleazar greeted Saul in the courtyard.

The men savored the lunch, but Mariam could barely eat anything. She didn't know what to do; who else knew about Eleazar's secret? Soon lunch was over and they headed back to Bethany.

Eleazar strained under the harness of the cart. He nudged Mariam with his walking stick. "You're quiet. Didn't you enjoy your visit with Elizabeth?"

Mariam kept her eyes on the road. "It was good to meet her—I mean, to see her again, now that she's older," she replied. "She seems sweet."

Thankfully Eleazar didn't bother her anymore. She knew that he had learned the moods of his sisters and knew it was best to let them both speak on their own terms. Recently he'd even told her that he missed the days when they played and talked as equals; now he felt completely inept around her and Marta.

Mariam attempted to clear her mind and asked, "How were your deliveries? Did you get everything distributed without any problems?"

"Yes. There was a large vase for the palace that had me concerned. It was very intricate, with tree branches and birds carved into the sides. John really outdid himself with that one. I can't do that yet, but I will soon. John says so." He beamed at that.

"If you live," Mariam muttered before she realized it.

Eleazar looked at her. "What?"

Mariam looked at her brother. "If you live," she said in a normal voice. "You could be taken along these roads and forced to work somewhere faraway. You could ... You could end up like Nathaniel and catch some terrible disease or worse."

Whew, she thought, *that was close.* She had almost let Elizabeth's secret slip.

Her brother rolled his eyes. "No one will bother me. I am the only man at home and I have to take care of you and Marta."

He said it as if it was fact, but she clenched her teeth, knowing that Eleazar was as subject to forced labor as any other man along the road—and she'd had enough of dancing around what had her stomach tied in knots.

"Elizabeth told me you are attending meetings in the city!" Mariam said, no longer caring if she betrayed the confidence. "She says you have joined the freedom fighters." Tears welled in Mariam's eyes.

"Oh, I see now ... but so what, Mariam! We need to fight! It is time for the Messiah to help us. If it's this Jesus, then he will lead us soon. Just watch."

"You need to watch your tongue, Eleazar. Remember, 'A fool vents his anger, but a wise man holds his tongue.' Do not be reckless with

your tongue or your actions." Mariam's dark
eyes held Eleazar captive between the boy that
he still was and the man that he longed to be.

Neither spoke the rest of the way home.

The evening air filled Mariam's senses with
the heady scent of jasmine, which she used to
mask the odor of the man who'd recently
stolen away back to his wife. The flowering
vine trailed across the eaves of the upper room
where she slept. At least she tried to sleep.
The hot air, the whispers through the village
of an uprising in Cana, the unrelenting
nagging in her mind of Eleazar's negligence of
the most important matter ... All of these
made Mariam toss again on the reed mat
under the window. It had nearly been a year
since she'd discovered Eleazar's covert
activities, but they still weighed heavily on her
heart and mind. At least she was better at
secrecy than he. She smiled to herself. Neither
Eleazar nor Marta seemed aware of their
sister's nearly nightly exploits.

A scream from the direction of Deborah's
house pierced the darkness. Mariam jumped
up and heard the terrifying sounds of men
being dragged from their beds and homes.
Angry shouts and orders to fall in line mixed
with the shrill cries of women. Mariam

grabbed a lamp and ran downstairs, knowing that their house was no safer than the next. She found Marta crying hysterically under the tree in the courtyard—and all around, silence. The attack had ended, over before they'd barely realized it had begun. Eleazar had been spared, but many men had not. Mariam swallowed down a lump, even as she heard Eleazar cursing from within the house.

"It is Jacob all over again!" Marta sobbed as she rocked back and forth.

Mariam tried to comfort her, stroking Marta's hair and holding her close. How well she remembered Marta doing the same for her when Mother and Abba died, but who had comforted Marta when Jacob had been taken?

With lamp in hand, Eleazar burst through the courtyard door. "They cannot do this!" he yelled. "We will hide along the road and take them back."

"No!" both women shouted.

John came running through the archway just as Eleazar was leaving. The old man grabbed him by the shoulders and spun him around.

"Eleazar! Stop." John's voice sounded quietly authoritative. "This is not the way. It is discipline that will bring you freedom, not flinging yourself madly into the night. Take your sisters to Abraham's house; he will protect you for now."

Of course Abraham's family would be safe, Mariam thought; he worked in the palace.

Eleazar looked like he wanted to argue with John, but he finally just shook his head and then motioned for his sisters to go with him. The three crept forward along the darkened street and walked along the shadowy edge of the houses. They saw Deborah's family weeping in the light from their doorway. Mariam wished they could stop and see Deborah, but she knew they had to keep moving. A man hiding in the shadows of the street grabbed Eleazar's wrist and mumbled in his ear, but Mariam heard every word: all of the men in Deborah's house had been taken, even twelve-year-old Zeb.

The story was the same throughout the village: candlelight silhouettes flickering on the walls, giving form to the sounds of despair.

After several minutes that felt like hours to Mariam, Abraham opened the door and ushered them inside. Mariam saw Helena and the children huddled together in the middle of the dark room.

"You're safe," Helena breathed as she grabbed the women.

Are we? Mariam wondered as her body sank into Helena's embrace. *Will we ever be safe?*

Still clutching Eleazar's hand and refusing to let go, Marta shook as she replayed the night's details. Her mind confused the night's raid with the one that always haunted her memories: the men bursting into the house, grabbing Jacob's clothes as he was pushed out the door and corralled with the other men, the torches meant to intimidate and frighten, the crying and wailing next door, the smell of fear that penetrated the streets, the broken doors and broken families. It was all too much, and Marta finally collapsed on a pallet that Helena laid out.

There was nothing to be done until daylight. The night smothered them with the smoldering smoke of misery and the poisonous vapors of desolation. Mariam wrapped her covering tighter and prayed for a way out.

*I know that there is nothing better for people
than to be happy and to do good while they
live. That each of them may eat and drink, and
find satisfaction in all their toil—this is the
gift of God.*
—Ecclesiastes 3:12-13

CHAPTER 17

Ginny had already opened the studio by the time I arrived. She was slab-building a tray on the wooden workbench. She had used a wooden tool to etch a small house and a tree with a tire swing in the middle of the soft clay. Now she was using flowers from Mrs. Hammond's garden to make imprints along the border.

"That's nice," I said.

"Thanks. It's for my brother's wedding. I'm going to stamp their names below the house," she said, looking at her work. "The house looks like the one they were looking at when I was up there earlier."

"I'm sure they'll love it. And adding their names is a nice touch."

"I have been taking orders for pie plates and cake pans with names embossed on them. They're good for potlucks and parties. You always know who should take home which pan." She smiled. "People fill out this form ..." She pulled one from a drawer. "... and then I mail the finished product to them a couple weeks later."

I nodded. "That sounds like a good niche market."

"Say again?"

"I mean, I haven't seen others in the industry doing that. It makes your pottery unique."

She eyed me. "That's a good thing, then?"

I laughed. "Yes, it's a good thing."

Ginny took a deep breath and sighed. "I thought it was. I hoped it was, anyway."

Then she went back to work. I watched her begin the stamping process until Mr. John came in.

"Don't be lollygagging, Jack," Mr. John said. "I've got a lot of work to get done. You sent me an awfully big order last week, young man."

"Yes, sir." I grinned. "Your stuff is selling like hotcakes. What should we start on first?"

We spent the better part of the morning checking inventory against the order I'd given to Christy. I missed seeing her at the register. Ginny had to keep running out to the shop when the tourists would roam through the aisles. Mr. John never got irritated when the customers asked to see the studio. He invited them in, answered questions, and made them feel welcome. It must have been good for business, because nearly everyone bought something.

During a slow period I took a few minutes to eat a sandwich out by the kiln. Mr. John was loading some glazed bisque ware for the final firing.

"You know, Jack, these pots are like my children. I build them, mold them, do all I can for them, but I cannot turn them into hardened ceramics. They must go through the fire. The fire burns hot—twenty-three hundred degrees—and the pots cry for relief, but I cannot remove the fire or there will be no finished pots. The pots have to stay in the fire for a few days, some for a week. The tiny particles of silica and spar transform gracefully and enfold the clay in beauty. I talk with the clay, and I talk with the fire, but I cannot stifle either one. The fire and I work together to form the finished pot."

I felt certain that Mr. John was telling me something important. I chewed on the crust of Aunt Rose's sourdough bread and pondered fire and clay. I began to understand what Ginny seemed to already know: being a potter was more than building with clay.

Daddy attended church with us in Paradox. He hadn't been back since Mama passed. The Hammonds were excited to see him, as were all of the local folks who had known Daddy and Mama as a young couple. Mama had been loved in Paradox, and so they loved Daddy by default.

After lunch Daddy drove back to Rome. I promised him I would come by one day during my vacation and spend it with him. I would even treat him to dinner at the Bumblebee Café since I was the one who just got a raise.

Sundays were resting days in Paradox. The aunts took their naps on the front-room couches with electric fans blowing gently over them. I dragged the hammock back under the shade of the pin oaks to get a little more air flowing and then settled down for a rest. My mind circled the camp several times but couldn't settle down with me. Finally I gave up on a nap and decided to go for a Sunday drive.

I left a note on the kitchen table, grabbed a few oatmeal raisin cookies, and headed out the door. I drove down the lane toward Paradox and then turned north onto Highway 27. I had the windows rolled down, and the breeze soon blew the busy haze out of my brain.

I switched on the radio and sang along. A family was out riding bikes, and I slowed as I passed by them on my left. I kept my speed down after that and just enjoyed the passing scenery. Pulling into the small town of

Summerville, I decided to stop for an ice cream cone at the Tastee Freez.

I was passing some young people enjoying their own treats when I heard, "Jack! What are you doing here?" It was Ginny. She and a young man broke out of the crowd and walked up to me.

"I just went for a drive and ended up here," I said. "What about you?"

"Clive asked me to drive over and have an ice cream," she said, motioning to the guy next to her, in his early twenties.

Clive smiled slightly and nodded my way. I raised my hand in greeting.

"Are you going out to see Reverend Finster?" Ginny asked me.

"Who?"

"Reverend Howard Finster. He's a local artist. He bought a little parcel of land outside of town and he's draining it to put in some sort of art garden. A lot of the art students at Bersher talk about his work. I thought maybe you knew about it." She shrugged. "We're headed that way, so you can follow us out if you want."

"No, that's okay. You and Clive have a good time. I'll see you tomorrow."

"You're coming in tomorrow? I thought you were on vacation."

"I am, but I thought I would put in a few hours and help Mr. John out."

"Okay, well, see you then." She waved and walked back to the little group of students.

I ordered my ice cream and ate it in the car as I drove back to Paradox. *Who is this Clive fellow,* I wondered, *and how serious are they?* Ginny hadn't seemed like she was attached to anyone before. I thought she was independent, looking to build a business. It just hadn't occurred to me that she might be involved with someone. The drive back seemed longer than the drive up had been.

Monday came and I burned off some of the brush piles that had built up at the back of the property. I started early before the heat became oppressive, but it still felt like I was the clay inside the kiln.

Seeing the small purple flowers growing along the edge of Aunt Lily's garden, I began to think of Mama. Why did she have to die so early, before Sam was even out of school? And I could have used her advice about working for Needler and Newman. I still wasn't sure it was the right fit for me. And what about Daddy? Why did he have to hurt all alone like that? He still had so much of his life left to live.

Then I thought about Mr. John's "children" and the fire. Maybe we were those pieces of pottery in the fire, being hardened by what we were going through in losing Mama. Maybe we depended on her too much. Maybe Daddy and Sam and I needed to lose Mama in order to become completed pots in our own right.

I finished burning the brush, poured water on the coals, and went inside for a bath. Aunt Rose was inside talking on the phone. I climbed the stairs and then relaxed in the cool tub of water. I changed into an old undershirt and threw on a plaid short-sleeved shirt with a tear in the pocket. I had brought several old shirts this time for helping at Mr. John's.

Downstairs Aunt Rose had fixed a lunch of egg salad sandwiches, pickles, and tomatoes with cottage cheese. I poured a glass of iced tea and swallowed it down in one draught.

"Oh, Jack, I'm sorry," Aunt Rose said. "I should have brought you out something to drink."

"That's okay," I replied. "I didn't realize how thirsty I was till just now."

"I was talking to Joe on the phone," she said as she poured her own glass of tea and refilled mine. "He invited all of us over tomorrow to a neighborhood picnic on the levee. He said we could watch the fireworks there and spend the night at his house."

"Really? Well that's awfully nice of him. It might be fun to see the fireworks. Some of my friends might be around."

"I don't know about spending the night, though. He invited Ginny to come along too. I just don't think that would look right." She looked at me.

"He invited Ginny? Why?"

"He enjoyed her company at dinner the other night, and he thought she might like to go into town for a change of pace."

"Hm. She might, but she was just in Summerville yesterday. I saw her with a young man; Clive was his name. She might have plans already."

"Oh. Well, I guess we can ask. No harm in asking, is there?" she said. "But you better let me or Lily ask. It wouldn't look right for you to do the asking."

I could only nod and smile; Aunt Rose was the perpetual proper Southern lady.

I finished my lunch and then walked over to Mr. John's. The sun was burning hot on my neck now, and I slowed down under the shady spots along the road. The door to the shop was propped open and a fan sat atop the sales' counter. I wiped my sweaty face with a hanky as I walked through the store and into the studio.

"Hi, Mr. John," I called as I passed into the studio.

Mr. John nodded and kept working on the wheel. He was forming and I knew better than to talk to him now. Ginny was attaching handles to pitchers with some slip and a wooden tool. I walked over and started helping her.

"Did you find the reverend yesterday?" I asked.

"Yes. He was quite interesting. He sees his artwork as his ministry. He preaches through his art. He's a little like Mr. John," she said, glancing in his direction.

"How so?"

"I don't know ... he just said things. He was talking to Clive about some of his photography. The reverend told Clive that the world is always bigger than one's own focus and that he ought to look through someone else's lens for a while. Just stuff like that."

"He does sound like Mr. John," I said, then chuckled. "Maybe they're brothers."

Ginny kept attaching handles, and I kept trying to think of something to say as I got started working. I wanted to ask about Clive but didn't know how. Finally I decided to throw caution to the wind—and to risk the wrath of Aunt Rose.

"Hey," I said in my best small-talk voice. "My dad wants to invite you over tomorrow for the holiday. He invited me and Aunt Rose and Aunt Lily. Seems he's taken a liking to you. So if you don't have plans, we'll leave about two o'clock tomorrow. There's a cookout on the levee and then fireworks afterward. Daddy says we can all stay the night at the house." I didn't dare look at her, but kept crisscrossing the clay with the wooden tool.

"That's so sweet," Ginny gushed. "I'd love to come, but is there really room for all of us at your house?"

"I think I am getting the couch, but you can have my room and the aunts get the spare room and Sam's old room. There's space or Daddy wouldn't have asked."

She just nodded and kept working, and I breathed a sigh of relief that she hadn't mentioned Clive at all.

We worked on small projects for the remainder of the afternoon. It was a restful kind of working; I didn't even feel like I was working, to tell the truth. The constant thrumming of the potter's wheel had a relaxing effect and the three of us working together made for a peaceful atmosphere. The quiet was only broken once by a customer traveling through from Alabama; she told us stories about her granddaddy's pottery back in the 1800s. I wondered again how long Mr. John had been making ceramics. After the older lady left, I gathered my courage and asked Mr. John, "How long have you been making pottery?"

Mr. John stopped to consider awhile. Holding his chin with his still strong but gnarled hand, he finally said, "I can't tell for certain. My papa taught me how to work with the clay, to mold it and fashion it. He was an expert, you know. He was very good at talking the clay through everything and getting the fire just right."

Ginny rubbed Mr. John's back and then gave him a little side hug. "I bet your papa was the best potter ever," she said quietly.

"Yes," Mr. John answered and then we went back to work.

Late in the afternoon I washed the clay from my hands in the work sink near the back door. Ginny joined me there.

She smiled at me. "I think I'd like to go with your family tomorrow if it is still okay. Should I call your daddy to accept?"

"No, I'll let everyone know," I said, trying to hide my pleasure. As I dried my hands on an old rag, I asked, "Do you want us to get you at two o'clock at the Hammonds'?"

"Yes, please."

And that was that: my first date with Ginny was set, even if she didn't know it would be a date.

After dinner that evening I broke the news to the aunts as we hoed weeds in the garden. Aunt Rose sounded mortified that I had been so forward with Ginny, and she seemed equally upset to find out Ginny had been so brazen as to accept. Aunt Lily smoothed it over by reminding Aunt Rose that it was Daddy who had done the inviting and that I was just the messenger.

"No harm done," Aunt Lily told Aunt Rose. Then she beamed at me and danced a little jig.

Independence Day dawned clear and cool in Paradox. I decided to do a little fishing on the riverbank and headed out early. I stationed myself against a river birch and waited for the fish to bite. It didn't take long. When Aunt Lily came down an hour later, my stringer was filled with shad and even two striped bass about five pounds each.

"Woo-wee, boy!" Aunt Lily whistled. "We're gonna have some good eating tomorrow. You about done? You don't want to fish it dry all in one day, you know."

"I was about to stop, but I'm not ready to head back just yet. I was enjoying the morning," I said, looking across the river toward the beaver dam.

The land on the other side of the river was turning into a wetland paradise for the beavers. A few water birds were starting to use the area for roosting.

"They worked so hard, I barely have the heart to destroy the dam," Aunt Lily said, gazing out at the same spot. "The kits are still too little to move on."

"Isn't there some way to move the water around the dam instead of destroying it? They always come back when you destroy it anyway."

"None that I know of; we destroy the dams and they build them back. That's the way it works."

We walked together back to the house and cleaned the fish in the cool shade on the side of the barn. Aunt Rose was puttering in the kitchen when I walked in to rinse the fish in the sink.

"Good heavens, Jack. I guess you didn't have to wait for fall after all," Aunt Rose said.

I looked at her and shook my head. "Wait for fall?"

"You threw the last batch back but said they would be ready by fall, remember?"

Aunt Lily entered the spacious kitchen and said, "I told you he would be back for fishing before that. Jack was meant for Paradox."

I laughed as I recalled that day; not even two months had passed. I had thought Atlanta was home, that I was content there. But now I was beginning to wonder if I had made the right choice to be at Needler and Newman. Aunt Lily was right: home was becoming a paradox, in more ways than one.

Aunt Rose packed a cooler to put in the boot of my car. She had made potato salad, cucumbers and onions, and baked beans to take with us to Rome. She placed my fish around some ice on the bottom so that we could have those for breakfast the next day at Daddy's house. Then we headed over to the Hammonds' to get Ginny.

I pulled up to the hardware store and found Ginny waiting on the porch swing. She waved and then ran into the house. By the time the aunts and I got out and opened the trunk, Ginny and the Hammonds were already walking toward us. Mrs. Hammond had a sack of tomatoes and squash to give to Daddy, and Mr. Hammond told the aunts to enjoy themselves.

"Don't worry about the house," he said. "We'll keep an eye on things for you."

"It'll only be one night," Aunt Rose promised as she clasped Mrs. Hammond's hands through the open window.

The aunts hadn't been away from the house overnight in years. I actually had been surprised that they agreed to go, but Aunt Lily said they wanted to assure Daddy that he was still part of the family. It was only right, she believed, to reciprocate the visit he had shared at their house.

Ginny started to climb in the back with Aunt Rose, but Aunt Lily told her to sit up front with me and keep me company. "We'll probably take a little afternoon nap," she whispered as she slipped into the backseat.

Ginny sat next to me, but kept her distance. She wore a soft-blue sundress and sandals, and she had her hair pulled back with a scarf to keep the wind from blowing it too much. We waved good-bye to the Hammonds and started toward Rome.

The two of us talked in the front seat about people and places we both knew in Rome. Of course we had many of the same professors at Bersher. Ginny went to the Methodist church when she was in school and so we knew some community folks too. We both agreed sharing a fresh loaf of bread from the Merita Bakery on

First and Sixth was the best breakfast on a chilly morning. The ride to Rome never passed so quickly.

I got another surprise when we pulled up and found Sam standing there on the porch. He yelled for Daddy and soon we were all on the curb grabbing bags and the cooler, passing out hugs and kisses. It had been years since we were all so congenial and easygoing. Mama would have been pleased—*was* pleased, I reminded myself.

Sam dropped my duffle behind the couch and carried the ladies' things upstairs. Just as I had figured, I was to be on the couch, but I hadn't expected to have a suite mate on the floor. It would be good to have Sam with all of us. After we settled everyone where they were to sleep, we all meandered out to the front porch to enjoy a drink and some conversation. A little later on, Christy swung by and added her own gossip.

"Did you hear there is a dance at the armory this evening?" Christy asked. "Some of the students at Bersher have formed a band and they'll be playing. Any of you want to go?" Christy asked, looking at me.

"I ... I didn't even know about it," I said. "We probably ought to stay here with Daddy and the aunts."

"Oh, we'll be fine without you," Daddy said. "You kids go out tonight and have a good time. Just be quiet when you come in. The old folks need their sleep."

Aunt Lily reached and gave Daddy's leg a little smack. "Ha! Speak for yourself, Joe," she said. "Lily Russell can keep up with anyone on a dance floor." She turned toward Christy. "What time will it be?"

"After the fireworks, Miss Lily; you will come, won't you?"

"That depends on the music," Lily said, "but we will come for a little while. Won't we, Rose?"

Aunt Rose laughed. "Well, Joe, you and I are younger than Lily. I guess we better go so she doesn't show us up."

So it was settled without any input from the "kids": we would all go to the dance.

The picnic started at five o'clock down by the levee. The town had set up tables and everyone turned out with food. Aunt Rose placed her offerings on the table along with everyone else's, and Daddy helped man the grills that had been warming since late afternoon. Burgers and hot dogs were pumped out as fast as the men could cook them.

It was a raucous event. People I hadn't seen since high school came by to introduce their spouses and children. Ginny held her own and even introduced some people to me. Christy went between her family and ours with ease, though she spent more time with me than with Sam.

Over a plate of watermelon, I asked Christy about her plans for the Peace Corps.

"I leave on Thursday. I'm not sure if I am excited or terrified," she said. Then, looking at Sam laughing with some of his buddies, she added, "I think I am more terrified for Sam, though."

Ginny looked at the two of us and shook her head, perplexed.

"Sam leaves this month for the navy," I said.

"Oh, well ... Jack will keep you informed about Sam when he writes," Ginny assured Christy.

"Will you write, Jack?" Christy asked.

I had not planned to write; it had never been my strong suit. But Ginny put me in a difficult position. I hated to tell Christy "No," so I touched her arm and said of course I would write.

The evening was spent playing baseball, the east end against the west end. Several kids had Frisbees and kickball games going as well. I realized this wasn't the sort of thing I had ever seen in Atlanta. There, I stayed in my apartment unless I was going out for work or for an evening at the cinema. I didn't know many of my neighbors, and I certainly had never played games with them.

Ginny sat next to me on a blanket, cheering on our team's first baseman at bat.

"I haven't done this in a long time," I said.

"You should do it more often. You look happy," she said, squeezing my knee.

"Maybe it's the company," I said, eyeing her.

"I'm sure it is. How could you not be happy with your family all together and Christy still here too? You'll miss her, though. We all will. I liked having her at the shop."

Her words confused me. Why had she brought up Christy? I was still pondering it over when Aunt Rose came by to tell us they wanted to watch the fireworks from Daddy's porch, so they were heading back home. Ginny and I both offered to help carry back the dishes, and soon the five of us were walking toward home. Sam stayed behind with Christy and her family.

A little ways down the sidewalk, Ginny looked behind us and asked, "Hey, where's Sam?"

Aunt Lily laughed. "I saw him heading over to the Landoffs' with Christy. I think he wanted to get some more visiting in before she leaves for Africa."

I caught Ginny out of the corner of my eye looking from Aunt Lily to me. Maybe I wasn't the only one confused.

Back at the house we cleaned up the dirty dishes and the aunts grabbed their sweaters from the upstairs bedrooms. We all went out on the porch and heard neighbors on their own porches calling to each other and to those still walking home in the twilight.

Daddy and the aunts called out some greetings of their own, but I just sat there on the step below Ginny, clenching my fists in my lap. Finally I took a deep breath, summoned my courage, and then looked at her.

"Would you like to watch from Clock Tower Hill?" I asked Ginny, extending my hand.

She didn't even hesitate; just smiled and said, "Sure," and so we bid the others farewell.

The night felt chilly for July. It had been a long, cold winter last year and, except for a few stifling days, the summer didn't seem to be able to heat it up like usual. We walked up the hill to the clock tower where several young couples were waiting for the show to begin. I was out of breath before we got to the top of the hill.

"Atlanta ... has made me ... soft," I said, wheezing. "I used to climb these hills like a billy goat."

"These are nothing!" Ginny laughed. "I come from the mountains northeast of here. Rome is only the toes of the foothills, hardly anything at all."

Ginny and I stationed ourselves on the stone wall between the tower and the sidewalk. We sat in the growing darkness, Ginny swinging her bare legs and me watching her. The first boom sounded before I could think of anything to talk about.

The crowd of young people oohed and ahhed. When the finale exploded over the river below, everyone cheered with plenty of yelling and clapping. Then most of the couples joined hands and started walking toward the armory.

"Time for the dancing to begin," I said. I hopped off the wall and did a little two-step.

Ginny laughed and asked, "Should we go get the old folks?"

I shrugged. "They know where it is. Come on; we'll walk down this way."

I led the way, following the flow of people down the sidewalk. Light streamed from the armory doorway and music blared out of some electric speakers near the stage. The band was made of six students from Bersher, including one in his ROTC uniform. The vocalist looked oddly familiar.

"Look!" Ginny said. "It's Clive's band! I never imagined when Christy mentioned a band from Bersher."

That's why he looked familiar. "You should go say hi," I yelled above the music.

"No, it would scare him. Aunt Lucy doesn't like that he is in a band," she said, but I didn't understand.

"Aunt Lucy?" I asked.

"Yes, his mother. The rest of the family might be Methodist, but Aunt Lucy and her family are definitely NOT." She laughed. "The last time Clive played, he got caught and Aunt Lucy made him go home every weekend for a whole semester so he could go to church with her."

"Soooo ... Clive is your cousin?"

"Yeah. What did you think?" She looked at me with sparkling eyes.

"That he was your cousin, of course."

I grabbed her hand and led her onto the dance floor. I never saw Daddy and the aunts, and honestly didn't think much of it, because Ginny and I danced until midnight when the place closed down. Walking home afterward, we saw Christy and Sam strolling hand in hand toward Broad Street.

"I guess you and Christy are not interested in each other?" Ginny asked quietly.

"No, she's interested in Sam, but I don't think it will go anywhere with both of them leaving. Sam isn't a letter writer either." I grinned down at her and put my arm around her shoulders.

"Sorry about that." She chuckled. "I thought you two were together."

The next morning Daddy was frying my fish and Aunt Rose was offering him advice when I walked into the kitchen. Stretching and yawning, I gave Aunt Rose a peck on the cheek.

"Good morning," I said to both of them at once.

"Good morning, Jack," Daddy said. "What time did y'all get in? I thought I heard someone at two o'clock." His eyes cut through me like he'd found out some crime of mine.

"Ginny and I came back after the dance, about twelve thirty. Sam was out later," I said, keeping secret his walk with Christy. "I didn't see you three at the dance." I smiled, trying to lighten the mood.

Aunt Rose hooted. "That's because Lily isn't as young as she thinks she is. We decided to hit the hay after the fireworks were finished. The old girl is still in bed!"

Just then Daddy's mourning dove flew at the window and startled Aunt Rose. She yelped and dropped the bowl of fish flour in the sink.

"Daggone it!" Daddy hollered. "That bird just won't go away."

"You haven't gotten rid of him yet?" I asked.

Soon everyone was up and talking in the kitchen. Aunt Rose pulled biscuits out of the oven and set a big bowl of cantaloupe on the table. Daddy placed the platter of fish on the red and yellow Formica table, and we all bowed in prayer. The bird pecked on the window the entire time.

"I'm going to go insane if that bird doesn't stop it," Daddy said.

"You know," Aunt Lily said, "some people think that a visiting bird is a messenger from beyond."

"Well, I wish it would give me the message and go back yonder," Daddy said. "It's annoying," he muttered.

The morning went quickly and the aunts were ready to get back home. We cleaned up the house, packed up our bags, and loaded the car by ten o'clock. Sam and Daddy stood on the porch waving when we pulled out, calling our good-byes through the open windows.

I dropped Ginny off at the Hammonds' place and then drove on back to the aunts'. I unloaded the car while Aunt Rose assembled some sandwiches and Aunt Lily looked over her garden. They were happy to be back home again.

I spent the next couple of mornings clearing out brush and weeds that had overgrown the old farm. Then in the warm afternoons I walked over to Mr. John's studio and practiced my pottery skills. Mr. John was always ready to teach and talk. I felt comfortable with him.

Ginny was always there too. We talked and worked together, but nothing was said about Christy or Clive. It just seemed better to leave it alone.

Sam called on Thursday evening to tell us that Christy had left for her training. He also had received his orders. He would head to Lake Michigan for Basic Training on the first of August, and after that he would go straight to Rhode Island for Officer Training School. He seemed more anxious than I had expected. Daddy talked to us for a little while too; he sounded agitated.

On Friday I changed the oil in the tractor and cut the higher grass in the meadow. The farm didn't have any livestock, so we didn't need hay, but Aunt Rose liked to keep it cut back. From the field above the house, I could see the spreading wetland on the other side of the riverbed. The beavers were getting out of hand.

During lunch I told Aunt Lily I had an idea for draining off some of the swampy land without destroying the beaver kits' home. I finished up my spaghetti and salad, and took the old farm truck into Paradox.

Mr. Hammond had long pipe piled behind the store. I bought several pipes and joint connectors and loaded the truck bed. Then I walked over to the studio to tell Mr. John I wouldn't be back in for a couple of weeks.

Ginny was dealing with some customers, helping them to choose colors and patterns for a pie plate. Mr. John was glazing some pieces at a work bench.

"Hello, Mr. John," I called as I entered. "You doing well?"

"Hello, Jack. Yes, it's a fine day today. The preacher called. His wife is in labor and he wanted to know if I could take over the sermon this Sunday." He smiled.

"Great," I said. "That will give me the chance to see you again before I head back to Atlanta. I'm going to do some work on the farm the rest of my time here, and then I won't be in the studio again for a couple of weeks."

"That's fine, that's fine. It's been nice having you so often, though. You will be a great potter soon." He patted my hand. "See you Sunday." He waved his brush to dismiss me.

I waved good-bye to him and Ginny, and then I drove back to the house and unloaded the pipes, transferring them onto the tractor's plank trailer bed. I grabbed an old pair of sneakers from the bedroom and then drove the tractor around the field to the old wooden bridge that crossed the river. I parked on the other side, ready to begin my experiment.

I spent all afternoon and evening clearing several holes through the beaver dam and inserting the pipes. I ran pipe from the wetland, through the dam, and into the river. Afterward I covered over the ends of the pipes with wire mesh so that the beavers wouldn't try to fill them in—and then I just had to wait to see if it would work.

The next evening Aunt Lily, Aunt Rose, and I walked down to the riverbank to see the progress. The pooled water was draining back into the river. I had placed the piping high enough that the wetland wouldn't be completely drained, but it also wouldn't ruin the land either. It appeared we would win the battle of the beavers.

"Jack, it sure would be nice to have a smart man like you around here on the farm," Aunt Rose said. "We need help to keep it up. The ice storm last winter and now the beavers just prove that we can't maintain the farm."

"Pshaw!" Aunt Lily said. "We're doing just fine, Rose. You act like we have one foot in the grave!"

Aunt rose rolled her eyes. "Calm down, Lily. I'm not saying we're ready for the glue factory just yet, but we do need help, and you know it. I had thought maybe Sam would move back to teach in Rome and take over the farm, but it doesn't look that way now. Of course he may not stay in the navy long ... and we still have a few good years left." She sighed.

"Well, at least you'll give us a few years," Aunt Lily muttered. "It's good to know you don't have the mortician's phone number memorized."

I laughed. "I have enjoyed helping out this week, and I bet Daddy would be willing to help if you told him what you need."

"Yes, Joe will help, but he's busy at Bersher. Something will work out, though. God always provides," Aunt Rose said.

The lightning bugs lit the path as we walked back to the house.

What medicines do not heal, the lance will;
what the lance does not heal, fire will.
—Hippocrates

CHAPTER 18

Time is never a friend to the disconsolate. Marta, Mariam, and Eleazar survived in Bethany with broken hearts and broken lives. Marta cloaked herself in mind-numbing preparations: cooking, cleaning, walking to the bakers, going to Helena's for some special herbs ... whatever could keep her mind and hands busy. Deborah and Mariam hovered nearby, always ready to do whatever Marta demanded.

Marta invited the women of Deborah's family to stay at her house, feeling there might be safety in numbers—and that perhaps Eleazar would go unnoticed in a future reaping. But the more time went by, the more Marta worried. She had no more energy for grief; only despair was left to her.

John joined them for Shabbat dinner not long after the night of terror that had claimed so many men from the village. John sat silently with Eleazar: an old man who had seen a lifetime of dying, and a young man who had witnessed too much already. John stared at the deep furrows that were already gouging themselves into Eleazar's brow.

"Marta is losing her troubles in her work," John said.

"No, she is hiding them in her work," Eleazar said. "I don't think she ever mourned Jacob, she was so busy with me and Mariam, you know. This has just stirred up all of those memories. She just cleans and cooks and prepares and works."

"Labor frees us from some bonds," John said softly as he patted Eleazar's back. "It takes discipline to find that freedom, but a deeper freedom is found in our bond to the Lord."

Eleazar shook his head. "How can we be free if we are bound? You make no sense." He sighed. "The bond Marta needs, and Mariam too, is the marriage bond. Abraham does not think he is able to keep the marriage bond for Jacob. I need to find husbands for them, but now the young men are all gone. I should have done it long ago."

"There is time for that. Right now you need to be gentle with Marta. I will watch over you and your sisters. You will keep working for me, and I will take care of you."

Eleazar's eyes grew big. "Are you offering to be Marta's husband?"

John laughed. "No, no. I have already been her husband and father and friend as long as she has been alive, but no, I am not offering to marry her. I am saying to live and to work and to rely on the Lord for whatever needs arise. He and I will take care of you."

The men that remained in Bethany met at Marta's tavern one night for dinner. After finishing the meal, Elijah took Eleazar by the arm and led him into the courtyard. Nearby, at the garden wall, Mariam decided not to go back into the house just yet. No, she shouldn't eavesdrop, but like Marta, she feared for Eleazar—and so she listened in as she eyed the men in the dim light of the lanterns.

"I know about your activities in Jerusalem," Elijah said.

Eleazar drew back as he caught his breath—even as Mariam raised a hand to her lips.

Elijah put a hand on Eleazar's arm. "It's alright. I want to help you and your sisters."

Eleazar paused, then said, "Thank you, but what do you intend to do?"

"Mariam is young and attractive. She needs a husband and should have been married off already—if Jacob would have noticed. I can help with that. She will be invited to parties at the palace," and he said "palace" with great meaning. Eleazar clearly did not miss the intent.

"Will ... Will she be safe?" Eleazar said. "Why not just marry her to someone now, in the village?"

Elijah put his arm around Eleazar. "She can get information in the palace, son."

What kind of information? Mariam wondered. But then she smiled. *What does it matter? I can go to the parties! I can find a husband. Yes ... Elijah will work it all out.* Relief flooded her heart and washed away the grief that had so completely filled it.

"Why are you going to Jerusalem?" Marta asked again as Eleazar and Mariam were finishing up lunch. "Doesn't John need you at the shop?"

Eleazar looked at her. "Marta, we will be fine. Mariam must be cared for, and going to see Salome will help her chances. Men will not think about her poor circumstances but will see a connected woman, someone who can help them get ahead in the world."

Mariam stifled a smile, knowing that Eleazar was not going to back down from getting her to the palace, no matter how much Marta had been complaining about it since he had first brought it up after his meeting with Elijah.

"But there are still men here in Bethany who would take Mariam for their bride," Marta said. "Why does she have to go to Jerusalem? It isn't safe. What if someone picks you up along the road?" Marta's voice cracked and trembled.

Eleazar shook his head and hugged Marta. "We will be back tomorrow. John will keep an eye on you."

Soon after lunch Eleazar and Mariam said good-bye to their sister, and they left for Jerusalem.

Mariam felt beside herself with happiness. She was going to the big city, to visit her old friend Salome, Elijah's niece. Salome had always been kind, even if her party invitations to Mariam had ended; surely at Elijah's insistence she would help Mariam to reconnect with old friends, with possible husbands. Of course, it would all be up to Eleazar in the end, but it was good of Elijah to help them this way.

The air smelled sweet and the sun warmed their shoulders. It was a perfect day for a walk to the city. Laborers worked in the fields along the road and their work songs drifted across the siblings' path.

Having kept quiet for as long as she could, Mariam said, "Oh, Eleazar, do you really think I can find a husband in the city? One who won't make me do all the work like Marta does? I want to be pretty again. I want new clothes and to stay clean and to eat good things. I'll invite you to our house, of course. You'll come won't you?" Mariam grabbed Eleazar's hand.

"Mariam, really. You will have a husband; don't be so shallow." Eleazar shook free from her hand. "You're putting the cart before the donkey, anyway. Be kind and friendly with Salome; she is your ticket to the palace and to Elijah's prospects."

"I wouldn't have to be this worried if Abba were still alive. He would have made sure that I was taken care of. Hmph … Jacob waited too long. I don't think he even realized I was old enough to wed, and now it is almost too late for me to find a good husband."

"That's ridiculous. You are only twenty-six. No one thinks you are too old to marry. There are many children still to be born."

"I know … you're right. It's just that all of my friends were betrothed early and didn't have to worry about what would happen to them. It's different for you. You are a man; you can do whatever you like!"

"Not everything," Eleazar said. "Now … remember at the dinner to listen to the men, even when they are not talking to you. Elijah needs information."

"I know, I know … nothing is free," Mariam said.

The dinner was delicious, but hardly the main attraction of the evening for Mariam. The women were dressed in colorful fabrics and gold jewelry. Elaborate braids adorned their heads and made Mariam feel inept and inadequate. The men's voices on the other side of the room only reinforced Mariam's belief that she was out of her element. She would never find a husband in this crowd. What man would be interested in such a plain woman as herself?

The men talked about their lands and harvests, and Mariam listened even when they droned on and on about the most boring topics. The grapes were looking good this year, though some believed the vine worms would still attack. One man in particular was worried about worms on all the vines: eggplants, cucumbers, squash. Mariam avoided his gaze; she didn't want a farmer. Finally the talk turned to taxes and became more animated—and Mariam became more attentive to their words. She was able to gather names of men who were considering not paying the exorbitant tax rates. They were preparing to fight back if need be. This was information Elijah would relish.

Near the end of the evening, Salome invited Mariam to attend dinner the following month, and Mariam gratefully accepted. She had been sure this would be her only night at the parties, but she had been given a second chance.

I need new clothes, though, Mariam thought. *Or else I may not get another invitation ... and then I'll have no chance at a husband ...* And the usual worries again drowned her mind in fear.

Travelers came and went at Marta's little inn. Her reputation as a superior cook spread far across the region, and many made it a point to stop on their way to Jerusalem. Of course the prices were less in Bethany than in the city, so people had an added incentive to stop before their final destination.

Mariam had managed to cover some of her expenses in the past by entertaining the male travelers, but she had decided to stop prostituting herself since Elijah promised to find her a husband. Still ... some fresh clothes would speed the process. Perhaps she could earn enough to get some new clothes before the next party, she decided one night when the inn had filled to capacity with travelers.

Mariam made sure to wash her face and brush her hair before dinner. A little dab of perfume on her hair added to the allure. She had long ago learned how to smile and laugh provocatively. The country men had no chance against her simple beauty and eagerness to please during dinner. Mariam had become a pro at exacting her own price for a night's pleasure and keeping it secret from Eleazar and Marta.

A couple of days later, Marta stopped her housework when Mariam walked in after a bit of shopping.

"Where did you get the money for that?" Marta asked. Her eyes narrowed as she looked at the bright fabric Mariam caressed.

"Elijah offered to help me," Mariam said. It was true that Elijah had offered to help her, but it was only through party invitations. The money had come through Mariam's nightly exploits. "I need new clothes to attend the parties in Jerusalem."

Marta frowned. "I don't think you should go to this next party. Jesus and his disciples will be coming through soon and I need the extra help. You know how large the crowds are whenever he visits."

"But I have to go to the party. Elijah is counting on me. He says soon Eleazar will be able to make an agreement with one of the men. Anyway, you don't know exactly when

Jesus will come and he always stays at least a week. I will be here to help for most of it."

"Of course she is going to the party," Eleazar said as he appeared in the doorway. "We have gained several men to our plans, and it is because of Mariam's listening ears. Several men have been talking about her too." Eleazar smiled at Mariam. "In this new clothing I am sure I can strike a deal with a wealthy man to care for her." He looked at Marta. "That will make it easier to find a husband for you."

"Well, don't expect to be pampered and served when you two come back," Marta said. "Dinner parties are work where I come from, and husbands are seldom any help with those." And she disappeared out the door.

Mariam just looked at Eleazar and shrugged.

The pathway to the pottery shed seemed more treacherous than usual. Marta picked her way down the slope of shards and then finally knocked gently on John's door. She had spent an hour walking through the olive grove, trying to pray as Jesus had suggested, but silence was all that came out of her. Perhaps John would be able to help.

The sight of the old family friend smiling at the door in front of Marta was the last straw in her resolve to be strong. She fell crying into his arms.

"What's the matter?" John asked, resting his chin on Marta's head.

She moaned. "I think Mariam is lying to me, and Eleazar is defending her. Oh, John, I hate to make accusations, but I think Mariam has lost her purity." The words choked out of her like weeds sprouting out of a garden wall. The strength that had sustained Marta was gone, and she hung on to John for dear life.

"Come in, Marta," John spoke quietly. "No one is here. It will be alright."

He drew her into the small shed and helped her down onto the bench at the table. John sat across from Marta and held her hand—*Just as Abba would have done,* she thought.

"Now tell me what you think and why," John said.

Marta took a deep breath and retold the tale of the comments she overheard from travelers, the tears that so often visited Mariam's eyes, and now the richly colored robes. She didn't want to believe it, but what other explanation made sense? Marta blamed herself. She should never have agreed to turn the house into an inn. Everyone knew the reputation of inns, she said; it was inevitable that something like this should happen.

John touched her arm. "No, Marta, you must not blame yourself. Mariam had a choice, and if what you believe is true, it was her decision to make. Now dry your tears. I want to show you something."

John dampened a towel from the washbasin and handed it to Marta. She wiped her eyes, and then he led her to the back of the shed.

"This is the clay that Eleazar and I harvested yesterday," John said, gesturing toward the floor with his hand, where the clay was laid out on wet cloths. "Do you see the grasses that are mixed into the clay?"

"Yes ... I think so."

"This clay is difficult to work with. We have to remove as much of the leaf litter as possible before we work with it. It isn't possible to use the wheel with this clay, but I mold it and use it for items like platters. The leaves and grasses burn off in the kiln and the clay becomes a useful product."

John held up a red platter with handles twisted into a rope. "This is made from that clay." He smiled. "Mariam has litter that needs to be burned off, but, Marta, she is still able to be useful and beautiful."

"But what man will have her once it is known that she ... that she...?" Marta asked, unable to bring herself to finish the thought.

"Do you not remember that Rahab was a prostitute, and she was a predecessor of King David? And what of Solomon who was born to an adulterous woman? Marta, God can use the platter for whatever purpose he desires. Mariam is still moldable clay."

Marta nodded, hoping—praying—that it could be true for her sister.

A light rain washed the dust from the small village as crowds streamed into Bethany in anticipation. The healer was back in town, teaching and healing. Eleazar had left Mariam in Jerusalem and hurried back to try to catch the show. He was sure Jesus would stay several days, but seeing the healings always made him ecstatic. Surely this man could overcome the Romans. The time was quickly approaching, Eleazar was certain.

"Eleazar!" John called from the studio door. "Eleazar!"

John's voice drifted across the crowds and caught Eleazar's attention. Eleazar noticed John standing in the door frame, motioning him to come over. Eleazar dodged through the crowd and made his way to the familiar potter's shed.

"The crowds are growing bigger," John commented as Eleazar drew near.

"Yes," Eleazar said. "Soon the healer will be made king and we will overthrow the Romans once and for all."

John grimaced. "Eleazar, you know that I—"

"I know, I know! You don't think that is what Jesus is going to do, but there doesn't have to be fighting. A man who can heal the blind, the crippled, even cast out demons, well, John, I figure there doesn't have to be any fighting. Jesus can just take over and that will be the end of it." Eleazar smiled.

Now John shook his head. "Eleazar, you are so young and naïve. There is no way the Romans will just hand over a kingdom to another man without a fight, even if it is against someone as powerful as Jesus. Death surely will take place, but it will be a death that brings birth."

Eleazar raised one eyebrow. "Death brings birth? None that I have seen."

"You are willing to die with these freedom fighters, are you not?"

"I am."

"That would be too easy, Eleazar. What you need to do is kill your beliefs about the Romans. Let your hostilities die and birth love in the soil that now grows hatred."

Eleazar wanted to argue, but John was his elder—and his boss.

"Will Jesus be staying at Marta's again?" John asked as he turned back inside the studio.

"Yes, he loves Marta's cooking, just like everyone else," Eleazar said, following John into the shack. "Elijah will be there, too."

"Mmm. Questionable friends will bring you to ruin, but there is a friend who sticks closer than a brother." John turned and looked at Eleazar. "Help me to unload the kiln, would you?"

"Now?" Eleazar asked. "But I wanted to see Jesus."

"It won't take long, and you said Jesus will be staying awhile. I need the help; I'm an old man!"

Eleazar laughed, and they walked out the back of the shed toward the domed kiln half-buried in the hillside. The freshly cut wood scented the air as the drizzle dissipated and then stopped. John opened the top door of the kiln and began to carefully pull out the cooled ceramics. He handed each to Eleazar, who inspected and then set them on a grate that would be carried to the shed.

John sighed. "I was afraid of that." He pulled out several fragments of broken pottery. "I knew there were some air bubbles in the clay on that one, but I hoped I had all of them out. The fire was too much for it in the end."

"That's the pot you worked on so long, John. I'm sorry," Eleazar said. "It's always frustrating to work so hard and then have it blow up in the firing."

"There is only so much the potter can do if the clay will not release its flaws. A pot can look great, but when the fire is set to it, the inner qualities are released. Remember that, Eleazar. Now go on to dinner with the healer and Elijah. Shalom."

Eleazar carried the grate to the shed for John and then walked the trail the women used to bring his lunches to him. The crowds used the main thoroughfares but Eleazar still stumbled across some of the travelers on his way up the path. He smiled at the thought that so many people would be staying at Marta's house again. He didn't have to worry about a husband so much for Marta if she could keep on providing so well for herself. And with Mariam well positioned thanks to the palace parties, it seemed as if everything was turning out perfectly.

*Wealth consists not in having great
possessions, but in having few wants.*
—Epictetus

CHAPTER 19

Sunday dawned clear and bright; a beautiful morning. Orange rolls and coffee waited for me on the porch.

Aunt Rose smiled as she poured my coffee. "I thought we would enjoy breakfast outside."

"It is a beautiful day," I said. "Tomorrow will be a letdown after this."

"We will miss you." Aunt Rose paused a moment and then added, "When will you be back?"

"Mr. John is still holding his end of the bargain, so two weeks is the plan."

"And are you only selling Mr. John's work?"

"No, I still have many clients all over the country. I actually seem to be doing better lately."

"That's not what I meant," Aunt Rose said, cutting off a piece of orange roll for me. "Are you selling any of Ginny's work?"

"Oh. Well, yes, she has sent some of her work in with the inventory from Mr. John, but it is all what he tells her to make. I haven't purchased any of her own original work."

"Is it not good enough? I was really hoping she would be able to make a go of it here."

"Actually I saw some of her original work last week and it was very good. She has a flair for the unique, but I think she needs some help with her business plan."

"Isn't that what you do?" Aunt Rose looked up at me. "Couldn't you help her figure it all out?"

"Well … I could try, I guess."

"You should talk to her about it." Aunt Rose nodded as she rocked.

The rest of breakfast was quiet.

We stopped to pick up Christy's granny before church. She was a frail, old woman but just as talkative as her granddaughter. The aunts enjoyed visiting with her while we drove over to the church.

I pulled over near the weather-beaten doors to drop off Mrs. Landoff as closely as I could. The aunts helped her out of the car and up the few stairs to the church. Ginny waved as she walked in with the Hammonds.

I parked in the grassy field near the back of the building and walked into the church alone. Mr. John was standing by the last pew and caught my attention.

"Jack, would you please read the scripture for the sermon today?" he asked.

"Of course," I said.

The song leader started the church service and Mr. John handed me a slip of paper with the scripture reference. I slid into the pew next to Aunt Rose, who was helping to bookend Mrs. Landoff opposite Aunt Lily and Daddy. They all smiled and nodded to me as they sang the ancient hymn. After three songs and the prayer, it was time for me to read.

I stood in the aisle next to our pew and flipped open my Bible. I grinned as I began to read: "'But now, O LORD, thou art our father; we are the clay, and thou our potter; and we all are the work of thy hand.' Isaiah 64:8."

"Thank you, Jack," Mr. John said from the pulpit and then began his sermon. "I know none of you are surprised to hear the scripture reference for my sermon." Everyone chuckled and twisted in their seats. "I am excited to take this opportunity to express my understanding of the relationship between the Father and his children, or the Potter and the clay.

"The most difficult thing for the potter and the clay comes at the beginning, in what is called 'centering.' Every piece of clay the potter makes on the wheel starts at the same place.

Each piece must be centered, must come into an alignment that allows the potter to work and the clay to mature. If the clay is not first centered, it will never develop into the work of art that the potter intends."

Mr. John paused and looked back and forth over everyone. "We all have a common center. We are all made by the same Potter and he positions us with the same shared center. We all long for a relationship with the Potter. We desire fairness and justice, not just for ourselves but for the poor and helpless. We long to receive mercy and grace and relish moments when we witness them. These yearnings come from our common center created by our common Potter."

He raised a finger. "But a potter is not completely in charge of the clay. Yes, I know that surprises you," he said as the congregation murmured. "The clay can yield to the pressures of the potter, or it can choose to be rigid and unbending. The potter may desire to make a delicate serving dish for a fine lady's table, but if the clay will not respond to the potter, it will likely end up being a basic serving dish.

"The basic serving dish has a necessary role, and it can be terribly important in its own right, but for that particular piece of clay, its true purpose and design will never be reached. It will always be something less than was intended by the potter.

"The clay has a choice to make. Many think that it is the potter who chooses what to form out of the clay, but in reality it is a mutual relationship of potter and clay working together to freely form what the potter desires. As potter and clay push against each other on the wheel, innumerable shapes and objects can be designed, but surprisingly the clay has to agree to the design as well."

Daddy and the aunts looked toward me as if for agreement. I nodded my head, remembering the times I had had to change my plan for a lump of clay.

"While the potter works on the wheel, he touches only one part of the clay at a time. But the clay continues to move around and around the potter's fingers. The whole piece of clay is affected even though only a small part of the clay is being touched. In our own lives we often don't see what the Potter is doing because we can't sit on the Potter's shoulder and observe the process, but once we are centered and formed, we look at every side of our pot and see the Potter's prints completely engulfing our being.

"Formation is not the end of the potter's job, however," Mr. John went on. "The potter must fire the kiln. The potter and clay can labor together to make a beautiful work of art, but the clay is not finished without going through the fire. The fire transforms the clay from a plastic, immature object into a solid, durable piece of art. The fire causes a death, but it is also a birth. The clay does not actually die; it lives on, transformed into the original vision of the potter, and truth be told, the original vision that the clay desired as well.

Mr. John spread his arms. "Some of us have been through the fire and we have been transformed into the beautiful work of art that the divine Potter intended. Others of us are still clay on the wheel, turning through the fingers of the Potter, being supported by the tension in his divine body. He offers his palm to support and guide us, his arms to protect, and his back to give us strength. The Potter is holding his breath, focusing closely and attentively to the formation of your clay. Will you yield? Will you center? Will you transform into that holy vision?"

The sermon ended as gently as it began, and I felt myself spinning slowly around as if I was a piece of clay freshly centered and waiting for the walls of my pot to rise.

It took a few days to get back in the swing of things at work. Orders had backed up over the holiday week, and I stayed busy focusing on getting them filled and shipped. Long hours spent on the phone made my back and neck ache with fatigue.

I tried contacting Santa Barbara again. My stomach lurched as the line picked up. "Hello, Heart of the Art. May I help you?" the voice asked in a singsong cadence.

"Good morning. This is Jack Sharp with Needler and Newman in Atlanta. May I speak with Mr. Carter?" I heard my voice shake as I spoke.

"One moment, please," the operator said before she put me on hold.

A few minutes later I heard a click and then, "Jack, it's good of you to call. Thank you for the pictures of your new client's work. I have shown them to our board and they are willing to try a few of the larger pieces. I think we can sell such unique items."

I glowed from the inside out. Mr. Needler would be happy to hear that I'd finally won them back.

Before I could reply, Mr. Carter said, "Our own potters are working on reproducing the pictures you sent me. When will you be able to get your potter out here to teach them his technique?"

I sat there for several moments with my mouth hanging open. "Excuse me?" I finally asked. "No, you don't ... I mean, the value of his work is that he is the only one who can make it. He won't be traveling to California to give away his secrets."

Now it was Mr. Carter who went silent. I heard him take a deep breath and say, "Then I'm afraid we can't use your potter. We are moving toward a more modern plan for commercial success. We can't afford each piece of work to take so long. I'm sorry, Jack. Let me know when you want to talk seriously."

Just like that, the line went dead. A headache began thrumming at the base of my skull and then plagued me the rest of the week. I was happy to see Friday evening finally come.

I decided a day of fishing was what I needed to relax and headed to Piedmont Park at daybreak on Saturday. I had fished a few times before in Clara Meer with some success. I packed a bag with apples and sandwiches and grabbed a bottle of Yoo-hoo from the fridge; as an after-thought I threw in a block of cheese for bait.

The morning was warm but a breeze kept me cool. I settled on the bank of the lake under a stand of oak trees. I cast my line and waited while I watched some ducks paddling several yards away. The quiet morning and fresh air had the desired effect, and the tension in my neck and shoulders finally began to dissipate.

Two older gentlemen were casting their lines from a rocky overhang a few hundred feet away. Occasionally I could hear snippets of their conversation floating across the water. I realized I was lonely and started thinking about Aunt Lily and my most recent fishing excursion. Then I wondered if the beaver family was behaving itself and if the water bypass was working.

My thoughts turned to Ginny and Mr. John, and I wondered how their week in the pottery studio had gone. Memories of Mr. John's sermon drifted back to me, and I mused over the idea of being a piece of clay. The idea that the clay has a choice to make in its design and purpose was new to me. I always thought the clay just was and that the potter exerted all of the force and creativity, but I also knew that sometimes the pot I envisioned was not the pot that developed.

Hmm ... I wonder if I am the pot that the Potter intended.

The old men burst into laughter, startling a small bird in the oak above me. I was frustrated that the fish weren't biting, as if they knew I was a mistake about to happen. I packed up my gear, chucked it into my trunk, and sped home.

I spent the rest of the weekend puttering around the apartment, cleaning, playing solitaire, and listening to a game on the radio. I tried calling Jimmy and some other office men to play a little poker, but no one could make it. I even called Daddy on Sunday afternoon, but he never answered. I looked forward to Monday just to break the monotony.

And it certainly did break that day.

Mr. Newman was waiting for me when I arrived on Monday morning.

He stood there with his arms crossed over his chest. "Jack, we have an issue with one of your sellers, a Mr. John Kadar."

Not waiting for me to reply, he ushered me into his office, where Mr. Needler sat waiting in a high-backed leather armchair. The room was well-lit, but seemed strangely dark as I entered.

"Have a seat," Mr. Newman said, motioning toward an empty straight-backed parson's chair near his desk.

I sat stiffly, wondering what this could be about and how they could possibly have an issue with Mr. John.

"Jack," Mr. Newman said, "you recently signed a potter named John Kadar."

"Yes, sir."

"He lives near here, I believe?" Mr. Newman asked.

"Yes, sir. He lives outside of Rome, near where I grew up."

"So you have more than a professional relationship with Mr. Kadar?" Mr. Needler asked.

Still not knowing where this was going, I decided to be nothing but honest and forthcoming. "Yes, I have known Mr. John most of my life, I suppose. Recently when I signed him to supply pottery, he agreed only on the condition that I practice pottery under him so that I would correctly represent his pottery and methods. I have been going back to Paradox every two weeks to learn from him.

I have gotten to know him better since then." I looked from Mr. Newman to Mr. Needler. "What is this about?"

Mr. Newman cleared his throat, and Mr. Needler crossed and uncrossed his legs. Mr. Newman shuffled through papers on his desk and then finally looked up at me.

"We have been contacted by an art dealer outside of Houston. It seems Mr. Kadar has an ongoing ceramics show at a venue there. The dealer claims that Mr. Kadar is copying another potter; that he isn't the creator of some of the pottery in the Houston show."

"What! Mr. John would never do that." I shook my head. "He doesn't need to copy anyone. His work stands on its own merit. I ... He is the best potter I have ever known." I felt my neck muscles tighten and my stomach lurch even as I tried to swallow down the anger about to explode out of me. "I ... I've seen him at work!"

"Jack, calm down," Mr. Newman said. "No one is blaming you or questioning your integrity. We just can't be selling knockoffs to our high-end clients if they aren't truly original designs."

I sat on the edge of the hard chair. "Where is the charge coming from?"

"The art dealer outside of Houston said he had recently been to Spain and purchased some antiquities," Mr. Newman said. "He said many of Mr. Kadar's items in the show are a copy of what he purchased in Spain. He implied even the signature is forged."

My chest loosened a bit at those words. "Now that I know is not true. Mr. John signs his pieces with a special mark, not with his name."

"A bird, by chance?" Mr. Needler broke in.

"Uh ... yes. It's his thumbprint and then he swipes it to make a flying dove."

"Well, then this should be easy to investigate," Mr. Newman said. "We can just test the fingerprints and see if they match."

My bosses probed me a while longer to get all of the information they needed. It was agreed that I would contact Mr. John and ask him to meet us in Atlanta. The art show in Houston had taken close·up photographs of the insignia and mailed them to Needler and Newman. I went back to my cubicle to call Mr. John.

The phone at the store rang four times before Ginny answered: "Hello?"

"Hi, Ginny. It's Jack. Listen, is Mr. John there? I need to talk to him."

"Yes, he's here. Is everything alright, Jack?" Ginny asked. "You sound odd."

"I'm fine. I just need to talk with Mr. John," I said quietly. *No need to alarm her,* I thought.

My mind was reeling trying to imagine an explanation. The aunts had said that Mr. John showed his work all over the world. Could the dealer in Houston have purchased some of Mr. John's work in Spain by mistake? Maybe someone in Spain was claiming the work was their own when it really was Mr. John's? It was all so ludicrous; Mr. John was the best potter I had ever met, and I had seen him work with my own two eyes.

"Hi, Jack," Mr. John's voice came across the line. "Do you need to place another order already?"

"No, Mr. John, I'm afraid it isn't good news. There are some allegations being made that you are forging some ceramics. I know it's ridiculous, but my bosses would like you to come to Atlanta and make a signature in the clay to prove it is your mark on the pottery we sell," I said, feeling like my tongue tripped over the words and the ideas that made no sense.

"What do you mean?" Mr. John calmly asked.

I explained about the dealer in Houston, the pottery exhibit he had seen, and its similarities to the ceramics from Spain, and finally the need to verify the thumbprint insignia. Mr. John surprised me by remaining quiet and calm, only offering an "Mmm, I see."

"I know you haven't done anything wrong, Mr. John," I said. "You are the best potter I have ever met and I know you do your own work. I'm so terribly sorry about this."

"Jack, it's okay. And you're right, I haven't done anything wrong. There's nothing to worry about. I will come down on the train tomorrow if that works for you."

"That will be perfect." I sighed. "I'll tell Mr. Needler and Mr. Newman."

The next day at 10:00 a.m., Jan at the front desk called me on the intercom. A Mr. John Kadar and his guest were there to see me. *Good, he brought a lawyer,* I thought, wiping my sweaty palms on my slacks.

I strode out to the front of the building and stopped short. Mr. John stood there—with Daddy chatting politely with Jan.

"Hi," I called out, trying to collect myself.

"Good morning, Jack," Mr. John said, walking up and shaking my hand. "I hope it's okay that I brought your father. He had told me he wanted to visit you at your office, and I thought this was a perfect opportunity."

Mr. John smiled and looked me straight in the eye. He held no grudge; this was no payback. Daddy truly wanted to visit and the time was expedient.

I read all of that in Mr. John's eyes and responded, "Of course it is okay. I'm glad you came, Daddy," I said as I clapped his back and lightly hugged him. "Jan, would you tell Mr. Needler and Mr. Newman that John Kadar is ready to see them, please?"

We rode the elevator to the top floor. I was surprised it could climb so easily with the weight I felt on my shoulders. Mr. Needler was waiting for us in the foyer. He shook hands with everyone before ushering us into the formal office I had been in just the day before. It still seemed dark and foreboding, as if an evil fog penetrated the walls and floor. I shivered in the imagined damp shroud.

"Good morning, Mr. Kadar," Mr. Newman said. "We're sorry about the situation but are pleased that you could meet with us so quickly to clear up the matter. Won't you please have a seat?"

Mr. John sat across from Mr. Needler and Mr. Newman just as I had yesterday. Daddy and I found seats on a bench along the wall. Daddy sat close to me and patted my knee, then gave me a reassuring smile.

Mr. Newman laid out the details of the business, then said, "An art dealer in Houston was recently in Spain where he purchased some antiquities; among them were some pieces of pottery supposedly from the Dark Ages. He brought the pottery back to display at the studio in Houston where you are also displaying ceramics."

Mr. John nodded.

"The dealer noticed some surprising similarities between your work and the relics he had purchased in Spain," Mr. Needler said. "The designs and items are quite unique, including an oil lamp that illuminates through pinpricks.

I sat up straighter: I remembered seeing that type of lamp in Mr. John's store.

"But most surprising ..." Mr. Needler paused. "... was the signature on the ceramics. Both the antiquities pottery and your pottery are signed using a thumbprint containing a swoosh that creates a dove in flight."

Mr. Needler eyed Mr. John and waited.

Mr. John seemed unruffled, sitting there in the smaller chair while the two younger men loomed above him at the desk, waiting for a response.

The silence lingered until Mr. Needler continued the interrogation: "Do you have anything to say to these allegations?"

"I'm sorry. What allegations?" Mr. John asked.

"That you have copied ancient relics and have sold counterfeit pieces!" Mr. Needler blustered.

"Who says I have?" Mr. John asked.

"The evidence seems to imply that you have," Mr. Newman said. "That is why we asked you here. If we could just take a sample of your thumbprint, we can test it against the relics. Then we will know if you have sold counterfeit pieces."

Mr. John agreed to imprint his thumb for the men. It was photographed and sent on to a detective for processing. Feeling disgusted, I took the afternoon off of work and showed Daddy and Mr. John around our offices and then Atlanta, at least the areas that I was familiar with. First I showed them my office, introduced them to Jimmy and some other colleagues, and then drove through Piedmont Park. I realized that three years in Atlanta had not amounted to much of a relationship with the city or its people. We ended back at my apartment for a short visit before they would have to head home on the train.

I placed some of Aunt Rose's cookies on a plate and poured some drinks.

"Mr. John, I am so sorry about all of this. I feel like it is my fault for getting you into that contract," I said, apologizing for the umpteenth time.

Mr. John shook his head and patted my arm. "Jack, I have done nothing wrong, so there is nothing to be concerned about. If they decide they don't want to contract with me any longer, then that is their prerogative. I can continue my work with or without them." He shrugged. "I do hope that their decision will not affect your desire to continue visiting me at the studio."

"I ..." But I didn't know what to say. I'd expected him to be offended by the allegations. I would have been, anyway. I finally managed to choke out a "Thanks" as I sat down with a sigh.

Meanwhile Daddy was studying the tomato plants in my windowsill. "Where did you get these, Jack?" he asked.

Embarrassed by their spindly stalks and underdeveloped fruits, I replied, "I bought them at Hammond's Hardware in May. I guess I should have had larger pots."

Holding a small orb in his fingers, Daddy said, "No, you should have planted them in the ground." He paused a few moments and then asked, "Jack, why are you here?"

I looked at Daddy. "What do you mean?"

"Why do you work at Needler and Newman? Do you enjoy it?"

Mr. John sat next to me at the kitchen table, drinking a cold Coca-Cola. I glanced at him, but he only waved his hand in front of him as if to say, *Go on, answer him.*

"I like seeing the new work people are producing and being a part of the art business," I said.

"But do you feel like you are doing what you should be doing?" Daddy asked.

I cleared my throat. "I'm successful, if that's what you're asking. I can't afford a house yet, but the time is coming. Some of my contacts are starting to pay off and I did just get a raise."

Daddy looked at me and then down at the tomato plants. "You know, Jack, when the Hammonds planted these tomato seeds, they expected tomatoes to grow. They never expected squash or green beans or cucumbers. And the Hammonds were right: tomatoes grew. Jack, if you had planted these in the ground, and tilled, fertilized, and watered them, you would have had an abundance of healthy tomatoes."

Daddy stopped and looked out the window. I was unsure what to say. I looked to Mr. John again. He shook his head, so I waited a while longer.

Finally Daddy continued, "Jack you were born a pottery seed, and you have grown to be a potter, but you haven't had very good soil." He paused and looked at me. "That's my fault. I thought you should be a businessman so you could support a family someday. Your mama knew better. She knew you should be a potter, but she allowed me to plant you in a small pot."

Daddy cleared his throat and then turned to Mr. John. "John, do you think if I transplanted this spindly, little potter he could still grow into a strong potter?"

"Why do you think I've been fertilizing him these last months?" Mr. John grinned at the two of us. "How about it, Jack? Would you like to learn at a master's wheel?"

"I'm ... not sure I follow," I said, looking at Daddy and then Mr. John.

"Give up this businessman façade," Daddy said. "Be a potter like you have longed to do the whole time anyway. You'll be better for it."

"But you always told me I couldn't make it in life as a potter. You said a potter can't support a family!" I nearly shouted. My world was swirling like wet clay on a wobbly bat.

Daddy nodded. "I was wrong," he said just above a whisper. "A potter working only as a businessman can't support a family. You are a potter first, not a businessman."

"I ... I wouldn't know where to start," I said. "Purchasing a kiln, renting a studio, finding clients. It isn't as easy as it sounds, Daddy. Tell him, Mr. John."

"You're right, Jack," Mr. John said. "Being a potter is a difficult endeavor. It isn't for the weak of heart. But would you like to try it?"

"Do you really think I can do it? Can I really support myself as a potter?" I asked.

"What does your heart tell you, Jack?" Mr. John said. "What do you feel when you are at Needler and Newman, and what do you feel when you are in Paradox at the studio?"

"I guess I feel frustrated at both places," I said. "My coworker—Jimmy, the one you met—he makes it all look so easy. He chatters with the clients and spins them in circles until they fall in his lap. I can't seem to do that. Instead I bite my fingers until they bleed and worry about meetings with my boss. I know good pottery, and I can sell what I buy, but I get frustrated trying to keep everyone happy. And in Paradox ... I feel at home, at ease, but I'm not always sure that I understand what is going on with the clay the way you do, Mr. John. I don't know all of the subtleties of working with clay yet."

"So you feel inept at both places?" Mr. John asked.

"Inept at Needler and Newman, yes. Not inept in the studio ... but unsure. I don't think I can make enough money on my own," I said quietly as I looked at the floor.

Finally the truth lay before me like a dried ball of clay: I was useless no matter what I did.

"What if I was there to help you, to guide you?" Mr. John said. "What if you started off with me? I can help you get centered, if you will."

"Well, I would be afraid to step out on my own. But what if I couldn't find enough customers at your place either? I need to eat all year, not just in the summer. At least at Needler and Newman, I know I'll get a paycheck."

"A man's calling is not to gather riches, but to serve those around him with what he has," Mr. John said. "Your calling is to become the pot that the Potter imagined. The clay and the potter work together; they yield to each other, listen to each other. If you are ready to yield and to listen, Jack, then you are ready to mold your clay into a potter."

We spent the next hour discussing possibilities and making plans. I was concerned about living expenses and start-up costs. Daddy said I could live with him until my business gained a reputation; he would be happy for the company. "Maybe your mother will stop nagging me," he said, then grinned.

When I dropped Daddy and Mr. John off at the train station, we had a strategy. I would submit my resignation that week and then join Mr. John in August at his studio. He would continue to apprentice me, and I would continue to look for buyers for him. Mr. John agreed that if all went well the first year, then he would make me a partner. I went back to the apartment to write my letter of resignation.

Those last days of July were a blur. Mr. Needler and Mr. Newman thought I was being too sensitive; they couldn't understand my desire to be a part of the creation process of pottery and not just a broker. Jimmy said he would miss me, and the whole third floor threw a going-away party. I spent my evenings packing and tying up loose ends, but mostly I dreamed.

The day before I packed my car and headed to Rome for good, I called Mr. John.

"Hello?" Ginny's voice rang across the line.

"Hi, Ginny," I nearly sang. "It's Jack. How are you?"

"Oh, Jack, I'm so glad you called," Ginny bubbled. "I wanted to ask you something."

"What's that?"

"Well, it isn't a proper thing to ask. Your aunts would have a fit if they heard me."

"I'm not too strict on Southern manners, Ginny. Go ahead and ask me ... whatever it is."

"I want to ask you ... that is, can you ... would you please take me to my brother's wedding?"

I hadn't expected that. I thought she was going to ask about joining the business Mr. John and I were setting up. Aunt Rose had told me to talk to Ginny about the business, to help her get started. This was a whole new matter, and it could be taken in so many ways.

"Why, Ginny, I'd be happy to take you to the wedding. Do you just need me to drop you off at your parents' house or will you need a ride back to Paradox as well?" I thought that was a safe way to let her clarify her intentions.

"No, Jack." She sounded so flustered. "I am asking if you will go with me to the wedding. You know ... as my ... date?"

"Well, Ginny, you're right about one thing." I laughed. "Aunt Rose would be mortified! But I would absolutely be pleased to accompany you to the wedding, my lady. How was that for Southern charm?"

Ginny let out a big breath, then laughed and told me we could discuss the details at the studio the next week. Then she called for Mr. John, and he and I finalized our business. I hated to hang up the phone for fear that all my future fortunes would be disconnected as well.

But what if I fail of my purpose here?
It is but to keep the nerves at strain,
To dry one's eyes and laugh at a fall,
And baffled, get up to begin again.
—Robert Browning

CHAPTER 20

At the palace Mariam averted her eyes as Ben and David walked into the room. They moved over to the men's area, seeming not to notice her. She had not expected anyone she knew to be a part of the celebration this evening. Elijah had spoken of many men, but none had been familiar so far. And she didn't want her reputation to disgrace this evening's events.

Salome and her cousin Justine sat next to Mariam, complimenting her new clothes and the gold ringlets around her arm. Elijah would be pleased when he discovered Mariam was so popular. Certainly a husband could be found now. She would live in the city and have servants to help with the work. She would

bear sons and her husband would call her
blessed.

After the meal everyone moved outside to
listen and dance to the music. Mariam hadn't
laughed so much in years. Sometimes a
traveler at Marta's inn would pay for a meal
with an evening of music, but Mariam was
always part of the clean-up crew and she
mostly just heard the concerts from the open
courtyard door. Now she was a part of the
festivities, and it felt glorious.

"He keeps staring at you, Mariam," Salome
said, then giggled.

"What? Who?" Mariam asked, looking
around.

"Joshua, the trader from Nain. He can't
keep his eyes off you." Salome giggled again.
"Too bad Eleazar isn't here. Perhaps a bargain
could be made while the man is so stricken.
Why didn't Eleazar come this evening,
anyway? I see Ben and David are here from
Bethany."

Mariam swallowed hard at the mention of
their names. "Jesus, the healer who has been
traveling around, is in Bethany. Eleazar
wanted to see him again. He will come back to
pick me up soon."

"Your brother said I should take you back to
Bethany."

Mariam turned at the sound of the familiar
voice. David approached the ladies.

"The crowds are too large for him to get
back and Marta needs help," David said. "I

passed him on the way here as he was headed back to Bethany, and he asked me to escort you back to Bethany. Will you be ready to leave soon?"

Mariam said nothing, unsure about leaving with David. It wouldn't look appropriate, but many people would be on the road and several from the party would be traveling the road together, she mused. If Eleazar had thought it the best way, then it must be.

"I will leave whenever you wish," Mariam replied, looking at her feet. She would have no one guess that she knew how to handle a man already.

"Then come along. I am ready to go. Thank you for your hospitality, Salome," David said.

The road was muddy from the afternoon's rain and heavy traffic. Mariam lifted her bright robes to keep them out of the filth.

"That's a good girl," David said, sneering. "Show everyone the goods."

"What?" Mariam gasped.

David leaned in closer. "Elijah needs us to raise some money for the freedom fighters. He said you could make quite a bit to help with the efforts." He smiled. "I know you've made a lot off me. How many nights did it take to pay for those robes?" He fingered the edge of her new cloak.

"I'm sure I don't know what you are talking about," Mariam said. "Elijah is helping Eleazar find a husband for me."

"A husband!" David scoffed. "Everyone in Bethany and Jerusalem knows you're a whore. No man would have you. And all of those travelers who pass through Marta's for the 'cooking'? They've been talking too. There will never be a husband for you."

Mariam came to a halt, feeling tears well up even as anger began burning in her heart. She thought Elijah a respectable man. He was an elder of Bethany. He wanted to help Eleazar and the other men to be real Israelites. Yes, lately more men had desired her services, but she didn't think she could have such a widespread reputation as David suggested.

She glared at David. "I can walk myself home, and don't bother coming by anymore." She stomped past David.

The rest of the walk to Bethany was as soggy as Mariam's spirits. She had never meant to sell herself, but life had not been working out the way it was supposed to. Abba and Mama were gone before she could really be provided for, and then Jacob was abruptly taken as well. Marta did the best she could, but with no family and Abraham's failing eyes at the time, there was nothing for it but to take matters into her own hands. Mariam's tears ran freely down her face as she struggled along the miry road, the mud sucking relentlessly at her feet like demons from hell pulling her down.

"There you are," a familiar, cheery voice called. "I was afraid I had missed you."

It was John.

Mariam glanced up, feeling relief—and fear. John had always been a family friend, but what if he knew? David said everyone in Bethany knew.

"John, what are you doing out here?" Her voice caught in her throat as she tried to hide her turmoil.

"Eleazar was still sitting with Jesus, so I decided I would come fetch you and surprise him," John said, looking her in the face. "But why are you crying, sweet girl?"

"Oh, John, I have ruined everything." She cried as she grabbed hold of his strong arms. "You know what I have done, don't you?" She looked straight into his eyes and saw everything clearly.

John only smiled at her. "You need to re-center your clay and go at it again, but you are not lost or useless as you imagine. Why don't we hurry? Marta will just be setting dinner in front of the healer. Perhaps he can help."

"Thank you," Mariam whispered.

"Mariam! Thank goodness," Marta cried from the stairs. "I need help in the kitchen. Deborah and Helena have both gone back home, and I can't keep up with this crowd."

"What can I do?" Mariam asked, anxious to avoid the conversation that must soon be had.

"Carry these platters up to the men, then come back and cut up some more onions for tomorrow's stew." Marta handed over the platters and hurried off to the kitchen.

Mariam carried the platters up the stairs and set them on the low tables in the dimly lit room. *Back to being a servant,* she thought.

"Do not be anxious about what you will eat or what you will wear," the healer was saying. "God knows you need to eat and you need to have clothes. He will take care of you. Look at the flowers of the field. They do not labor and yet the Lord clothes them better than any finery of the greatest kings."

This didn't sound like the talk Mariam so often heard in the inn. Usually the men were talking about politics, overthrowing the government, or how the vineyards were doing, or just as often they were complimenting her to get into her bed. Mariam stopped in the large room to listen.

"Becoming rich is not the blessing you think it is," Jesus continued. "It is more important to be a servant. Sell your possessions and give to the poor, and your Father who sees what you are doing will bless you abundantly."

How true, Mariam thought. *I gained wealth, but lost myself. It has been a curse, not a blessing.*

Mariam found a quiet corner and settled down to listen. The men were asking the healer questions, and he was answering them with confidence and authority.

"Sir," one man asked, "I try to follow the commands of the Lord, but I never seem to succeed. What can I do?"

Jesus said, "A man had a fig tree, but it never produced any figs. Finally he went to his caretaker and told him to cut down the tree. But the gardener was sure there was something good inside the tree. 'Please let me try one more year,' he begged. 'I will tend it carefully and fertilize it. If after this year it does not yield fruit, then you may tear it down.' So the owner gave his permission. You need to tend to your life as if it was that tree, fertilizing and pruning where necessary."

"But what if it is only one or two figs that the tree bears?" Mariam heard herself ask. "Will the owner still destroy the tree?"

The men glanced back at her, and Mariam herself wondered what had possessed her to speak in this crowd of men. But ... honestly she didn't care that she had done it.

"The Father," Jesus said, "was willing to spare Sodom for only ten people. He will take your fig harvest and turn it into a feast. As Scripture says:

'Trust in the LORD with all your heart,
and do not lean on your own understanding.
In all your ways acknowledge him,
and he will make straight your paths.
Be not wise in your own eyes;
fear the LORD, and turn away from evil.
It will be healing to your flesh
and refreshment to your bones.
Honor the LORD with your wealth
and with the firstfruits of all your produce;
then your barns will be filled with plenty,
and your vats will be bursting with wine.'

"If you will start by giving that first fig to the Father, he will multiply it until your tree cannot hold all of the figs," Jesus said as he smiled at Mariam.

Just then Marta rushed into the room. "Mariam! You are supposed to be helping me in the kitchen. Sorry, my lord, she has forgotten her place. She won't bother you anymore."

"Marta, Mariam's ears are beginning to open. Let her listen and worry about the kitchen later. We will be fine if there are no onions in the stew tomorrow."

Eleazar stood then and took each sister by the arm. "Thank you for speaking to us, Rabbi. Enjoy your stay and we hope to hear more later," he said and then ushered the women out the door and down the stairs.

In the kitchen Eleazar glared at Mariam. "Did you walk home all alone?" he asked. "It is not safe for you to be on the roads alone."

"And yet here you are still at home," Mariam shot back. "Instead you send that piece of trash, David, to walk me back!"

"What! I didn't send David to get you," Eleazar said. "What are you talking about?"

"David said you asked him to walk me home because the roads are so full with crowds to see the healer. He said Elijah wanted me to sell myself to make money for the freedom fighters. He also said Elijah never intended to help you find a husband for me!" Mariam started crying again.

"How did you get home?" Marta asked.

"John found me ... He walked with me ... I was safe," Mariam said between sobs.

Eleazar narrowed his eyes and turned toward the stairs. Elijah was up there, Mariam knew—a member of the party, a welcome guest, a friend to her brother. And Mariam knew what was racing through Eleazar's mind. She grabbed him by the hand and cried, "No, Eleazar. Leave him be. I deserved no better." Then she poured out her troubles to Marta and Eleazar even as she felt a fig leaf sprout in her heart. It was a start.

Each day is a little life:
every waking and rising a little birth,
every fresh morning a little youth,
every going to rest and sleep a little death.
—Arthur Schopenhauer

CHAPTER 21

I arrived at Daddy's on a Friday evening to discover that he had made room for me in several cabinets and closets. "I didn't know what you would need," he muttered. "It's going to take awhile for us to get used to this, I suppose, now that you've been on your own for so long," Daddy said as he looked around the bedroom I had occupied as a child.

"You've been alone for quite a while yourself, Daddy," I said. "We will both have to make adjustments."

"I didn't know if you would have eaten before you came, so I have some ham sandwiches made up in the kitchen, and Mrs. Landoff sent over a chocolate cake when she found out you were coming. She said you wrote to Christy." Daddy smiled at me with eyebrows raised.

"I promised her I would write and thought I better do it before I get busy with Mr. John. What about Sam? Has he written or called her?"

"A few times." Daddy chuckled. "Come on down and eat."

Saturday and Sunday flew by, and I didn't sleep a wink on Sunday night. When the six o'clock bells at the First Baptist Church finally played "Beautiful Garden of Prayer" on Monday morning, I jumped out of bed and threw on my clothes in the dawning light. I heard the paperboy making his deliveries and grabbed the *Tribune* off the steps while the coffee percolated on the stove. Daddy came down in his robe and slippers and joined me for a cup of coffee.

"I guess you didn't sleep well," Daddy commented as he sipped his hot coffee.

"No, I keep wondering if I did the right thing. I'm excited, but it's all so ... uncertain," I drifted off.

"I guess the question is: Are you willing to give up what you already have in order to get what you truly want to have?" Daddy paused and we both stared into our mugs.

"It's a little late to decide that now." I chuckled. "I don't think I have anything left to give up at this point."

Daddy stared into his coffee a little longer while I jiggled my leg nervously and ate a bowl of cold cereal. "I would say you have been sleeping for a few years, Jack. You have been alive, yes, taking in everything around you, and I imagine you have even learned a lot about the business end of pottery, but you haven't been fully awake. I know you feel fuzzy-headed after a sleepless night, but today you are awake. You'll still use a lot of what you learned at Needler and Newman, but now you will actually love your work."

I picked up my coffee mug, inhaling the strong aroma. Daddy was speaking deeply again and I needed to concentrate to take it all in. I consciously stopped my leg and awaited his next remarks.

Finally he continued, "Love requires risk, Jack. Love will transform you, but like Mr. John says, you will have to yield to it. Do not think love is easy; never think that. You will have to go through the fire, Jack, just like your pots, and be transformed. Love is alarming, sacred, and beautiful all at once, but it isn't easy. I'm glad you are chasing your love, Jack." Daddy looked up at me.

I smiled, dumbfounded. "You must be reading more poetry, Daddy," I said and grinned. "Thank you."

I passed Hammond's Hardware just as Ginny emerged on the porch steps. I waved from the car and drove the last hundred yards to my new employer's. Mr. John and I were to be associates, but I still felt like he was the boss. Pulling into the small dirt parking lot, I turned off the radio and offered a wordless prayer.

Ginny knocked on the window as I sat there in the quiet morning. I turned to open the door and she stepped back.

"Good morning, Mr. Jack," she mocked me as she curtsied.

"Jack is just fine, Ginny. I'm really nervous," I said, "so please don't tease me today."

The morning felt chaotic as I attempted to decipher Mr. John's inventory system. Ginny helped as best she could, but the filing system for orders was a shambles, and I couldn't make heads or tails of the purchasing slips. I felt overwhelmed and terribly anxious.

Aunt Rose and Aunt Lily brought a sack lunch by for each of us at noon, and at Mr. John's insistence, the five of us sat under the trees in the lawn chairs to enjoy a little fresh air. The break from paperwork and the distraction of chitchat eased the knot that had been growing at the base of my neck since early that morning.

After lunch Mr. John encouraged me to turn back to the wheel. "Remember the reason you changed jobs, Jack. You need to center," he

said, implying that more than throwing clay
was involved.

The week sped by. Early mornings were
spent learning a new system and making
improvements, lunches were eaten with the
aunts and sometimes the Hammonds joined us
as well, and then the afternoons were
blissfully peaceful as I further developed my
centering and throwing skills. Daddy was
eager to hear about my day and he often
cooked dinner for both of us, though he
assured me that wouldn't continue once the
fall semester started. Before I knew it,
Saturday was dawning and I had a date with
Ginny.

I dressed in one of my Needler and Newman
suits with a wide green necktie and a crisp
white dress shirt beneath. Daddy whistled
when I came into the kitchen for my morning
coffee. I managed to eat a slice of cinnamon
toast, but I had to admit I was a bundle of
nerves. Daddy saw my hand shaking as I lifted
the hot coffee to my lips.

"So you like Ginny, do you?" he said quietly.

"I think so, at least so far," I said. If it had
been Mama asking, I would have explained
that Ginny was a novel idea to me. She was
independent and opinionated, but still
feminine and gentle. She was attractive, but I
liked her best with clay spattered on her work
apron and her hair falling around her face.
And the way she answered the phone at the
store always sent an electrical charge down

my spine. I definitely liked her, but I didn't know what to do about it with all of the changes I was going through just then. "Yeah," I said, then sighed.

Daddy never looked at me; he continued to stare at his coffee cup, sending swirls of steam above it. "You like her better than a kick in the head?" he asked.

I snorted. "Yeah, better than a kick in the head. What happened to the poetry, Daddy?" I sure missed Mama.

He shrugged. "I guess all my poetry concerning the females of the race was spent on your mother." Just then our mourning dove hurtled toward the window with a loud bang. "Maybe you should ask the bird," Daddy said.

"Birds and bees, you know, maybe that would be a good idea." I laughed. "I better head out. I told Ginny I would get her at the bus station."

"Have a good time," Daddy called as I passed Mama's picture in the hallway.

Ginny was waiting outside the bus depot. She held a wrapped gift in her hands and wore a trim green dress and short heels. Her hair was loosely curled, cascading down her back, and I thought she was beautiful. I jumped out of the car to open the door for her.

"Wow! You look great," she said. "I hope you didn't buy anything new."

"No, these were my work clothes at Needler and Newman."

"Well, that has certainly changed." She laughed. "You look really nice, Jack."

"Mama always said special places deserve special clothes. I guess your brother's wedding is a special place," I said, climbing back in my side of the Chevy. "Now how do we get to this wedding?"

We drove through town and headed northeast. Soon trees flanked both sides of the roadway, and the curves blocked my view. I slowed down as we passed through some leftover morning fog. As the car started climbing the mountains, I said, "You're right. Rome is just the toes of these foothills. I didn't realize you were such a mountain girl."

Ginny didn't respond. Staring out the passenger window, she chewed the inside of her cheek for the next twenty minutes.

"I hope I didn't offend you," I said. "I didn't mean anything by calling you a 'mountain girl.'" I glanced over at her.

"I know." She let her shoulders sag. "I'm a bit sensitive about it. Some of the girls at school say things about the uncivilized, backward mountain people. I didn't dare ask any of my school friends to take me today. The thing is, I often feel the same way. You'll see for yourself today at the wedding."

Now it was my turn to be quiet. So Ginny didn't really want me to take her to the wedding; she just didn't want friends to be the ones to take her. What was I supposed to think? Did that mean we only had a working relationship, that she saw me as an older man, an employer? I had thought the Fourth of July trip to Rome was a beginning for us, clearing up the Christy and Clive misunderstandings, and then she'd ask me to this wedding as her date ... but now I wasn't sure what to think. The rest of the ride felt solemn, contemplative.

I drove up the rocky road that led to Ginny's family home. We stopped partway up the hill to open a painted wooden gate and then Ginny closed it behind the car after I drove through.

"Daddy raises goats and sheep," Ginny said, climbing back in. "They pasture between the main road and the house."

A short distance later we passed through the last gate and entered the lawn area of the homestead. Children were running everywhere, and several young women waved from the porch. I could hear Ginny's shallow breathing next to me.

"Ready or not," she mumbled.

We parked next to all of the other cars. The young women flocked around the Chevy, kissing and hugging Ginny. She grabbed the wedding present out of the backseat and then introduced me to all of the ladies, mostly cousins, but also some high school friends. Several were obviously expecting; they seemed to make Ginny uncomfortable, although they didn't say anything wrong that I could tell.

The wedding ceremony was to take place in the small church we had passed about a mile back down the road. Large groups were assembling to ride there in the backs of trucks. Ginny asked to excuse herself, pointed me toward one of the trucks, and then headed into the house. Now I felt totally confused and befuddled. I thought I'd been invited to accompany Ginny because she liked me. Then it was implied that I wasn't even a friend, and now she didn't want to go down to the ceremony with me? What had I been thinking?

At the church I sat on the groom's side near the back. People glanced my way, but no one stopped to ask who I was or how I knew the groom. It definitely felt awkward. About twenty minutes later Ginny walked in, whispered a "Thank you for coming" to me, and then sat up front where she belonged with the family.

The groom and best man waited at the front of the church. I could see the family resemblance. The groom had the same auburn hair and fair skin as Ginny, but his eyes were dark, and he was built heavier. The pianist began the wedding processional, and soon the whole thing was over. We all bunched up in the truck beds again and headed back to the house.

The wedding reception was held on the hillside by a large fishing pond. Several quilts and blankets had been laid out for the little ones to be corralled on, and a few wooden chairs sat nearby for the older people. Stumps and wooden beams formed benches for the younger people to use. The preacher drove

Ginny's grandparents down to the pond to begin, and the bride's parents drove her grandparents in their car.

Tables had been made out of sawhorses and long boards. The wooden planks threatened to break under the weight of the feast. Fried chicken and country ham biscuits filled large platters. Bowls of fresh corn on the cob and other garden vegetables, casseroles, scalloped potatoes, gelatin salads with cabbage, pineapple, or fruit cocktail, and of course banana pudding with vanilla wafers made it a true smorgasbord.

Surrounded by the gifts, the wedding cake sat atop the dining room table that had been brought to the pond for the occasion. Ginny's brother and his new bride stood near the table, greeting people as they arrived. They seemed deliriously happy.

Ginny found me standing underneath some shade trees. She gave a sad frown. "You're having a bad time."

"I just feel a little out of place," I said. "I don't know anyone, including the bride and groom."

"Well you should meet my brother. Come on; I'll introduce you."

Her brother, Phillip, greeted me warmly. "It's so nice to meet Ginny's boss. She talked all about you when she came home this summer. Of course you weren't her boss then. How is the new job going?"

We talked for several minutes about owning a business and the risks involved when Ginny's dad walked up behind us.

"At least you will be able to find a real job to pay the bills," he said to me. "Pottery don't pay the bills. You plan on having a family?"

"Daddy!" Ginny said. "That's none of your business. And pottery can pay the bills."

Her father ignored her and kept his eye on me. "Girls can waste a little time on nonsense like pottery and painting, but men's work requires more than that."

I nodded. "I would have agreed with you three months ago, but I've come to realize that we each are made for a purpose, and trying to reach that purpose by going the wrong direction is futile. I believe I have the business education and experience along with the creative passion to make this work." I actually managed to stay calm as I defended myself.

"But what about Ginny?" he asked. "She needs a man who can do more than chase a dream; she needs someone who can take care of her and the babies."

"Daddy!" Ginny gasped, turning bright red. "Jack is my boss. And I have enough talent and gumption to be a potter and support myself. I don't need a man!"

"You ain't got no more gumption than a nanny goat in a hailstorm! You're just a girl: a girl that ain't got no business staying away from home all year and gallivanting off to spend the night at some man's house." He glared at me. "Clive told me all about it," he spat, looking from me to Ginny and back again.

By now all the guests were looking everywhere but at us and trying hard not to appear to be listening. Ginny's eyes brimmed over as she looked around at her family.

"I wish the best to you, Phillip," she said, then forced a smile for her brother. "Jack, would you please take me home?"

"No, I won't," I said, now feeling incensed at the implications. "Mr. Toliver, Ginny has done nothing improper. She stayed with my family over the holiday, but she slept upstairs with my elderly aunts, and my brother and I slept on the couch and floor downstairs. She was there at the invitation of my father who had met her earlier and was impressed with her manners and intellect. He saw her for the woman that she already is." I turned and took Ginny by the elbow. "Now I will escort you home." As we passed by her brother, I said, "I'm sorry for the scene."

He gave a small nod and we walked to the car. Ginny was sobbing before I shut her door.

I decided to let Ginny choose the direction of our conversation while I drove her back to Paradox. She evidently thought silence was the best choice and stayed that way for an hour. Finally she breathed deeply.

"Jack, I'm sorry you had to be a part of that. Daddy just doesn't understand how things are changing. He doesn't like women working and making decisions. I'm sorry he insulted you."

"Ginny, your daddy loves you, and he wants to protect you. He doesn't say those things to hurt you; he truly believes he is helping you," I said as light dawned on my own past. "Your father had dreams for you, and probably for himself, and they aren't working out the way he expected or hoped. But you should be patient. Sometimes fathers change their minds." I grinned.

"Maybe," she said. After a short pause she continued, "Jack, it's not just the pottery business that upsets Daddy. He wants me to get married and have a family. He thinks I am being too worldly going off to college and driving with a man for hours at a time. He doesn't seem to understand that I have no aspirations to marry or have a family. At least not anytime soon. I want to be a potter and that's it." She looked at me.

"That's good, because you are a great potter."

We talked shop the rest of the way to Paradox. When I dropped Ginny off at the hardware store, she opened her own door and said a quick good-bye. The decision was unspoken: we would be employer and employee.

*The beginnings and ends of shadow lie
between the light and darkness and may be
infinitely diminished and infinitely increased.
Shadow is the means by which bodies display
their form. The forms of bodies could not be
understood in detail but for shadow.*
—Leonardo da Vinci

CHAPTER 22

Marta meandered through the olive grove, remembering the happy times she and Jacob had shared there. Jacob had been a talented mason, creating buildings of strength and delicate beauty, but he had also been an artist. It was he who had made the stone scroll benches nestled under the olive trees along the south wall. Heading in that direction, Marta saw the form of a man kneeling near the bench under her favorite tree.

As Marta drew closer, she saw that it was the healer.

He looked up and smiled. "Good evening, Marta. Have you come to pray after all?"

"I was enjoying the quietness," Marta said. "My husband and I used to walk here in the evenings."

Jesus nodded, taking a seat on the bench. "There is not much quietness at a tavern. It's good to get alone; being alone is the only way to realize that you are never alone."

"What do you mean?" Marta asked as she sat at the far edge of the bench.

"Surrounded by people, noise, and work, it is often easy to feel forgotten and alone. You have to take care of others, live for someone else, and think about what will happen to you. In the midst of all of that worry, you feel like no one understands your dilemma, your problems. Sometimes you think no one cares about you at all."

"Yes." Marta nodded. "Especially since my husband died, I have felt all alone, even though I am surrounded by people."

"But here in the quiet, you realize the Father is still watching over you. You are not alone, Marta."

Marta looked away, but did not hesitate in making the decision to trust this Jesus enough to share her heart. "When Abba and Mother passed away and left me and Jacob with Eleazar and Mariam, I never felt alone. Jacob was so equal to it all. He was a good man. But then he was taken away from me and I was left all alone. I know the Lord is still there, but he doesn't seem to notice me." Marta sighed.

"Why are you here?" Jesus asked Marta.
"Why did you walk to the olive grove this
evening?"

"I guess I was hoping to hear Jacob. We
used to come here and dream together. Now I
only have nightmares and I don't know what
to do. I truly am alone," Marta whispered as
tears fell, making her cheeks glisten in the
twilight.

"You don't hear because you don't know who
to listen for," Jesus said. "Don't listen for
Jacob. Listen for the Lord; he is waiting to
speak to you."

Jesus stayed a while longer, sitting in
silence, and then quietly walked into the
deepening darkness. Marta hardly noticed as
she struggled to breathe in the thick storm
clouds that gathered in her mind. *Mariam is a
harlot and Eleazar could be tried as a traitor.*
Where had she gone wrong? She hadn't felt up
to the task without Jacob. If only Jacob hadn't
been taken away, none of this would have
happened. She never would have opened a
tavern. Eleazar would not have been corrupted
by the freedom fighters who went from town to
town stirring up trouble. And Mariam would
not have been corrupted by the men who spoke
so alluringly to her sister's pride. But the
decisions they made were theirs to make. Even
if Jacob had lived, there was no way to know
that her brother and sister would have made
good decisions.

"Lord, where do I go from here?" she asked aloud.

"Marta?" John's voice broke the still night and a bird flew from the tree. "What are you doing out here, daughter?"

Marta startled and jumped from the bench, its cold hardness leaving an ache in her back. "I was talking ... with Jesus," she said, looking around.

"Are you sure?" John asked. "You seem to be alone." He smiled.

"John, you are never alone, even when you are alone." Marta grinned. "I think I will head back to the house. I need to talk to Mariam. It's time to move on."

A bright moon slid from behind a cloud and lit the path back home.

Months passed by without a word from Elijah. Eleazar stopped attending the meetings in Jerusalem and the small villages. Marta no longer hosted the Bethany men's meetings; instead the men chose to gather at Shimon the Leper's house. Mariam had not given up her "business" completely, but she depended on it less and less, choosing instead to glean in the groves and fields when Marta could spare her. Then she sold her produce on market days.

Jesus came several more times to the tavern, always bringing crowds with him. It was a healthy income for Marta, but more than that, it was a time to listen. All three became friends with the healer, loving him for more than his goodness to Abraham and the income that he generated. They loved him for the healing he brought to their broken spirits. Life wasn't perfect, but it seemed to be improving.

John had given Eleazar a lesson in cutting and molding this morning and he had completed his first vanity vase. Eleazar was proud of the delicate designs he had outlined and removed from the leather-hard clay. Now the morning fog had lifted and the spring sun was warming the pottery shards that lined the path as he walked back home for lunch. Mariam was whitewashing the sleeping rooms to clean out the winter soot and dirt, and could not be spared to bring him his lunch. Suddenly a searing pain grabbed his calf—and then he spotted a black cobra rearing back for another strike. Eleazar fell headlong into burning darkness.

*It is not light that we need, but fire; it is not
the gentle shower, but thunder. We need the
storm, the whirlwind, and the earthquake.*
                —Frederick Douglass

CHAPTER 23

One evening in late August at Daddy's house, I received a phone call from Jimmy. He said he was being reckless to call me, but he had heard some rumors at work and thought I should know. The authorities would soon be coming for Mr. John. There were questions about his legitimacy.

I tried calling Mr. John several times, but he never answered. I slept fitfully that night and headed into the studio before dawn the next morning. No one was around yet, so I started chopping firewood for the kiln. The exertion helped relieve the stress I was feeling. Soon Mr. John emerged from his small house.

"You're up early. Everything alright?" he asked, sipping his hot coffee.

"I'm glad you're up," I said, slamming the axe into an upright log. "Jimmy called me from Needler and Newman last night."

Mr. John nodded.

"He says the authorities are coming for you. They are questioning your work. I didn't get all of the details. What are we going to do?"

"Jack, I told you I haven't done anything wrong. There isn't anything to do," Mr. John responded. His calmness only set me further on edge.

"But, Mr. John, what if they arrest you? What if they take you away?"

"It will all work out, Jack. Trust me. Chop some more wood if it helps. We have a lot to get fired for that order you made in Boston." Mr. John walked back to his house.

Late in the afternoon, as Ginny and I worked on the wheels and Mr. John talked with some customers, a burly man in a three-piece suit came into the shop. He approached Mr. John and handed him a letter. Then he waltzed out of the studio as quickly as he had appeared.

Ginny looked at me and raised her eyebrows. I finished off the walls on the pot I was throwing and then washed in the utility sink. I found Mr. John outside in his lawn chair reading the letter.

"What is it, Mr. John?"

He handed the letter to me. It was an official letter from the government. Preliminary tests showed that the fingerprints on the relics and on the sample Mr. John provided at Needler and Newman's offices appeared to be the same prints. They were requesting Mr. John's presence at the federal courthouse in Atlanta the following week.

"Oh, Mr. John, I feel like this is my fault," I said. "What will we do?"

"Jack, how many times do I have to tell you it will be okay?" Mr. John smiled at me.

I couldn't understand his calm demeanor. I would have been shaking in my shoes, asking about lawyers, planning an escape, anything but accepting the news as if it was a Christmas card from a neighbor down the street.

I drove Mr. John to Atlanta on Monday. I wore my best suit and tie. Mr. John wore a plain black suit and tie; he didn't own anything special. On the way down we discussed how business was going and the new sales I was helping to make. The business did seem to be improving, though it was still summer and the tourist season was strong. I felt optimistic that in a year or two, I could manage to move out of Daddy's house.

Eventually the discussion turned to Ginny. "Do you see Ginny staying on?" Mr. John asked.

"Mm, I don't know. She heads back to school in another week, and I guess she'll be pretty busy then. Maybe she'll do an additional internship with another potter. Of course she couldn't do any better than you, Mr. John."

"That's kind of you, Jack, but I meant after Ginny graduates. I think she has what it takes to be a great potter. She could be good for your business ... *and* your life."

I felt surprised to hear him say that. Mr. John had never mentioned my love life or intentions toward any girls. Of course our lunches with the aunts were always filled with good-natured comments, but nothing serious was ever said.

"I ... don't think Ginny is interested in a romantic relationship," I said. "And I think it's pretty clear she wants only a working relationship with me in particular."

Ginny had been cool toward me ever since the wedding. She was polite and respectful, but she usually went back to the Hammonds' for her lunches, found excuses to work in the store when I was in the studio, and barely ever spoke to me when we did have to work closely. She had even asked us to use her given name, Virginia. I decided I had misread the Independence Day and wedding "dates." She had seen me only as a nice guy and an employer.

"When you are forming a pot, you try to make the outside mimic the inside of the pot, right?" Mr. John asked.

"Yes," I said, unsure where this was headed.

"If the outside is different than the inside surface, you have a heavy pot. It is a sign of bad craftsmanship."

I waited a while longer, but Mr. John seemed to be finished. I just didn't understand this guru stuff. I had known Mr. John off and on for a long time. Over the summer I had gotten to know him very well, I thought. Here I was driving him to the federal courthouse, putting my own career and new business on the line, and he was going to throw out pottery analogies that made no sense?

"I don't know what you mean by that," I finally said. "Are you saying something is wrong with Ginny?"

"She is still being thrown, Jack; a soft piece of clay being formed by many potters: her father, her classmates, even you. But the most important Potter, the one who can feel inside her and outside her, is the one who must make them match. She needs help guiding herself through that process. You were very nearly a bottom-heavy pot too, but look at you now with your walls rising and forming again. You will soon be ready for the fire. Ginny could use some of your experience, Jack."

I hadn't thought about being a mentor to Ginny, but Mr. John was right. I knew what it was like for your father to be disappointed in your choices, to try to steer you in one direction. I knew how scary it was to step out in faith that you were doing the right thing, but still feel the shakiness of the risk involved.

"You're right," I said, but my voice caught in my throat.

At the courthouse the polished lobby greeted us, cold and stark. A receptionist pointed us toward the stairs and we climbed the curved staircase to the second floor. A small office was reserved for international affairs, and my stomach lurched as I realized this was an Interpol issue. The frosted door glass was labeled for the department head; we knocked gently on the door.

"Come on in," called a man through the door.

Mr. John opened the door and walked into the small office. I hesitated in the doorway, unsure if I should really be a part of this. But Mr. John was my friend. He had taught me so much. I owed this to him at least. I closed the door behind me; there was no going back now.

"I'm John Kadar," Mr. John said, extending his hand to the man behind the desk. "And this is Jack Sharp. We work together." Mr. John motioned toward me.

The man looked at him and scratched his head. "I was expecting a foreigner," he said.

Mr. John chuckled and shook his head.

"I'm Greg Walton," the man said. "Sorry, have seats, please," he said as he shuffled papers off of the chairs in front of his desk. His appearance was as disheveled as his office. "I don't get many people in here."

"Now let me review your case, Mr. Kadar," he said as he pulled a manila folder out of his desk drawer. "Oh, yes, you voluntarily gave your fingerprints to a company here in town that represents your wares across the country. You are a potter, correct?" Mr. Walton looked at Mr. John over the papers.

Mr. John nodded.

"Another company in ... Boston? Is that correct?"

I wasn't sure if the man was trying to trap Mr. John in a lie or if he really didn't know what was going on.

"No, sir, Houston," Mr. John said.

The man checked something off on the paper with a pencil. "Houston," he muttered. "The accusation is that you have sold your pottery under the pretense of it being archaeological relics. The sales occurred in Madrid and the items were shipped to Houston. Have you ever been to Madrid, Mr. Kadar?"

"Yes," Mr. John said.

Mr. Walton waited for an explanation, but Mr. John didn't offer any.

This is not a time for your silent treatment, I thought.

"Mr. Kadar has traveled many places to display his craftsmanship," I said. "He is a well-known potter."

The man cleared his throat and looked back down at the papers. "Yes, well, it seems that the signature mark on the relics purchased in Madrid is the same mark that your Mr. Kadar uses." He paused to look at some more papers in the file. "The odd thing is that your mark uses a thumbprint to create a bird and so does the one on the relic. That is surprising. The relics date from the 1200s, but the real anomaly is that the actual print designs of the thumbprints match. That is why you are being asked to be printed officially. It's just protocol. I really don't think anything will come of it." He smiled and looked at the two of us.

Mr. John waited patiently while the agent prepared the slides that would be used for the fingerprints. He explained that they would be sent on to an international pool of fingerprints to see if anything suspicious popped up. They would also be sent to the dealer in Houston to have the relics examined by a professional. The whole process would likely take several months, he told us.

We ate lunch at a little diner across the street and then headed back to Paradox. I kept the radio on to avoid the stifling silence that promised to engulf me. How would I manage a new business with this hanging over our heads? Mr. John napped beside me, oblivious to the danger that threatened. I felt like one of Mr. Toliver's nanny goats in a hailstorm.

And they will look to the earth, but behold,
distress and darkness, the gloom of anguish.
And they will be thrust into thick darkness.
—Isaiah 8:22

CHAPTER 24

Deborah found Eleazar unconscious on the side of the path to the potter's, his leg swollen and angry. She ran for help, but most of the able-bodied men were still gone from the village. Marta and Mariam rolled Eleazar into a blanket and tried hoisting him back to the house. Even in their adrenaline-rushing state, he was too much for them. John heard their cries and came running from his hut.

The venom flowed quickly through Eleazar. Helena was called to use her knowledge of the medicinal arts that would relieve the stinging poison. She came with her herbs and oils and slathered the snake bite. Eleazar drifted for several days in and out of consciousness, spinning dizzily like a mound of watery clay refusing to rise on the wheel.

The sisters sent to the villages searching for Jesus. If he would only come, they knew he would heal their brother. Surely the Lord would not visit another calamity on this small family. The healer had to be found!

It had been less than a week since Eleazar had happily walked up the trail toward home. Now he could not hold on any longer; a happier home he was sure to find. He let go of Marta and Mariam's hands even as they grasped him, clawing at the bedclothes, his arms, his face. Desperately refusing to let Eleazar leave yet knowing from experience that nothing could make him stay, the sisters fell into John's embrace.

Hope is the only bee that makes
honey without flowers.
—Robert Green Ingersoll

CHAPTER 25

The rest of the summer flew by. In September a letter arrived from Christy; she had flown to Ghana and was enjoying the first few days getting used to her surroundings. She wasn't homesick yet, but she would certainly enjoy some letters, she said. Sam didn't write us or call, but we expected that to happen during Basic Training. Ginny went back to Bersher for her senior year. Daddy went back to work and had to sit on several new committees. I began eating dinner with the aunts and staying in Paradox a few nights a week to save some gas money. A restive routine formed.

Then Aunt Lily contracted a stomach bug at the end of September, so I offered to mow the grass for her. It was late enough in the year that this would be one of the last mowings of the season. I pushed the reel mower out of the barn and started walking the length of the house. My mind wandered as I fell under the hypnotic turning of the reel.

Four short months ago I had come to visit the aunts. I'd been playing into a guilt trip that Aunt Rose piled on me. I arrived stressed and disheartened by my job at Needler and Newman. Then I went fishing, slept in a hammock, listened to beavers, and watched lightning bugs, and most importantly I met Mr. John. I made friends with Daddy, and with Sam and Christy, and even with Ginny. I exchanged the stress of Atlanta for the quietness of Paradox. Not that there wasn't stress here too, what with the investigation concerning the pottery relics and Mr. John's work, but I was restful in a deeper sort of way. Maybe that was the paradox of Paradox: I was willing to give up everything in order to gain the one thing I'd never had—peace.

Cucumber vines escaping the confines of the garden lay across my mower's path. I stopped to circle them back into the garden. I looked over Aunt Lily's garden, nearly dead now with depleted harvest. Some small cucumbers and tomatoes held on, but frost would be here in a few more weeks and that would be the end of them. I gathered them in my shirt front and picked my way through the rest of the garden. At the end were Grandpappy's flowers.

Marigolds still bloomed, but most of the summer flowers were gone. In their place were bright blue asters growing in bunches. Their fragile-looking petals surrounded the yellow bulbous centers. Aunt Lily had planted the asters I'd brought her. Grandpappy and Grandmama had not had the strength to move on, but Aunt Lily had seen that it was time.

I set the vegetables on the porch steps and wandered down to the riverbank. The evening light was fading and a large moon was rising over the beaver dam. My piping system had worked all summer, and the field on the other side of the river was high with autumn grasses. The neighbor would be mowing the last hay soon, so I thought perhaps I should clear the pasture one last time for Aunt Rose. I realized that I was taking over responsibility for Aunt Rose and Aunt Lily. Daddy was doing what he could—*But,* I thought, *maybe Paradox is my home.*

Woe to him who strives with him who formed him, a pot among earthen pots! Does the clay say to him who formed it, "What are you making?" or "Your work has no handles"?
—Isaiah 45:9

CHAPTER 26

Eleazar's body was wrapped in spices and linen cloths, and Abraham allowed that the family tomb should be opened for Eleazar. Heaviness in Marta's chest threatened to suffocate her as she oversaw the burial that placed her brother and her husband side by side, and then the tomb was sealed. Hand in hand, Marta and Mariam trudged back to the tavern, followed by the friends and family who were there to help mourn.

Loud wailing and singing filled the upper room. Marta stopped hearing it after the second day. Her head throbbed from the constant noise, the grief, the despair. Surely the Lord was punishing her for something. Perhaps it was because she had lived so long in the shadow of death that she had ignored the life that was happening all around her. But why did Eleazar have to be the one to suffer? He was so young, so full of courage, so ready to take back the land for the Lord. It wasn't fair. Where was the Lord's justice?

The mourners continued to come in droves, reminding Mariam that her brother was gone and so was her future. She had loved him greatly, but now she was completely alone. Mariam knew now that she would forever be a prostitute, and soon her disgrace would become common knowledge. There would be no hope of a husband now that Eleazar was gone. There would be no sons to bless her, no one to care for her when she was old.

Days had passed and with them came a growing conviction that all days should end. Mariam knew that Marta's prospects for a husband would be ruined, if they hadn't been already, by the public knowledge that her sister was a disgraced woman. Mariam fingered the alabaster jar of perfume that she had been saving for her wedding. She couldn't live knowing that she was the cause for both their ruined lives. She set down the jar of perfume and twisted her hands around the brightly colored robe she had worn that last night in Jerusalem. How appropriate that the item she had been sure would bring her a new life should now bring about her death. She gently caressed the fabric, then folded it neatly and placed it at the end of her sleeping mat. She would retrieve it later for one last walk in the olive grove.

Marta wandered to the cistern, looking for a cool drink to ease the burning anger and despair that consumed her. Groups of mourners were milling about the courtyard sharing bits of gossip when Marta overheard Deborah and her mother.

"Jesus was seen along the road. He should be here soon," Deborah whispered.

"Such a shame," her mother clucked. "If only he had been here last week, before it was too late."

Marta ran forward and grabbed Deborah by the shoulders, then shook her. "Who saw Jesus? Where along the road? Take me to him—now!" she half-pleaded, half-commanded.

With a small nod Deborah led Marta in and out of the throng weaving along the crowded road until they met Jesus walking toward them.

"Why?" Marta shouted, falling at the healer's feet. "Why did the Lord take my brother? It was me; it was my fault. Eleazar should not have been punished for my sins!" The tears that had been dammed behind the pain tore down the levee wall and flooded Jesus's feet. "If you had only been here, my lord, Eleazar would still live," she sobbed.

Jesus bent down and took Marta by the hands, pulling her to her feet. "Dear Marta, your heart has been shattered into midnight. Take me to our brother," Jesus whispered.

Marta looked up at Jesus's face, expecting a rebuke for her outburst, but only love and sorrow met her gaze. Squeezing Jesus's hands, she turned toward the tomb. They walked in silence, needing no words. The crowd that always accompanied Jesus fell in quietly behind the two, solemnly marching toward the great abyss of pain and sorrow that had enveloped the young woman for the last week.

"Here ..." Marta choked back the sobs that threatened to overwhelm her. "Here is the place where our brother rests. If only you had been here earlier, I know you could have saved Eleazar." The accusatory tone had disappeared. The icy anger and malice that she had felt toward the Lord Almighty melted as tears flowed unchecked down her cheeks. What was done was done.

"Where is Mariam?" the healer asked. "I would like to see our sister."

"I'll get her," Deborah said, but Marta raised a hand.

"No, let me find her," Marta said as she watched the trail of tears tracing the curves of Jesus's face.

She ran off to retrieve her sister, trying hard not to fan the flicker of hope that rose in her breast.

A black cloud of fear and determination hovered around Mariam's shoulders and fingered her slender throat. She was absentmindedly picking at a bowl of beans with Helena when Marta found her in the upper room.

"The healer is here! He has come, Mariam. He wants to see you. Hurry!"

"What? What do you mean?" Mariam asked.

"Jesus has come at last. He is waiting for us at the tomb," Marta said.

"It is too late." Mariam began to tear up again, but she rose and followed Marta. "Always too late," she muttered.

The road to the tomb was crowded with mourners for Eleazar and with the crippled and diseased that always followed on Jesus's heels. Marta sped through them, barely noticing Elijah among the crowds. Elijah had paid his respects to the sisters, as any town elder should do, but Marta and Mariam had not welcomed him or his family to the vigil wake that continued through the week.

Jesus was waiting with his disciples when Mariam and Marta burst through the pack of people. Jesus turned to embrace both women at the same time. His gentle familiarity was so unexpected that all Mariam could manage was a weak, "If only you had been here, my lord, our brother would not have died."

"Your brother will live again, Mariam," the healer said.

"I know he will live in the resurrection, but for now he is lost to us." And the misery that had knotted her shoulders and tied up her heart grabbed her by the throat. Now she knew for certain that all hope was lost.

"No, Mariam." He turned away from her. "Marta, tell the men to open the tomb."

"But, my lord, it is too late to say good-bye now. He has been there four days already," Marta said.

"Open the tomb," Jesus commanded with quiet dignity.

Abraham was standing nearby and nodded to the men in the crowd, ordering them to roll away the heavy rock that had been fashioned by Jacob to cover the family grave.

Then Jesus, wiping tears from his eyes, called, "Eleazar, come out!"

Mariam glanced at Marta's wide eyes and open mouth, her own expression certainly reflecting the same confusion. Did he not believe that Eleazar was truly dead? Who ever heard of raising someone from the dead? There were rumors, of course, that this healer had done it, but after four days in the grave? It just couldn't be.

And then the familiar laughter that had taunted the sisters for nearly twenty years burst from the tomb as their brother walked out to greet them.

Shake off your dust; rise up, sit enthroned, Jerusalem.Free yourself from the chains on your neck, Daughter Zion, now a captive.
—Isaiah 52:2

CHAPTER 27

Early in October, Mr. John, the aunts, and I went to the Coosa Valley Fair together. It was a warm autumn day, and we enjoyed looking at the 4-H exhibits, the Ladies' Auxiliary canned goods competition, and the art exhibits. I was chewing on a candy apple when I saw a pottery booth next to the Rotary display.

At the booth Ginny was visiting with some older ladies, showing them her pie plates and cake pans. She looked good, better than I remembered. I walked behind the display to eavesdrop on her.

"They're great for church potlucks," she said, "because you always know you have the right dish when you go home."

"I lost my best platter at a family reunion," one of the ladies said. "I guess I would need it with my full name. We have three Lindas in the family," she said as she elbowed one of her friends.

"I can do that," Ginny said. "You just fill out the form with whatever you want it to say, and I will have it done in a few weeks. Then I'll ship it straight to you."

Two of the women filled out forms and paid Ginny, then they wandered off to the decorated cake displays. Ginny was filing the forms and money when I walked into sight and cleared my throat.

She looked up and smiled. "Jack! Hi! How is Mr. John?" Her face grew serious. "I heard there was more trouble with the show in Houston."

"He's fine, acts as if nothing ever happened. It's supposed to take several months to get the final results of the tests, but the agent was confident that nothing will come of it. I'm hoping so," I said and then pointed to her booth. "How are sales going for you?"

"Pretty well really," she said. "I may need a little help, actually." She peered at me.

"Oh?"

"I was planning to fill the orders with my school quota requirements, but I have so many orders that I don't think I can convince the school to let me continue using their equipment. Do you think I could fill a couple of kilns at the studio? I would give you part of the profits for payment."

"It's fine with me, but you need to talk to Mr. John too," I said, feeling happy that Ginny would be back around.

"Well, actually," she said, "I already asked Mr. John. I ran into him for a few minutes at school last week. He said he was helping your father with an Arts and Sciences committee project. Anyway, Mr. John said it wasn't up to him and that I had to talk to you."

I blinked. "What? Really? Why didn't you call, then? Of course you can use our equipment. You're a very good potter, Ginny. I'm sure we could even find some more work for you if you wanted it."

She smiled. "Hey, are you hungry? I was just going to get a burger and fries at the Lions Club booth. Want to join me?"

We walked across the fairway while men called for me to win a prize for "your gal." We ordered burgers and sodas; Ginny said she only wanted six fries, so we shared an order. Sitting across from each other at a picnic table, I couldn't help thinking I had been missing this. I'd never had time in Atlanta to visit with a pretty girl at the fair, or anyone at the fair.

"Jack, I spoke with Mr. John about more than just coming out to use your equipment," Ginny said, avoiding my eyes. "Mr. John has a knack for knowing what needs to be said ... you know?" she asked and then paused. "He told me that I was hungry for things that appear to be at odds."

I nodded. "Mr. John often says strange things. Do you know what he was talking about?"

"I think so. He said that people have many appetites that need to be satisfied; not just for food, but also for money, approval, pleasure, even power. Mr. John said I was trying to feed my hungers, but I was never satisfying them. He said all of those hungers come down to just two things: a desire to have freedom and a desire to be bound."

I wasn't sure what all of that meant, but I thought this was a good time to be patient and listen. Ginny looked out over the fairway and took a deep breath. She seemed to gather her thoughts, looked at me, and then looked away again with a shrug of her shoulders.

"Jack, I want to be a potter, a really good potter. I always thought that meant I needed to completely focus on my craft. Focusing on anything else would mean that pottery wasn't as important as I thought it was." She looked at me.

I smiled slightly and nodded, but stuck to the plan of patient listening.

Ginny went on. "I thought if I was interested in a man, in having a family, then it would mean my daddy was right: I was only made to be a wife and mother. But I think what Mr. John was saying is that I can't ever be free to be the best potter I can be until I also admit that I need other things too."

"Like what?"

"You sure don't make this easy," she grumbled. "Okay, you remember the platter I made for Phillip and his wife? With the house and the flower petals?"

"Yes," I said, happy to answer something confidently.

"I designed that from a happy place. Phillip had shown me the house when I was back home. He talked about his plans, about Rachael, about the beautiful view from the front room. I felt free making that platter because I love Phillip and Rachael, and I am excited to add her to our family. You see?"

I thought I had caught on—and felt my heart sink. "So Mr. John is saying you will only be free when you have peace with your family, when you're united. You want to move back there, don't you?"

"For Pete's sake, Jack. I'll only find freedom when I admit I need to be united with you! You're not very good with subtlety, are you?"

I felt my face blush and I could only smile. "I guess I get my ability to understand women from my father. So are you asking me to marry you, Ginny? Because I don't know that I am that modern of a man." I winked at her.

"Jack Joseph Sharp! You're going to make me regret this aren't you?" She tried to act angry, but I knew better. A sparkle was playing at the edge of her eyes, forcing her freckled nose to crinkle up.

"No," I said, "Ginny, I would love to get to know you better, even date you, but you have to understand that I can't support a wife and family yet, especially not with this question of Mr. John's authenticity hanging over the business."

"That's just it, Jack." She took my hand. "I don't want to be taken care of. I want to be in a partnership, where we both need each other and support each other. That's what Mr. John was talking about: the hunger for freedom and the hunger for unity."

"Sounds like we better start eating," I said. "How about some cotton candy?" I asked as I rose and took her hand. "Only I hope you share it better than you did the fries. I know you ate more than six, young lady!"

The thief comes only to steal and kill and destroy;I have come that they may have life, and have it to the full.
—John 10:10

CHAPTER 28

The men gathered at Shimon the Leper's house, celebrating Eleazar's miraculous recovery. Jesus ignored the platters of delicacies being passed around, choosing instead to observe Eleazar.

"You have been granted freedom, Eleazar, a new birth. Will you accept it?" the healer asked.

"I have been granted life, my lord, and, yes, I accept it gratefully," Eleazar replied as the men clapped him on the back and laughed in renewed relief and joy.

Jesus continued staring at Eleazar. "The freedom fighters are not the way to achieve freedom, Eleazar. It is only through death that you will be free to live."

Eleazar looked up. "You sound like John the Potter. John once told me that death would bring birth, but I still don't see how that can be."

Jesus smiled. "John is wise and an excellent potter. You should spend more time with him, learning. Use your death to bring about change, change that turns everyone you meet to the Father. Then they, too, may be born anew."

"I still don't—" Eleazar cut his words short at a commotion at the door.

An obscured woman carrying a bundle of brightly colored robes was pushing her way into the house and past the obstinate servants. "You are not to come here!" a male servant ordered.

"I must see Jesus. I have to tell him," came the familiar voice, raised in defiance.

Eleazar could only smile: *Mariam.*

"Tell me what, Mariam?" Jesus motioned to the servants to let her in.

As soon as Mariam eyed Jesus, she rushed to him. Eleazar watched as she placed the cloak in Jesus's lap, then fell weeping at his feet.

"You are my only hope," she cried. "You have turned my despair into gladness. The days of death will darken my pathway no more. I will sing to the Lord."

Her words jumbled together, dancing between mournfulness and laughter as she poured the alabaster jar of perfume on Jesus's feet and wiped them with her hair.

Shimon sneered. "Perhaps you haven't heard yet what kind of woman is touching you," he said to Jesus.

"I know who is touching me: a woman who honors the Lord. A death has occurred and a life has been born, one that smells of perfume and figs." Jesus smiled at Mariam and touched her shoulder. "You will go out with joy, Mariam. The hills will break out in song as you journey through life. Never again will you find only barren darkness. Thank you for your gift."

He dismissed her with gentle words, leaving Eleazar and the others sitting in stunned silence.

I am a most noteworthy sinner, but I have cried out to the Lord for grace and mercy, and they have covered me completely. I have found the sweetest consolation since I made it my whole purpose to enjoy His marvelous Presence.
—Christopher Columbus

CHAPTER 29

Mariam was kicking the wheel as Eleazar coned the centered clay. John had invited her to help in the pottery studio to give her some honest income. She enjoyed watching the men form beautiful objects out of clumps of muddy clay. She, too, was beginning to learn the arduous process of centering the clay.

"You cannot force the clay to center," John had told her as he held her hands in place applying pressure to the backs of her palms. "There are good reasons for the clay not to center: the moisture may be wrong, or the clay perhaps too cold, or even the bat may have warped. But if the clay will cooperate and come as close to center as possible, the potter can work with it. The clay has to agree to work with the potter, though."

Mariam had smiled when she heard that. Her clay had been royally messed up, but now she had been wedged and was yielding herself to the Potter. *Someday,* she thought, *I will be a vessel worthy of my King.*

"What are you doing now, John?" Mariam asked from the stand by the wheel.

John brought over the leather-hard pitcher he was working on. He showed it to Mariam as she continued to kick the wheel for Eleazar.

"See, my finger marks are all around the inside of the pitcher," he said as he turned it for her to look at. "My fingers mold the inside of the pitcher as it turns on the wheel. The outside is affected by many forces. I can cut it, carve it, use a molding tool, lots of things, but the inside will always bear my fingerprints. I also sign the outside of my work where the fingerprints aren't so obvious, so there is no question about who made my pieces."

John showed her his thumbprint on the base of the pitcher. Then he took a small piece of bone and cut around the smudged print to form a flying bird.

"Why a bird, John?" Mariam asked.

"It's a dove, Mariam. Doves bring reassurance. The pitcher was made by me, by my own hand."

I determined never to stop until I had come to the end and achieved my purpose.
—David Livingstone

CHAPTER 30

The bright lights and sweet smells of the autumn carnival began wedging together the clay of our lives. We both knew that it wouldn't be easy, this living life as you are intended. No one guarantees a porcelain Ming vase is what you get when you follow the Potter's lead. Many days our experiences produced plain terra cotta flowerpots. Some days only offered kilns of broken pieces.

We were married a year after Ginny graduated. The aunts were ecstatic when we bought the old Sidler place next to theirs. The village was still called Paradox, but our home made it Paradise. Our pottery business didn't seem to suffer from the scandal surrounding Mr. John's identity. Long after our wedding we finally received a letter apologizing for the delay. It seemed the experts decided that thumbprints in fired clay could not be correctly identified and the coincidence of the similar signature was just that: a coincidence.

Ginny and I worked together to create a market for our unique items, and the business thrived. Daddy admitted he'd been completely wrong: a potter *can* support a family, especially when he has a wife like Ginny. Mr. John stayed on at the studio for several years, teaching me and Ginny about clay and potters and life. And then one day he said he would be leaving.

"I will return ... soon," he said as he clapped me on the back and then hugged Ginny. "I need to take care of some business, but I'll be back."

"How long will you be, Mr. John?" Ginny asked with one barefoot, freckled kid on her hip and another behind her skirts.

"It's hard to say," he said quietly, staring at Ginny. "Jack," he said turning to me, "remember that a potter needs fire to finish the pot. Fire is necessary to create the beauty. Good-bye, son." That was the last thing he ever said to me.

The years passed with a steady rhythm, like the thumping of a potter's wheel. Our walls raised and we grew strong. Beautiful designs were carved into our hardening sides as Sam and Christy joined in marriage, bringing peace to Daddy until fire destroyed Sam years later in the Vietnam War. The anger and depression came back to rest in Daddy's aching chest.

After the war Christy moved to Vietnam and opened the Chester and Sam's Home for War Orphans. She invited Daddy to join her after he retired. Together they helped write new lives of pure poetry.

Daddy died in 1983; we brought him back to Rome and buried him next to Mama. I swear I could hear them talking the minute he was placed by her side. The aunts had already joined Mama on the other side of the river five years before. Aunt Lily and Aunt Rose were laid next to Grandpappy and Grandmama in the Paradox cemetery where flowers grow in the spring.

Our family continued to grow with those flowers through the many seasons of life, and we turned back to the land that had supported my people for five generations. I collected clay along the creek banks, thinking of Sidlers' crisis that had unearthed the beautiful clay that would be centered, molded, and then fired. Sometimes the fire would be strong and short. Sometimes it would burn slowly and intensely. In some cases the fire would be applied several times to make a glaze more beautiful. Mr. John was right: a pot is never finished without the fire ...

Rome, Georgia: 2004

"Grandpappy?"

Claire gently touched my arm. I traced the signature thumbprint bird again and turned away from the window. Twenty-year-old Claire stood before me looking so much like Ginny that it took my breath away. The auburn hair, pale skin, and the twinkling green eyes reminded me of her grandmother, gone these past six years, taken by the cancer, though never silenced.

"Yes, Claire?" I asked, returning from my long reverie.

"Where do you want the ceramic relics placed? Dr. Johnson said to ask you," she said, holding a crate of fragile shards from Hebrew University.

"On those shelves over there," I said, motioning toward a large wooden case.

I held the piece of ancient pottery gingerly in my hand. The fragment was worn smooth by time and use. It was a part of the traveling exhibit that I had convinced Bersher to host. The packing box labeled *Ancient Jerusalem* still lay open on the counter.

Claire came back from placing the box on the top shelf. "You look sort of flummoxed, Grandpappy. Did you find something special?"

I smiled. "Yes, Claire, I did. Something very special."

I placed the signature shard gently in the display case as a dove flew from the windowsill.

OTHER BOOKS BY TRACI STEAD

Coming Winter 2016
The Doctor of Dunstable Plains,
Volume 2 in *The Spirit* Series

Also by Traci Stead
Devotions of a Gerbil

AUTHOR BIO

Traci Stead is a Christian wife, mother, volunteer, and all-around mountain girl. Transplanted from West Virginia into the sandy soil of the North Carolina coastal plain, she often escapes to the mountains by train or by brain. Sipping a cup of tea, visiting with family, and rocking in the porch chair is her idea of living the high life.

Traci believes stories of real life are the best tales to tell. Though she often writes fiction, the stories are all true.

You can get to know Traci better at www.TraciStead.com.